Praise for Martha Wells and the Books of the Raksura

"Martha Wells' Raksura books are dense, and complex, with truly amazing world building, and non-human characters who are quite genuinely alien, yet still comprehensible and sympathetic. The characters, particularly the protagonist, Moon, are compelling and flawed and likable. The plots are solid and fast moving. But it's the world that really astounds. There is a depth and breadth and sheer alienness here that I have rarely seen in any novel. Shape-shifters, flying ships, city-trees, six kazillion sentient races, floating islands, and on and on and on."

—Kelly McCullough, author of the WebMage series and the Fallen Blade novels

"Using its alien protagonist to explore the politics of gender and belonging, this is a fascinating read for SF readers looking for something out of the ordinary."

—*Publishers Weekly* (starred review)

"*The Cloud Roads* has wildly original worldbuilding, diverse and engaging characters, and a thrilling adventure plot. It's that rarest of fantasies: fresh and surprising, with a story that doesn't go where ten thousand others have gone before. I can't wait for my next chance to visit the Three Worlds!"

—N. K. Jemisin, author of *The Hundred Thousand Kingdoms*

"Filled with vivid action and memorable characters, *The Cloud Roads* is a terrific science fiction adventure story with a heart. I read it eagerly and look forward to its sequel with great anticipation."

—Sarah Prineas, author of *The Magic Thief*

"It reminds me of the SF/F fantasy I read as a teen, long before YA was categorized. Those books explored adult concepts without 'adult content'; the complexity of morality and the potential, uncaring harshness of life. This story's conclusion satisfies on all those counts as well as leaving me eager for the sequel."

—Juliet E. McKenna, *Interzone*

"There's so much to like here: multiple sapient species sharing a world (or NOT sharing) with complex gender roles, wildly differing societies, and varying technologies. This is rigorous fantasy without the trappings of European medievalism. And most of all, it's riveting storytelling."

—Steven Gould, author of *Jumper* and *7th Sigma*

"Martha Wells' books always make me remember why I love to read. In *The Cloud Roads*, she invents yet another rich and astonishingly detailed setting, where many races and cultures uneasily co-exist in a world constantly threatened by soulless predators. But the vivid world-building and nonstop action really serve as a backdrop for the heart of the novel—the universal human themes of loneliness, loss, and the powerful drive to find somewhere to belong."

—Sharon Shinn, author of *Troubled Waters*

"Wells . . . has created a new world of dragonlike shapeshifters and human tribes that could serve as the background for future novels in this exotic setting. Concise storytelling and believable characters make this a good addition to most fantasy collections."

—*Library Journal*

"*The Serpent Sea* is a wonderful and spellbinding sequel to *The Cloud Roads*, which was one of the best fantasy books of 2011. It gloriously continues the saga of the shapeshifting Raksura."

—*RisingShadow.net*

"A rousing tale of a lost boy who finds his way home and discovers that he has a role to play in saving the world. High-octane fight scenes nicely contrast with Moon's emotional growth and developing romance. Genre fans looking for something different will find this just what they needed."

—*School Library Journal Blog*

"With these books Wells is writing at the top of her game, and given their breadth, originality, and complexity, this series is showing indications it could become one of the landmark series of the genre."

—*Adventures Fantastic*

"I loved *The Serpent Sea*. It's extraordinary story telling with engaging characters in an enchanting world I want to visit."

—Diana Pharaoh Francis, author of the Path and Crosspointe series

"I loved this book. This has Wells' signature worldbuilding and wholly real character development, and her wry voice shines through. I can't even explain how real the world felt, in which each race and city and culture had such well-drawn back story that they lived on even outside the main plot."

—Patrice Sarath, author of *Gordath Wood* and *Red Gold Bridge*

"*The Cloud Roads* is a terrific fantasy novel that stands out due to imaginative worldbuilding, accomplished writing and engaging storytelling. For everyone else, *The Cloud Roads* is a proud example of what the genre is capable of producing."

—*Fantasy Book Critic*

"Another excellent and wonderful view into the universe of the Three Worlds and its fascinating inhabitants."

—*SF Signal*

"First off, the world revealed within this story is nothing short of amazingly detailed and intriguing. . . . you'll find this an imaginative and engaging novel."

—John Vogt, *Examiner.com*

"This novel is a must-read for any sci-fi fan. Moon is a delightful character and a great focal point for the story. The world the author has created is wonderfully complex and vivid and has wonderful layers of characters, cultures and creatures."

—*Portland Book Review*

"Wells remains a compelling storyteller whose clear prose, goal-driven plotting, and witty, companionable characters should win her fans among those who enjoy the works of writers such as John Scalzi and Lois McMaster Bujold."

—Matt Denault, *Strange Horizons*

"*The Serpent Sea* is a worthy sequel to *The Cloud Roads* and it features all of the strengths (fantastic world-building, great story, awesome characters) of that first novel. It is so easy to fall in love with this series and the reasons are manifold."

—*The Book Smugglers*

"I really loved Book 3, which wound up as my favorite book of the trilogy. . . . I'll be pushing it on everybody who loves great writing, ornate worlds and wonderfully-drawn nonhuman characters. And I am also looking up Martha Wells' backlist, right now."

—Rachel Neumeier, author of
Lord of the Changing Winds and *Black Dog*

"This is the type of Fantasy series I absolutely love—and highly recommend as a worthwhile series to read and fall in love with. . . . *The Siren Depths* closes the series really well."

—*The Book Smugglers*

"The first two books, *The Cloud Roads* and *The Serpent Sea*, were excellent, but in my opinion *The Siren Depths* is an even better and more satisfying book, because it takes the series to a whole new level of depth."

—*RisingShadow.net*

"*The Siren Depths* has more of what I've come to love about the Books of the Raksura—a compelling story, great world-building in a unique setting, and lovable characters with very realistic problems. In my opinion, it's also the most satisfying installment in the series."

—*Fantasy Café*

"Truly inventive and stunningly imaginative world-building perfectly melded with vivid, engaging characters make the Books of the Raksura one of my all-time favorite science-fiction series."

—Kate Elliott, author of The Spiritwalker Trilogy

"Martha Wells writes fantasy the way it was meant to be—poignant, evocative, and astonishing. Prepare to be captivated 'til the sun comes up."

—Kameron Hurley, author of *God's War*, *Infidel*, and *Rapture*

STORIES

of the

RAKSURA

Other books by Martha Wells:

The Element of Fire
City of Bones
The Death of the Necromancer
Wheel of the Infinite

Fall of Ile-Rien Trilogy:
    The Wizard Hunters
    The Ships of Air
    The Gate of Gods

The Books of the Raksura
    The Cloud Roads
    The Serpent Sea
    The Siren Depths

Stargate: Atlantis
    SGA: Reliquary
    SGA: Entanglement

Emilie and the Hollow World
Emile and the Sky World

Star Wars: Razor's Edge

STORIES

of the

RAKSURA

VOLUME ONE: THE FALLING WORLD &
THE TALE OF INDIGO AND CLOUD

MARTHA WELLS

NIGHT SHADE BOOKS
NEW YORK

Copyright © 2014 by Martha Wells

All rights reserved. No part of this book may be reproduced in any manner without the express written consent of the publisher, except in the case of brief excerpts in critical reviews or articles. All inquiries should be addressed to Night Shade Books, 307 West 36th Street, 11th Floor, New York, NY 10018.

Night Shade books may be purchased in bulk at special discounts for sales promotion, corporate gifts, fund-raising, or educational purposes. Special editions can also be created to specifications. For details, contact the Special Sales Department, Night Shade Books, 307 West 36th Street, 11th Floor, New York, NY 10018 or info@skyhorsepublishing.com.

Night Shade Books™ is a trademark of Skyhorse Publishing, Inc.®, a Delaware corporation.

Visit our website at www.nightshadebooks.com.

10 9 8 7 6 5 4 3

Library of Congress Cataloging-in-Publication Data is available on file.

Edited by Jeremy Lassen
Cover design by Rain Saukas
Cover art by Steve Argyle

Print ISBN: 978-1-59780-535-3

Printed in the United States of America

CONTENTS

CONTENTS

THE FALLING
WORLD

The night before Jade left for Ocean Winter, Moon had a stupid argument with Chime.

"You're going?" Moon asked, startled. Jade would be taking five warriors with her, which was usual for a queen making a visit to another court, but he hadn't thought Chime would be one of them.

Chime looked up, worried. "You don't want me to go?"

They were in the greeting hall, the heart of the Indigo Cloud court's colony tree, sitting near the pool fed by a narrow fall of water that streamed down the polished wood wall. The hall lay at the bottom of the huge well that spiraled through the center of the tree, stairways criss-crossing upward, leading to overhanging balconies, and the soft illumination coming from shells spelled to glow that formed part of the decorative inlay. When they had first arrived here nearly a turn ago, the place had been desolate and empty; now it was busy with warriors flitting around the upper levels and Arbora bustling back and forth, storing away baskets of roots. One of the more important harvests had ended today, so there was going to be a gathering to celebrate it, and to wish Jade luck on her trading trip.

Moon shrugged. "No, no, it's fine if you go. I just thought . . . You aren't normally excited about leaving the colony." He had been certain that Chime would use the fact that Moon wasn't going as an excuse to stay behind as well. Five changes of the month ago, when they had returned from Opal Night, Chime had acted as if he never wanted to leave the court again. A normal warrior would have been honored to go on a trip with the court's sister queen, but then Chime wasn't a normal warrior. Moon wasn't a normal consort, either, and that was one of the reasons why they had been drawn to each other.

"I know. I'm not." Chime ran his fingers through the water at the edge of the pool, startling a few tiny flying lizards who had taken up residence there. He was in his groundling form, where he had dark bronze skin, fluffy light hair, and usually a stubborn expression, though now he just looked thoughtful and a little worried. When he shifted, he would be a

3

dark reflective blue, with a gold sheen under his scales. Moon's groundling form was much the same, lean and angular, with dark bronze skin, dark hair and green eyes. Chime continued, "But I'm hoping that if I talk to the Ocean Winter Arbora, they'll let me into their libraries." He shrugged uneasily. "It's an older court. Maybe they'll have something on Arbora who change into warriors."

"Something that Opal Night didn't have?" Moon asked, and tried not to sound skeptical. Opal Night was one of the oldest courts in the Reaches, possibly the oldest one, and Chime had been all through their libraries.

Chime sighed, partly resigned and partly annoyed, as he was well aware of all these objections. "I know. But Opal Night's always been a prosperous court, as far back as their histories go. Their recorded instances of this—" he waved at himself "—happening were all secondhand from other courts. Ocean Winter is old, but it's never been as big. I'm just hoping they have a firsthand account somewhere."

Moon said, "Or a firsthand account of how someone got changed back." Shifting was what defined a Raksura; you were either an Aeriat—an infertile warrior or a fertile consort or queen, who shifted to a winged form—or an Arbora who shifted to a wingless form but still had the colorful scales, the razor claws, the tail, the spines, and the other things that made you Raksura. But before Moon had come to Indigo Cloud, Chime had been an Arbora mentor, and had shifted one day and found himself a warrior, gaining wings but losing the powers of healing and divination that only Arbora mentors had. He had never been reconciled to the change.

At Opal Night, Chime had found mentions of Arbora transforming into warriors, and confirmation of what they already knew, that it only happened to courts under pressure from disease, food shortages, or reduced population. He hadn't found any mention of mentors-turned-warriors having odd flashes of insight or being able to hear things they shouldn't. Chime had had moments where he knew upper air dwellers like cloud-walkers or sky-sailors were passing overhead, and sometimes he could hear a distant rumble that might be the voices of the mountain-trees.

Chime had left Opal Night with little more knowledge than he had started with, and a promise from some of the mentors to send word to him if they stumbled on any more information in their own searches. Moon didn't think he was going to get anything better than that at Ocean Winter.

Chime poked absently at one of the lizards, which hissed at him and fluttered its wings. "I'm a fool, I know that too."

"I don't think you're a fool. I just . . . have a lot of experience with looking for things without much chance of finding them, for turns and turns." Moon had been orphaned as a fledgling and grew up outside the courts, not even knowing he was a Raksura or what a Raksura was. Being found and hauled away to Indigo Cloud had been filled with revelations, some of them disturbing. He didn't regret any of it now, but he could sympathize with both the need to dig into the unknown and the urge to leave things as they were.

Chime grimaced. "You found what you were looking for."

"It found me, a long time after I gave up." Moon watched the Arbora, mainly Rill, Weave, Snap, and Bark rolling out the mats and cushions across the hall floor where everyone would sit for the gathering. The air was filled with the scents of baking flatbread, spiced roots, and other treats. He had never thought he would have a home of any kind, let alone one like this. He had trouble imagining wanting anything else, now. Maybe he didn't have as much sympathy for Chime's problem as he should. Chime had grown up with this, knowing who he was, protected by a large number of affectionate and quarrelsome Raksura.

"So I should give up?" Chime didn't sound impressed. "And somehow the answer will just show up?"

"No." There wasn't much resemblance between the two situations, after all. "But I think . . . " Moon realized he was about to tell Chime that he should give up, just accept what had happened to him. It sounded like good advice inside his head, but he had the feeling that once he said it, it would sound terrible. "I don't know what I think." And if it was making Chime feel better to search for answers, then he didn't want to discourage him.

"I think you think I'm wasting my effort."

"No, I don't think that. It's not like you have other things to do." Chime stared at him, and Moon thought, *why did I say that?* He seemed to have lost what little ability he had had to talk to people. "That's not what I meant."

Blossom called out, "Come on, we're ready!" and Chime pushed to his feet and stalked away before Moon could say anything else.

☾

"I said something stupid to Chime," Moon told Jade later in her bower.

"You had an argument?" she asked. It was long after the gathering, and she was sitting on a fur mat, sorting out jewelry to take with her tomorrow. Just because Indigo Cloud had the upper hand in this alliance didn't mean Jade didn't have to try to impress the reigning Queen of Ocean Winter. Not that Moon thought Jade needed anything but herself to impress anyone with. Like all Raksuran queens, she had no groundling form and could shift only between her winged form and a wingless shape that looked more like an Arbora. Her scales were blue, with a silver-gray web pattern. Behind her head, the frills and spines formed an elaborate mane, reaching all the way down her back to her tail.

Ocean Winter had already visited Indigo Cloud for a formal greeting between courts. The sister queen had come with her consort, and it had all been very correct and dull. Now Jade was going to return their visit so they could work out the details of a trading agreement between the two courts. Since the alliance between Opal Night, the most powerful court in the Reaches, they had had more greetings and requests for alliances than they could handle. Ocean Winter was not a particularly prestigious court, and Jade had decided it was better if Moon didn't accompany her, so as to make it clear just which court was the one begging for a trade alliance.

Moon put the kettle on the heated stones in the bowl hearth set into the floor. Mentors could spell stones and plants and other objects to make them produce light or heat, something else important to the court that Chime couldn't do anymore. "I don't think you can call it an argument when one person says stupid things and the other just stares at them."

Jade looked up, lifting one scaled brow. "I think you can call that an argument."

"I talked to him later at the gathering, and I think he was over it, but . . . I don't want to tell him he should stop trying to find out more about what happened to him." Chime was increasingly obsessed with exploring what it meant to change from a mentor to a warrior, and the strange and erratic flashes of insight he had were sometimes helpful, and more often just taunting reminders of the mentors' skills and powers he no longer had. "But . . ."

"But you think he should stop."

"Yes. I do." Moon shook his head. He knew he was a fatalist. He had spent most of his life not expecting to be particularly happy or comfortable, looking for the basics of shelter, food, and company that wasn't actively trying to kill him. Maybe he just didn't understand what Chime was really looking for or why. But Moon had gotten the answers he had needed from Opal Night, so maybe he was right that he didn't understand Chime's situation as much as he thought he did. "Maybe that's just me."

"I don't know." Jade sighed. "This court has had so many changes in the past few turns, but nothing has been as strange as what happened to Chime when he changed." She gathered the jewelry into a heap and set it aside. "He's going to have to work it out for himself, to try to find a mental place where he can live with it."

"So you think I should just shut up."

Jade smiled. "I think you should shut up and come over here."

Later, half-asleep and sated, Jade sleeping on top of him with one leg still pressed possessively between his thighs, Moon decided Jade was right and he should just keep his mouth shut about it. Chime would be leaving tomorrow with Jade and the others, and by the time he came back there would be other things to talk about. Moon's opinion wasn't going to change, and Chime needed to work this out for himself.

☾

TWENTY DAYS LATER

Moon circled the pond. Maybe he should bring the Sky Copper clutch out here to teach them about drains, since that was apparently going to be the main concern of the Indigo Cloud colony for the rest of their lives.

Snap surfaced with a spray of muddy water and gasped. "I think I see the problem."

Blossom sighed and rubbed the bridge of her nose. "I think I see the problem, too." She was an Arbora teacher, and rightfully should be inside doing something more important, but had been dragged out here to give her opinion. Moon was out here just because he was bored.

Bramble and Blaze, both female Arbora hunters, flicked their spines in a particularly disparaging way. Blaze said, "We've heard that before, Snap."

Snap shook water and mud out of his frills, spraying Moon and Blossom. "This time I'm sure!" He took a deep breath and went under again.

Blossom brushed the mud off her scales and said, "I hope he's right about this. We don't want to lose those lower platforms."

Moon ignored the mud and absently raked his foot claws through the grass. They were on one of the colony tree's higher platforms, the great dark wall of the tree's trunk looming behind them. The sunlight was green-tinted from the spreading canopy hundreds of paces above their heads, and it held the other wild mountain-trees at bay, so they formed a large clearing around the colony tree. The platforms were made by intertwined branches and heavy vines and turns of windblown dirt, now supporting gardens or fields or whole forests of smaller trees. This platform hadn't been replanted yet and was too overgrown with grasses and wild saplings to tell what it had once been used for. Blossom thought it was too high up in the tree for root vegetables or orchards, and that it might once have been a pleasure garden, with elaborate plantings and water features. Now it was just waste ground, buzzing with clouds of gnats that hung in the humid warm season air of the suspended forest. Whatever this platform had once been, Snap, one of the Arbora in charge of the colony tree's ancient, extensive, and recalcitrant drainage system, thought the pond here was a key element in the blockages they were trying to clear.

Moon just wished there was something to do that was a little more distracting.

He looked up and realized that everyone was staring at him sympathetically. Blossom smiled. "They'll be back soon."

Moon tried not to twitch at being read so easily. He said, "I'm not worried." Jade had taken not only Chime but her clutchmate Balm, plus Song and Root, all of whom were Moon's best friends in the court. She had taken Coil, one of the reigning queen Pearl's warriors, with her as well, but Moon wasn't attached to him. When they had first left, it had been easier to resign himself to missing them. Now that he was expecting them back any day, he was just restless and impatient.

Then Bramble said, "Hey, how long has he been down there?"

Moon glanced at the water, where a few bubbles broke the surface. Too few bubbles.

Blossom's eyes widened in horror. She dove in head first and Moon jumped in after her.

The pond was deeper than it looked, the water clouded and muddy. Moon followed the thrashing down to the bottom and found Blossom in the process of extracting a struggling Snap from a hole in the wall of the pond. All Moon could see was churning mud and struggling bodies. He caught hold of a root and felt Blossom's claws rip at a bundle of smaller roots and debris jammed into a channel outlet. The bundle must have trapped one of Snap's arms. Blossom had managed to loosen the debris and partly drag it out of the channel, but Snap still struggled to free himself. Moon used his longer reach to work his way further down the channel, got a better grip on the roots, and wrenched backward at the same time as Blossom.

The obstruction came loose with a rush of more muddy water, and all three of them shot to the surface. Moon shook mud out of his head frills to find Bramble crouched on the edge of the bank, hissing urgently at him. "Moon, Moon, stay down!"

He blinked at her, but sunk lower down into the water so most of his head was concealed. Snap coughed and sputtered as Blossom dragged him up onto the bank. "You idiot," she said, shaking off the root tendrils trapped in her spines. "You could have—"

Blaze, standing and facing away from the pond, hissed at her to be quiet. Moon lifted up just enough to get a view past her.

Five strange warriors and a queen were landing on the platform about thirty paces away. Moon hissed under his breath and sunk further down under the water, so only the top of his head and his muddy frills were visible. What a time for visitors to arrive. Consorts were expected to behave in certain ways, which didn't include sloshing around in muddy ponds clearing drains.

The group wasn't attempting to approach the pond. Raksuran etiquette demanded that strangers be greeted by a female warrior, so they were politely ignoring the two hunters and Blossom, who had just punched Snap in the stomach, apparently to help him bring up the last of the muddy water he had swallowed.

Two warriors from Indigo Cloud's patrol circled and then dropped toward the platform. They landed at an angle so the visitors turned toward them and away from the pond. It was Serene and Sand, both warriors of Jade's faction, and their slightly fixed expressions told Moon they knew he was here.

Moon debated staying underwater, but as the only Aeriat who had matte black scales, consorts were distinctive. It was much harder to tell the difference between a consort and a warrior in their groundling forms, and Moon's clothes wouldn't betray him either. He had come out here expecting to help with the work, so was wearing an old pair of pants cut off at the knees due to the acidic red mud patches on the lower garden platforms, and a light-colored shirt with tears and stains acquired while playing with the kids. And he had left his consort's jewelry in his bower. He decided to chance it, and shifted to groundling.

Bramble edged sideways as Moon pulled himself out of the pond, sitting where she could partially block the strangers' view of him. Moon crouched on the bank to wring the muddy water out of his shirt, keeping his head down. Serene had just shifted to groundling to greet the strangers, and was young enough to show her nervousness at the responsibility. She had the coppery skin and reddish curly hair that ran in one of the Indigo Cloud bloodlines. She was dressed in a light shirt and pants, wearing only some copper bead jewelry, but then she obviously hadn't expected to be doing this when she had come out this morning. "I'm Serene, of Indigo Cloud."

The foreign queen was young too, with emerald green scales and a gold web overlay. Her jewelry was moderately impressive, with a belt and pectoral that were all polished opals to keep from competing with the brightness of her scales. There were three female warriors in the group, all larger and more physically impressive than Serene. One stepped forward and said, "I'm Muse, of Ocean Winter. Our daughter queen has come to greet your queens, and to discuss trading between our courts."

Moon froze. *Ocean Winter?* Bramble hissed in surprise. Blossom and Snap stared, startled. Blaze turned to Moon, drawing breath to speak, but Blossom thumped her in the shoulder and she subsided. Sand looked confused, and Serene frowned, and started to say, "But our sister queen—"

Moon caught her eye and gave one sharp shake of his head. Serene swallowed the words and finished with, "—is not here, today, and—

But of course our reigning queen will greet you, if you follow us to our greeting hall."

Muse consulted her queen with a look, got a nod, and told Serene. "We're happy to follow you."

Serene and Sand leapt into flight and the Ocean Winter group followed. They all flapped up to catch a draft and ride it down toward the knothole of the colony tree.

The Arbora all turned to Moon at once. Blossom whispered, "What does it mean? Are they lying about what court they come from?"

Bramble's spines rippled worriedly. "Maybe they left before Jade arrived."

The timing was wrong. Unless this group had been making a tour of foreign courts, or had decided to sit out in the forest for days, that just didn't make sense. Moon pushed to his feet. "Get back inside. Pass the word to the others, tell the Arbora to get off the platforms for now, and warn the warriors that something might be wrong."

The visitors had reached the knothole and disappeared inside it. Moon shifted, bounded off the edge of the platform, and snapped his wings out.

A few flaps took him down to one of the largest platforms, tucked up against the trunk of the tree. When they had first arrived here it had been a weedy overgrown plot of encroaching jungle. Now it was covered with neat beds filled with roots, berry vines, and tea plants. There weren't any Arbora working out here today, most of their efforts being concentrated on the other still overgrown platforms. The bridges and ladder structures all connected here, since it had a doorway into the trunk. During the day while the Arbora were out working, the heavy wooden plug that sealed it would be open.

Moon took the paths through the beds and bounded through the round doorway. The young soldier who sat nearby on guard duty leapt to her feet and hissed in reflex. "Something wrong, consort?"

Moon paused to say, "A daughter queen from Ocean Winter just arrived to talk about trade with us."

She stared. "But . . . Oh." Her expression went grim as she realized the possible implications. "I'll send someone to tell Knell!"

"Tell Stone, too!" Moon had already turned away, headed down the nearest passage into the colony. He was tempted to look for Stone first, but he knew if he didn't go straight to Pearl she would be furious. And he needed Pearl's temper working for him right now instead of against him.

He took the back way up, half-climbing, half-leaping up one of the winding stairs that paralleled the central well, past the carvings formed out of the smooth wood, detailed depictions of plants, huge landscapes, stylized images of the wind, of Aeriat in flight or battle or Arbora at work. He went all the way up to the passages that joined the queens' and consorts' levels. There was a back way into Pearl's bower from here, though Moon was reluctant to use it. He didn't like using the front way that led from the queens' hall either, but he didn't want to risk being seen by the visitors yet.

He took the back passage into Pearl's territory, shifting to groundling as he passed the carved arch of intertwined warriors and Arbora that guarded the anteroom. This was only the second or third time he had seen these rooms, but he didn't take the time to look around.

He stopped in the doorway of the main room, which held a lavish bathing pool and in the back, a large hanging bed draped with fine fabrics. Pearl sat in the center of the room, near the hearth bowl, on a pallet of furs and cushions. She was in her winged form, not her Arbora form, so she wasn't all that relaxed, despite appearances. It made it much less awkward that she wasn't alone. Her new consort Ember sat beside the hearth, pouring out tea, and some warriors sat nearby, Drift, Floret, and a few others. But not River.

Moon cleared his throat, which was as close as Raksura got to the groundling customs of knocking or clapping your hands or stamping a foot to request entrance to someone else's space. He knew Pearl wasn't going to like the fact that he was wet and muddy, but he didn't care.

Everyone in the room stared at him. The warriors' expressions ranged from dubious to anticipatory amusement. Ember just set the teapot down and looked worried. Pearl flicked a spine in annoyance. Her scales were brilliant gold, overlaid with a webbed pattern of deepest indigo blue. The frilled mane behind her head was like a golden sunburst, and there were more frills on the tips of her folded wings, and on the triangle-shape at the end of her tail. She eyed Moon. "What have you done?"

Moon stepped further inside. "A daughter queen from Ocean Winter just arrived."

He didn't have to explain what that meant. Pearl's spines flared and she uncoiled and came to her feet in one motion. "With what news?"

Moon said, "They said they were here to talk about trade."

Floret hissed in realization, and the other warriors stirred uneasily, the amusement giving way to confusion. Pearl's spines twitched in suspicion and speculation. Moon felt a rush of relief that he didn't have to explain the implications. Pearl was so deliberately difficult at times, it was hard to remember that she was a battle-hardened reigning queen. Pearl said, "Someone send to the Arbora, tell the ones working outside to come in—"

"I did that already," Moon interrupted, then wished he could swallow the words. Surely there was a more diplomatic way to say it, but he had no idea what it was. Drift, pushing to his feet to take the message, froze.

Pearl hissed in reflex, then flicked her spines again. "Did the strangers see you?"

"No. Serene greeted them—"

Footsteps pattered behind him as Heart, the chief of the mentors, arrived in a rush, sliding to a halt when she saw Moon. She was young for her position in the colony, and was a particularly beautiful Arbora, with dark amber skin and bronze-colored hair in her groundling form. Moon finished, "I tried to signal her not to mention Jade. I think she understood."

Heart said, "She did. No one's said anything. The Ocean Winter warriors are acting as if nothing's wrong, as if . . . " She hesitated, threw a glance at Moon. "As if Jade and the others never got there."

More noise in the passage as Knell and Vine arrived, both hastily shifting to groundling as they saw Pearl. Knell was one of Chime's clutchmates, though he didn't much resemble Chime. His groundling form had dark hair and his skin was more brown than bronze. To Moon's relief, Stone shouldered past them. He stepped up next to Moon, but didn't say anything, just watched Pearl. Like Moon, he was lean and tall, and a consort, but unlike Moon he was very old, though his groundling form didn't necessarily show it, unless you knew what it meant when the color of Raksuran groundling skin faded to gray. He had one bad eye, partially blinded by a white haze across the pupil.

"Did the foreign queen bring a consort this time?" Pearl stepped around the cushions, her claws clicking on the polished wood floor.

"No. But she's young," Heart said. "The Ocean Winter daughter queen. Younger than Jade. Maybe she doesn't have one yet."

Pearl hissed under her breath. "Has there been any word from the patrols?"

Knell said, "No one's reported anything unusual."

Vine added, "I was just out there. All the Aeriat patrols are circling the clearing. No one's missing."

Pearl turned to Floret. "You and Vine get out there, take the patrols and make a search of the area outside the clearing. Don't be obvious about it."

Floret gave her a nod and hurried out with Vine. Moon twitched, wanting to follow, but he couldn't be in two places at once.

"But why would Ocean Winter want to war with us?" Ember said. He was young, delicate, and perfect, where Moon was gawky, awkward, and strange. He had stayed seated on the cushions, and set the teapot aside. "They're an ally with Sunset Water and Emerald Twilight, too. We're also tied to Opal Night, and all their allies. It doesn't make sense."

Pearl tilted her head in acknowledgement, which Moon was glad to see. Ember had a better understanding of court politics in the Reaches than anyone else in Indigo Cloud. Pearl said, "We'll see what they say when I greet them." She nodded to Stone. "I'll want you there. And you," she added to Moon, while he was frantically groping for a good reason to include himself in the group. She eyed him with disfavor. "Just clean yourself up first."

☾

Moon raced up to his bower, jumped in and out of the bathing pool, and threw on a good set of clothes. The shirt and pants were black, because that was easier to match jewel colors with and consorts often wore dark colors. He added the sash with the red woven through it and his consort's bracelet and had to fight down a surge of despair. *Don't panic. You don't know anything yet.*

He made it down to the consorts' passage to the queens' hall, a small chamber with walls carved with scenes of Arbora building platform bridges in the suspended forest, framed by towering mountain-trees. It was meant to be a private retiring room for consorts, where they could compose themselves before joining any gathering in the larger hall beyond. Moon found Stone waiting there, his head cocked to listen. He hadn't bothered to change clothes, or put on jewelry, but then he never did. Stone said quietly, "They just got up here."

Moon nodded. He could hear a faint murmur of voices, Serene making polite stilted small talk with Muse, the Ocean Winter warrior. It was Serene's first time to greet visitors from another court, and it must be even more nerve-racking to do it under these circumstances. Moon whispered, "Aren't you going to tell me it's nothing, that they're fine? That one of the warriors got hurt, and it delayed them?"

"After twenty days?" Stone snorted derisively. "Not likely." But he gave Moon's shoulder a rough nudge. "Whatever happened, Jade can handle it."

That was what was worrying Moon. That whatever it was, Jade hadn't managed to deal with it and return yet.

Ember came down the steps into the passage. He had changed clothes too, though there had been nothing wrong with the ones he had been wearing. He said softly, "Pearl is about to come out." Watching Moon with sympathy, he added, "I'm sure they're fine."

Moon took that in the spirit that it was meant and just nodded tightly. Stone didn't acknowledge Ember at all, and Ember just eyed him warily and didn't say anything. It wasn't that Stone didn't like Ember, so much as that he was completely indifferent to Ember's existence.

They heard Pearl's voice as she came out of her bower into the queens' hall. Ember slipped past Moon, waited exactly long enough at the entrance, then stepped into the hall. Moon didn't need to see to know Ember had arrived at the seating area at precisely the same moment as Pearl without appearing to hurry, and was now seated gracefully on a cushion behind her. Usually Moon got to witness this performance, since

Jade as sister queen was supposed to greet visiting queens first, and Moon would have been out there with her.

Stone waited a moment to give Ember time to get seated, then started out. Moon followed.

Moon usually found it awkward and unnerving, even when Jade was here, to walk out into the hall under the scrutiny of a foreign queen. Now he was just impatient. One side of the queens' hall looked out into the colony tree's central well, with the open gallery of the consort level above it. There was a fountain against the inner wall that fell down to a shallow pool, and above it a huge sculpture of a queen with outspread wings stretched out across the walls to circle the entire chamber, meeting tip to tip. The queen's scales, set with polished sunstones, glinted faintly in the soft light.

On the ring of cushions facing the Ocean Winter queen and her warriors were Pearl, Ember, and Heart, with several of Pearl's favored warriors scattered behind her.

As Moon took one of the cushions behind Stone, he caught the Ocean Winter queen eyeing him surreptitiously. Moon set his jaw and didn't snarl. He could hear faint sounds echoing up from below, the voices of the Arbora and warriors, louder than usual at this time because everyone had been called inside.

Pearl introduced him. "Moon of Opal Night, first consort to Jade, our sister queen." She tilted her head to indicate the foreign queen. "Garnet, daughter queen of Ocean Winter."

Garnet inclined her head, and betrayed a trace of nerves as she settled her spines. She said, "We came primarily to continue the talk of trade begun during the earlier visit by our sister queen. We heard from her that you were interested in trading for seedlings and grains. We have those in abundance, but we are a small court and lack—"

"Is that the only reason you came?" Pearl interrupted.

Garnet frowned, and her warriors tensed, startled. "We also want to formalize our alliance. We heard from other courts you were much interested in trading partners."

"Which courts?"

"Sunset Water, to name one." Garnet flattened her spines in an effort of self-control. "If that information was not meant to be shared, I apologize." She hesitated, then admitted, "But we also wish to begin trade as soon as possible. We have more crops than we know what to do with but very little woven cloth."

Pearl sat back, flicked a spine. "Why didn't you bring a consort?"

Garnet's spines stiffened in offense, but she kept her voice under control. "I haven't taken one yet." Her gaze went from Pearl to Stone and Moon, to Heart, as if she was realizing that there might be something to their attitude besides the usual structured rudeness of a strange court. "What is this? If you have changed your minds about an alliance between our courts—"

Calmly, Pearl said, "If you're lying, I'll rip you apart."

Garnet surged to her feet and snarled, "Try it."

Moon moved before he knew he meant to, shoved to his feet and shifted to his winged form in one motion. His spines flared, his wings half extended, his snarl echoed through the open well of the tree.

Heart, the warriors, and Ember flinched in startled reflex. Stone didn't move, and neither did Pearl. Garnet's spines shivered in reaction. Her gaze went from Moon to Pearl, now more shocked than angry. She said, "What is it? Lying about what?" Her voice was rough.

Moon growled low in his throat. *She's playacting.* But deep in his heart, he knew a Raksuran queen that young could easily fake anger, but not the dismay and frustration of the unjustly insulted.

With the same lazy calm, Pearl said, "Moon, sit down and be quiet."

Moon lashed his tail and sank down to sit again. After a moment he managed to shift to his groundling form. Garnet took a deep breath and sat down as well, her gaze still fixed on Pearl.

His expression completely opaque, Stone said, "Tell her."

Beside Pearl, Heart said, "Yes. I don't think she's lying."

One of Garnet's warriors hissed, and Garnet quieted her with a look. She regarded Pearl again, no less angry but a great deal less confused. "What do you think we've done?"

Pearl said, "Twenty days ago our sister queen, Jade, left for Ocean Winter with five of her warriors to make arrangements for the trade alliance we had discussed when your sister queen visited two changes of the month previously."

Garnet's eyes narrowed. "Twenty days . . . We left six days ago and saw nothing of them. How do I know this is true . . . ?" Her gaze went to Moon and the words trailed off.

Moon didn't know what he looked like, but it must have convinced her. Garnet shook her head impatiently. "We haven't seen your sister queen. She did not arrive at our court before we left. I don't know what proof I can offer."

Pearl tilted her head thoughtfully. "Perhaps you wish to leave immediately, to return to your court to ask if anyone has seen her."

Garnet didn't fall for that. She said, "I assume that would only confirm your suspicions. In your place, it would certainly confirm mine." She hesitated, then said, "You can keep me here as hostage, and send someone to our court to search."

Her largest female warrior hissed a protest again, and actually reached to touch Garnet's arm. Garnet shook her off impatiently.

Pearl flexed her claws, their jeweled sheaths catching the light. But she said, "That is . . . wise of you."

Moon stirred in frustration, wanting to object or argue. *Even if we left for Ocean Winter now, they've had days to hide the evidence.* But a reluctant part of him found Garnet's sincerity convincing.

Garnet said, "All I can say is that Ocean Winter wants and needs alliances and trade. There is no advantage we could get from attacking you." She flicked another look at Moon. "The regard your court is held in by Opal Night is well known. Ocean Winter has no desire to make enemies."

Pearl eyed her for a long moment, and Garnet didn't flinch. Then Pearl flicked her claws. "If you will leave the hall for a time, we will discuss our suspicions, and your generous offer."

☾

Pearl sent Garnet and her warriors to the guest quarters, with a guard of warriors and soldiers to watch them and make sure they stayed where they were put. Bone, Bell, and Knell had arrived at the queens' level by that point, and joined the conference. Bone was the leader of the hunters' caste, and his heavily muscled groundling form showed the signs of age and past desperate encounters. He had white hair and an ashy cast to his dark bronze skin, and a ring of old scar tissue around his neck where something had once tried to bite his head off.

Bell was another of Knell and Chime's clutchmates, and the leader of the Arbora teachers' caste. He had the same dark hair and skin as Knell, and the same height, but was a bit slimmer.

They waited until Serene returned to report that the guests were safely ensconced and had seemed to settle in without protest.

Stone broke the uneasy silence. "The foreign daughter queen was right. There's no reason for them to attack us."

Moon had gotten to his feet to pace. He had managed to stay in his groundling form, but he had to move. Even though he wasn't sure he believed it, he said, "They could take whatever they want instead of trading for it."

"They don't want the damn cloth." Pearl's voice was an annoyed growl. "That's just their excuse. They want an alliance."

Moon stopped to stare at her. "How do you know?"

Pearl flicked her claws at Ember, who said, "They're a small court, and they've had setbacks. They've had trouble getting consorts. Indigo Cloud is small and new to the Reaches, but you already have two powerful allies." He leaned forward. "It's not what you have now that they're interested in. It's what you'll have in the future: consorts from Emerald Twilight's and Opal Night's primary bloodlines." Ember spread his hands. "It might be twenty turns before there are young Indigo Cloud consorts available, but the suit of a queen from a longtime ally is more likely to succeed. So they meant to become a longtime ally."

Moon shook his head and walked to the edge of the hall, looking down into the central well. Spell-lights gleamed a warm yellow-white from balconies and doorways all the way down to the greeting hall. Cool air flowed up the well, laced with the scents of green plants and wet earth, clean water, bread baking, and a myriad of Raksura. Not enough to even come close to filling the huge colony tree, but there were a few more than there had been when they had first arrived here.

He wanted Ocean Winter to be guilty because then he would know exactly where Jade and the others were, and it would only be a matter of finding a way to get to them. If Ocean Winter was innocent, then it meant something had happened on the way there. And that meant the best chance was that there was nothing left to find but bone fragments.

Knell said, "We'll know more when the patrols send word. If it's really just the Ocean Winter Queen and her five warriors, then there isn't much chance this is a trick."

Moon stepped off the edge of the platform, shifted and snapped out his wings, and drifted all the way down.

☾

Moon ended up in the bottom of the tree, below the Arbora's work rooms and storage areas. The passages here were more cave-like, the walls rough wood with no carving, the floors knobby and uneven underfoot. He was sitting on a landing near the edge of an open channel that curved down a set of rough stairs. Water rushed down it, mostly obscured by curtains of moss, then dropped to vanish into an enclosed pipe which diverted waste water down into the roots. The water was drawn up naturally through the tree, then tapped at various points to use for drinking and bathing. Most of it left the tree through the waterfall that fell from the knothole, but some of it was diverted down here, for the lower level bathing rooms and for flushing the latrines. When the drains worked the way they were supposed to.

The channel was flowing fast and the smell wasn't obtrusive, though it attracted gnats and beetles. There was no one else down here.

A faint scrape from above was his only warning. He looked up to see Stone's big black winged formed snaking down the stairwell, his claws catching in nooks and crannies. Stone's winged form was far larger than any other Raksura Moon had ever seen; tip to tip his wings were more than three times the size of Moon's twenty pace span. Raksuran queens and consorts grew larger and stronger as they grew older, and as line grandfather to Indigo Cloud, Stone was very old. Stone sank down onto the stairs and shifted all in one motion, flowing into his groundling form.

Moon said, "Word from the patrols?"

"Not yet." He sat down next to Moon. He was the closest thing Moon had ever had to a father, the one responsible for finding Moon in the wilds of the east and bringing him to Indigo Cloud.

"I should have gone with her," Moon said. He figured that was what Stone had come down here to say, and he wanted to get it out there first.

But Stone said, "We won't know that until we find them. Maybe you would have just been more of a hindrance than usual."

Moon couldn't handle optimism at the moment. And it didn't sound as if Stone expected the patrols to find Ocean Winter warriors lurking in the outskirts of the clearing, either. "You mean if they're dead, then it's a good thing I'm still around to keep the alliance with Opal Night." He didn't even know if that was true. He had no idea what happened to consorts whose queens died before they made a clutch. It was the clutch that made a consort part of a court, not just being taken by a queen.

Stone hissed in more than his usual level of annoyance. "You're good at feeling sorry for yourself, but I don't want to hear it just now."

Moon snarled and pushed to his feet. Stone caught his arm and yanked him back down. Stone said, "The question is, are you going to help me go after them?"

Moon's heart thumped. "Will Pearl try to stop me from going?"

"Not this time. This isn't a normal situation, and there's no daughter queen to lead the search." Moon knew his expression was dubious, and Stone gave him an exasperated look. "Pearl is Jade's birthqueen, remember?"

Sometimes Moon didn't remember it. It was hard to remember that Pearl and Jade had been disagreeing on things long before Moon had come along, that because they fought didn't mean Pearl wanted Jade dead. His nomadic past had made him used to thinking of relationships as temporary and fragile. "Who should we take with us?"

Stone frowned, but when he spoke it was clear he had already been making plans. "I want to bring some hunters. Chances are whatever happened, it was when they camped for the night. Hunters will be better at picking up trails and traces on the platforms."

Moon rubbed his eyes, trying to banish all the images of what that "whatever" might be. The warriors he trusted most, Chime, Balm, Song, and Root, were with Jade. "I want Floret and Vine." They were experienced at travel away from the court, and good fighters.

Stone grunted agreement. "Keep thinking. We'll need twice as many warriors as Arbora, so they can switch out carrying duties. And a mentor."

A mentor to scry for them and help find the way, and for healing. *And to keep us from falling into whatever trap caught Jade*, Moon thought.

☾

Moon was climbing the back stairway, on his way up to the queens' hall, when River stepped out of a cross-passage.

Moon was in groundling form and had a moment to wonder if this was an ambush. It wouldn't be the first time. When Moon had first arrived at the court, he and River would have been happy to see each other dead, and even though the dislike was no longer actively violent, they would never be friends. Before Moon's bloodline had been traced to Opal Night, River had made it plain that he thought a feral solitary of a consort was bad for the court and a waste of Jade's time. But it couldn't be an ambush now; River was in groundling form too, tall and slim with coppery skin and dark hair, and he was alone.

Queens took warrior lovers all the time, but Pearl had turned River away because he had, for many turns, taken the place of a consort. Now that she had a real consort again, there was no place for River. He was still in Pearl's faction, but he seemed to have lost much of his status in the court. The politics of status between warriors of different factions and alliances within the court was more difficult to navigate than inter-actions between any species Moon had ever encountered before, and he still didn't completely understand it.

"What?" Moon demanded. River had clearly been lying in wait here for him, knowing Moon tended to take this secluded stairwell that led up through the bowers when he wanted to avoid the central well.

River said, "I want to go with you. To look for Jade and the others." As Moon stared, he added, "You know why."

"I don't know why. I don't think about you, I don't care about you, nobody does."

That wasn't meant to refer to the end of River's time in Pearl's bed, but River clearly took it that way. River's voice tightened, and he said, "I have more experience than the others. I'm a better choice."

Pearl had sent River to follow them to the freshwater sea, on the trip to recapture the colony tree's seed, and he had come with them to the leviathan. They had been in a great deal of danger and all the warriors involved had proved themselves under pressure. Floret and Vine had gone on that trip too, which was why Moon wanted them now. Drift had been there as well, but Moon hated him worse than River. He said, "It'll be a good chance to give the others some experience."

River hissed in derision. "You're going to trust Jade's life to idiots who have never left the court before?"

"Better idiots than you," Moon said, but River's assumption that Jade was alive made his heart pound a little faster. It was stupid, since River knew no more about what had happened than anyone else, but it still made Moon feel better.

River snapped, "You know you can trust me to fight for the court. That's all that should matter." He hesitated, then set his jaw as if it took effort to get the next words out. "If I'm passed over, everyone will know that I'm nothing in this court."

Moon rubbed the bridge of his nose, and managed not to say that was River's own fault for trading so much on his relationship with Pearl that too many of the other warriors were happy to see him lose status. He hated River and River hated him, but they had fought together before, and River had argued, but never refused to obey Jade. And after their trip through the leviathan's insides, Moon knew River wouldn't break when confronted with the unexpected.

He didn't distrust the other warriors, but he needed to concentrate on finding the missing, not wonder if the warriors were going to listen to a consort in a crisis, or if they were going to do something stupid because there wasn't a queen to keep them in line. He didn't know that River would listen to him all the time either, but at least River wasn't stupid.

He growled, "All right. If Stone agrees." That last was pointless, since Stone's indifference to River's presence or absence was even more complete than his indifference to Ember, but it gave Moon the option to change his mind.

River hissed, partly in relief and partly in some emotion that clearly wasn't gratitude. But he said, "Thank you."

Moon snarled at him and went on up the stairs.

☾

As the sun set, the warriors brought the word that no sign or scent of any attack had been found in the colony tree's immediate vicinity. Moon wasn't surprised.

Moon was in the queens' hall to hear the news, with Stone, Pearl, Ember, a dozen warriors, and the Arbora caste leaders Bone, Heart, Bell, and Knell.

Floret finished describing the search and sat down, watching Pearl uneasily. Pearl was on her feet, facing the central well. She said finally, "So there is no attack."

One of the warriors in the back of the group stirred. Floret ignored him, but Pearl tilted her head in his direction. "Yes?"

Band, a young male warrior with more mouth than brains, said, "Just because they aren't out there today doesn't mean they aren't on their way. Maybe they meant to arrive after the foreign queen left."

Moon saw Floret give Vine a look of long-suffering annoyance, and Vine returned it. Apparently they had been hearing this from the younger warriors all during the search.

Knell twitched around to face Band and said, "As soon as the Ocean Winter party arrived, we'd know something was wrong. We would be on the watch for an attack. It doesn't make sense for them to plan to arrive later." He glanced at Pearl. "It doesn't make sense for them to send a queen in here at all, if they meant to attack."

"It doesn't make sense for them to plan an attack at all," Pearl snapped. She paced a few steps, lashing her tail. "And I don't believe they have."

Moon didn't believe it anymore, either. It had just been a faint hope to cling to, to make the terrible day bearable. He said, "I want to leave tomorrow, to go look for them."

Pearl turned to face him. One brow lifted in ironic comment, she said, "I know. You and Stone have already been recruiting warriors and Arbora to go with you."

Stone growled under his breath and started to speak, but Moon said first, "If we'd waited, you would have been angry about that, too." In Pearl's current mood, direct honesty seemed the best defense. "You know there isn't time to waste."

Pearl's spines twitched at his tone, and for an instant he was afraid she was going to say that there could very well be plenty of time, since the chance that Jade's group had survived was almost negligible. But she said, "I can't leave a consort in charge of a court."

Moon stared, taken aback. Even Stone looked a little startled. The warriors on the other side of the hearth looked horrified.

Ember said anxiously, "We're talking about Moon, right? Moon in charge of the court? Because I don't think I should be left in charge of the court."

It had occurred to Moon that Pearl might want to stop him from going, but it had never crossed his mind that she might want to go in his place. He hesitated, realizing it did make sense. Pearl was faster, stronger than Moon, her senses more acute. She and Stone working together would be a powerful force. But Moon would be stuck here, with no idea what was happening, unable to affect the search. *Maybe that's for the best*, he thought, though it hurt. Maybe he was too emotional, and it would cause him to make bad decisions. Pearl's record for making bad decisions wasn't so great either, but in this maybe her perceptions would be clearer than his. He swallowed down the protest and the lump in his throat, and managed, "You could. I'll do it. I'll stay, if you want to go."

The scaled furrows in Pearl's brow deepened as she considered it.

Then Heart said reluctantly, "Pearl, you can't. We have to let Garnet go eventually, and the word will spread everywhere."

Knell added cautiously, "And if something happened, and you didn't come back . . ."

Bone sounded reluctant, but seconded Knell. "With you gone, Moon would have to fight half the idiot warriors in the court. Not that that would be a bad thing, necessarily, but wearying for the rest of us." He added, "We can't chance leaving the court without a reigning queen. We just can't do it."

"'We?'" Pearl said with a hint of a growl, but Moon could see the moment had passed. "Very well." She regarded Moon again. "You leave tomorrow morning."

Stone pushed to his feet. "Then we have a lot to do tonight."

☾

Pearl called Moon and Stone to the queens' hall in the late evening. Moon had expected to be summoned for an argument about something at some point. But when they arrived, Pearl was facing Garnet and one of her warriors.

Uneasy, Moon took a seat beside Stone. Floret, Vine, and a few other warriors were seated behind Pearl. Behind Pearl's back, Floret leaned out and tried to give Moon some sort of warning signal involving lifted eyebrows, but he had no idea what she meant by it.

With something that might be malice or irony, Pearl said, "Garnet has a request."

Stone sighed. Moon eyed Garnet warily. She said, "I know you are planning to retrace your queen's route to Ocean Winter. I want my warrior Venture to accompany you." She gestured to the female warrior seated at her side, who was big, broad-shouldered even for an Aeriat, with copper skin and light-colored curling hair. She gazed back at Moon, her expression cool and confident.

This was an easy decision. Moon said, "No."

Garnet was taken aback. She turned to Pearl, who tilted her head in a way that clearly said, *he's not my consort.*

Talking to Pearl, Garnet said, "Venture is the clutchmate of our reigning queen. She will be helpful to you in your search, and if it takes you into Ocean Winter territory, she can explain your presence to our patrols."

Moon said, "And betray us at the first opportunity, if you're lying."

Venture's expression tightened, and Garnet's face worked as she struggled not to react. Garnet said finally, "The consort speaks freely."

Pearl's spines flicked once in amusement at Garnet's discomfiture. "It's his bloodline. His birthqueen is Malachite of Opal Night." She added dryly, "She also speaks freely."

Pearl had a love-hate relationship with Moon's recently discovered lineage. She hated that an older and more powerful queen than herself had a proprietary interest in Moon, but she loved to use Opal Night's patronage as a diplomatic club on other courts. Every court that might consider crossing Indigo Cloud was well aware that they weren't just dealing with a small struggling court recently re-established in its ancestral territory, they were dealing with Malachite, the Terror of the Western Reaches.

Garnet bared her teeth briefly at the implied threat. She said, "Allowing my warrior to accompany him will be a sign of good faith on your part."

"I don't have good faith," Moon said, "so why should I show signs of it?"

Garnet said pointedly, "Good faith on your reigning queen's part."

Pearl abruptly tired of the game. In a tone that meant that she was not interested in further arguments, she said to Moon, "Take her with you."

Moon set his jaw, but he had had a moment to consider that there had to be a reason Garnet wanted Venture to go with them. If Venture tried to sabotage the search party, then Moon would have proof that this was a plot by Ocean Winter. He said, "Yes, Pearl."

Pearl regarded him with narrowed eyes.

((

Moon and Stone spent the rest of the evening in the sitting area in the consorts' bowers, sending for various warriors and Arbora to talk to them about the journey, and waiting for word from the mentors.

The debate about how many warriors to take had been a serious one. Moon asked for twenty, though he didn't think Pearl would agree; that number came too close to leaving the court short of warriors, which they couldn't afford to do whether Ocean Winter was really their enemy or not. Pearl refused, but not for that reason. "If we send so many into Ocean Winter's territory, they can take it as an act of war," she said. "Then they would have a legitimate reason to attack us, if we can't prove they had something to do with Jade's disappearance. If they did, it may have been their plan all along." She added, "There's a reason we usually only send five warriors on trips to strange courts."

Moon conceded this point reluctantly, and they ended up with nine warriors: Floret, Sage, Serene, River, Drift, Sand, Aura, Briar, and Band. Sand was in Jade's faction, Aura and Briar were young female warriors who hadn't really picked a faction yet, and Drift was Drift. Moon had wanted Sage, who was also in Pearl's faction but was an easygoing older male who had never given Moon any problems. Pearl insisted on keeping Vine, since Moon was taking Floret, and Vine was good at keeping the younger males in line. Band was one of the younger males who needed to be kept in line.

Many of the hunters had volunteered to go, but Bone had chosen Bramble, Strike, Plum, Salt, and Braid. "They're the best trackers," Bone told Moon and Stone. "Sharp eyes and sharp noses." He squeezed Moon's shoulder, but didn't add any reassurances. They both knew too much about the dangers of the Reaches.

And then there was Venture. Moon wasn't sure what her purpose was, but he was fairly sure it wouldn't be to help them find Jade and the others.

When it was late and the colony was mostly quiet, Stone said, "Go get some sleep."

Moon shook his head. "I don't think I can."

"Do it anyway." Stone gave him a shove that was half annoyance and half affection. "We fly tomorrow."

So involved in planning the trip, Moon had almost forgotten that part. He left, grudgingly.

He didn't want to go to his own bower and he didn't want to go to Jade's or Chime's. Those rooms, empty except for the lingering traces of their scent, would just emphasize their absence.

And he didn't want to think about a future where their scent was all that he had left of them.

So Moon went down to the teachers' hall and then to the nurseries.

The nurseries were as familiar a place as Moon's own bower; more so, because he spent more time here. He stepped through the door with its carvings of fledglings and baby Arbora at play into the big low-ceilinged chamber. The spelled shell-lights lit a maze of smaller rooms opening off the main area, which held several shallow fountain pools for washing and playing. Everyone was asleep, the younger fledglings and babies curled up in nests of furs and blankets on the floor, along with the Arbora who watched over them.

Blossom, sleeping near the doorway, woke as Moon stepped inside and started to sit up. He motioned her to go back to sleep, and stepped past her to head for the room at the back of the nurseries.

In a cubby carved out of the wall, the Sky Copper clutch slept in a nest of blankets. Rill slept only a few paces away. She cracked an eyelid as Moon sat down, then subsided as she saw it was him.

After a few moments, someone stirred and then Frost crept out. She sat next to Moon and curled against his side. "I wish I could go with you."

It wasn't a surprise that the news had spread among the fledglings. "I wish you could come, too." Within the past couple of months, talking to Frost had become less like negotiating with a small angry hostage and more like talking with Spring, the female warrior fledgling from the last clutch of Amber, the sister queen who had died before Moon came to Indigo

Cloud. Frost was turning from child into adolescent, but also settling into the court. Moon said, "You're a little too small yet."

"I know." Frost sighed. "I can't wait until I'm big enough to go off to rescue everyone. Then you won't have to do it."

That was a dire thought. "Hopefully when you're big enough, everyone won't need rescuing so often."

Frost gave him a pitying look, as if Moon's unreal expectations made her sad but she wasn't going to try to disillusion him. She tugged on his arm. "Come sleep with us."

Moon followed her into the cubby where Bitter and Thorn were curled up. Moon took a blanket from the stack against the wall and lay down next to them.

Sleep was still elusive, but at least here he could relax, surrounded by the scents and soft sounds of the court's future.

☾

Moon woke before dawn with Bitter tucked up against his chest. He disentangled himself and eased away without waking the fledglings.

As he went up the back stairwell, he could hear the court stirring, earlier than normal. He ran into Heart in the interior passage to the queens' hall. She looked hollow-eyed and tired; she and the other mentors must have been scrying all night. Before he could ask, Heart reported, "No one sees death. We can't see what happened, but we don't see death."

"Do you see us finding them?" Moon asked.

Heart reached up to put her hands on his shoulders and said, "Not yet. But you know how this works. Sometimes we have to be . . . closer to the event, to get anything useful."

"I don't know how this works." Moon stepped back, putting a tight lid on his seething frustration. "Did you decide who's coming with us?" They were taking a mentor, both for scrying along the way and in the hope that Jade and the others were stuck somewhere with too many of the group wounded to transport.

"Merit will go." Heart pushed her hair back, betraying some frustration. "I wish I could, but—"

"I know." Heart was chief mentor and they needed her here. This wasn't like the journey to find the seed, where Flower had been their best hope. And Merit was the second most powerful mentor in the court. "It's a good choice."

Heart pressed her lips together for a moment, then met Moon's gaze. "Take care of him. I know he can help you find . . . whatever happened."

Moon just nodded. Mostly what he wished at this moment was that Flower was still alive. He didn't want a mentor he needed to take care of, he wanted a mentor who could take care of him and anyone else who needed it.

((

Not long after dawn, they gathered in the greeting hall, and Moon checked over the supplies everyone had collected. Even though they were bringing a mentor, Moon made sure everyone had flints to start a fire with, plus blankets, dried meat for emergencies, waterskins, and cutting tools. Even Band didn't need to have it explained to him that if he was separated from the others, it would be stupid to die because he didn't have anything to carry water with or no ability to start a fire.

Merit had prepared a pack with an extensive collection of dried herbs and powders, most for making medical simples and a few to help with augury, and the other things he needed for healing. "Where's your blanket?" Moon asked him. "And some spare clothes?"

Merit blinked, looked around as if he had misplaced them, then said, "Oh, I forgot."

As Merit hurried away to pack another bag, Moon rubbed at the incipient headache in his temple. Merit wasn't a fool by any stretch of the imagination, he was just intensely focused on his duty as a mentor at the moment. Moon would probably have to put another Arbora in charge of him to make sure he ate and slept regularly.

He looked up to see Venture watching him with bemusement, as if it was a very good joke to see a consort pretending to have any idea what a long journey might be like. He ignored her, since from Garnet's comments he was certain Ocean Winter knew of his origins, so Venture was just trying to deliberately provoke him.

Most of the court had gathered to see them off, but Moon was surprised to see Pearl drop down from the queens' hall. She usually didn't bother to watch anyone leave the court, no matter how important the trip.

The warriors had gathered, the Arbora had decided who would carry them, and Stone was already outside on the knothole's ledge when Pearl stopped Moon with a claw on his arm. Her voice low, she said, "Bring them back."

Moon felt his heart thump. Everyone had been carefully preparing him and themselves for the worst. He said, "I will," putting all the conviction he could into it, even knowing it might be a lie.

Pearl stepped back, and Moon led the others away and into flight.

☾

By agreement, Stone flew ahead to scout the most likely route Jade would have taken to Ocean Winter and look for signs of camps. Stone could fly much farther and much faster than Moon or the warriors, so he could search much more territory in a day than they could, crossing the path they thought Jade would have taken. His senses were far more acute, as well. They knew Jade had been in no hurry, and would probably have camped each night, and there would be evidence of that.

Flying through the suspended forest was normally a fascinating experience, with mountain-trees grown in all sorts of bizarre shapes, their platforms of entwined branches supporting small forests of their own, with waterfalls, pools, herds of different grasseaters, colonies of treelings, and all sorts of animals and strange fungi and plant growths. Now Moon was just impatient to keep going, to get out of Indigo Cloud's territory as quickly as possible.

Warriors should be able to fly most of the day without stopping, but because six of them were carrying Arbora, Moon called a halt three times, to let the Arbora stretch and rest briefly and so the warriors could trade carrying duties. Moon knew from personal experience that being carried in flight was uncomfortable, so at the first stop it was a relief to find that the Arbora were taking it well. Bramble and Braid had actually fallen asleep, and the others, having never been so far from the colony, were too interested in the scenery to mind the discomfort.

Stone still hadn't returned by the time the light started to fail, so Moon found a platform they could camp on for the night. It was a relatively small one in a large and gnarled mountain-tree, with a pool collecting runoff from the trunk. Several large spreading fern trees had taken root on it, and the grass had been recently flattened by a herd of grasseaters who must have reached it by one of the masses of entangled vines and roots that formed bridges from the other platforms.

As soon as they were set on their feet, the hunters spread out to search the platform for signs of dangerous predators. Moon sent Sand and Aura up into the fern trees to keep watch and made the warriors stay put until Bramble signaled it was safe.

With the hunters in charge, the minimal camp went together fast, including a dirt hearth and shelters constructed from stretches of fabric made water resistant with tree sap. There weren't any rocks handy, so Merit used chunks of mountain-tree wood that was too old and hard to burn, spelling them for fireless heat.

Moon sent River, Drift, and Briar with two of the hunters, Plum and Salt, to take a kill from the grasseater herd on a lower platform. He wanted to keep them all fed at every opportunity, to be prepared for anything. Once they were gone, Moon shifted to groundling, but he was so tense it didn't help much to lose the weight of his wings.

He paced on the flattened grass near the hearth. The other warriors distributed themselves around the camp, stretching and talking quietly. Floret stayed near Moon, as if waiting for instructions. He wished he could think of some.

Bramble brought the water kettle and set it on the wood to heat. Then Venture strolled up. She said, "You've done well today, consort."

There was no rational response to that, so Moon didn't make one. Bramble, crouched near his feet, hissed deep in her throat.

Venture asked Floret, "Are we waiting here for the line-grandfather?"

Floret, rather pointedly, asked Moon, "Moon, are we to wait here for Stone?"

Moon nodded, still lost in thought.

Floret told Venture, "Yes, we're waiting for the line-grandfather."

Venture gave her an ironic nod. "The consort spoke freely at the court, with a reigning queen present. Why not now?"

Floret tilted her head, annoyance turning to something more dangerous. Venture clearly had opinions about young consorts who thought they were qualified to lead bands of warriors and Arbora. But then young consorts who had never been feral solitaries normally would never have left the court without a queen to protect them, either the queen they had been taken by or a close relative. From Venture's point of view, Moon's presence here was foolhardy, rash, and scandalous, and Pearl was worse for allowing it. It was a valid point of view for a Raksura, except that Moon was tired of hearing about it. He said, "Venture, why are you with Garnet?"

A flicker of surprise and something else crossed Venture's expression. She said, "Queens are always accompanied by female warriors. Maybe with your background you haven't had that explained to you—"

"Queens are accompanied by their clutchmates. You're supposedly the clutchmate of the reigning queen. Did she not want you? Or does she not trust Garnet?"

Venture stiffened in offense. A queen usually kept any female warrior clutchmates close by; they were important advisors and companions. If Venture was with a daughter queen, then either the reigning queen didn't like her or she was meant to keep an eye on Garnet. Floret and Bramble watched her with fixed expressions. Bramble, in groundling form, flexed her shoulders as if raising spines she didn't have at the moment; under her sleeveless shirt her muscles rippled.

Venture showed her teeth briefly. "I was sent to Garnet as an honor to her," she said, and walked away.

Floret and Bramble both relaxed. Floret muttered, "If I said something that idiotic, Pearl would slap me so hard my fangs would fly out."

Bramble, dipping the metal travel cups into the tea, snorted. "I guess it's no fun for her to scratch when someone scratches back. Why did she ask you about Stone, Floret?"

Floret sat beside the hearth. "She's pretending she thinks I'm in charge to make us angry."

Bramble took Moon's wrist and put a cup in his hand. "Oh, wonderful. It's lovely enough having her along without that."

"I know. It's not as if we can't argue and fight on our own, we don't need an outsider poking us."

She was right about that.

Merit came to the hearth, carrying his pack, and Moon asked him, "Can you do an augury?"

Merit nodded. "I'll get started right away."

☾

Just before the light failed entirely, River and Drift and the others returned with two kills, big furry lopers. "We only need one," Moon said. They had all eaten that morning, and he didn't think an easy day's flight was enough to make them that hungry.

River dumped the second carcass and shook blood out of his frills. "Stone's coming back here tonight, isn't he?"

It was all Moon could think about, so he wasn't certain how he had forgotten that Stone was going to need to eat too. "You're right," he said.

River stared at him blankly, apparently having prepared a defense that now he couldn't use. Moon turned and went back to the hearth.

It was full night when Stone arrived.

Moon sensed him first, the near-silent movement of air over big wings, the sudden cessation of calls and hums and chirps from the night-dwelling insects, birds, lizards, treelings, frogs, and other creatures. A moment later the sentries hissed softly.

Merit had spelled some moss and wood for light, and Moon pushed to his feet as Stone's big shape appeared at the edge of the platform. Stone landed, shifted to groundling, and crossed toward the hearth.

Moon found himself holding his breath. Stone said, "I found their first camp."

"But not them," Moon said. He was half-expecting the tension in his chest to ease a little, but it didn't.

"No. No sign of any trouble, either. The firepit and latrine were covered, nothing left behind. No blood scent." Stone stretched and rubbed the back of his neck. "I searched all around it, down to the forest floor."

Moon reminded himself the goal today had been to pick up their trail, and Stone had done that. No one had really expected that they would find anything so soon.

☾

Stone returned to his winged form long enough to eat, then shifted back to groundling and joined Moon at the hearth. Floret, Serene, and Bramble sat nearby. The other Arbora and the warriors who weren't on guard duty kept a distance, some still eating and others already retiring into the shelters to rest.

Stone took the cup Bramble handed him and said, "How did it go today? Any trouble?"

"No." Moon knew he meant Venture. She had gone into a shelter with Aura and Band. "The only thing she could do is delay us. I'll leave her behind if she tries." He had thought Venture might fake an accident and claim to be too hurt to fly; if so, she had better be able to display an open wound or a broken bone.

Stone didn't comment on that. "I'll start out again after I get some sleep." He took a sip of tea and winced.

Bramble said, "It's good tea. You're too picky."

Stone ruffled her hair. "I'm a delicate consort."

Stone lay down on a blanket by the hearth, since he only meant to sleep for a few hours. Moon went into the little shelter the Arbora had built for him, mainly because he needed some privacy from the others. He could feel everyone staring at him, wondering what was going on in his head, if he would break down.

When Bramble crawled in after him, he said, "I want to be alone."

Bramble said, "Floret told me to sleep with you."

"What?" Moon stared at her.

"To keep Venture from trying anything," she explained.

Moon needed a chaperone about as much as he needed another arm. "I'll rip her head off if she tries anything," he said, exasperated.

"She doesn't know that." Bramble cracked her knuckles suggestively. "It's my job to make sure you don't have to rip her head off."

Moon said, "Are you serious?"

"We tossed lots for it and I won." Bramble handed him a blanket.

Moon threw the blanket down. "Fine. I'm not having sex with you." It was something many groundling races would have found inexplicable, that Moon would be considered compromised by the close presence of an infertile warrior from another court, but not by Floret, an equally infertile warrior and not by Bramble, a fertile Arbora. It didn't make much sense to Moon, either, at times.

Bramble pretended to look hurt. "I'm too proud to beg." With a little exasperation, she added, "Strike will be in here too, and the others right next to us." She sat cross-legged, facing him, and said seriously, "You need to let us protect you. Just let us worry about it, so you and Stone can worry about finding the others."

Moon rubbed his forehead, trying to get past kneejerk annoyance and think. "Why would Venture come after me? It would just make Ocean Winter look worse. If Ocean Winter isn't responsible for Jade and the others disappearing, it doesn't make sense."

Bramble said, "Venture might think we're lying about Jade's party being missing, that we're just trying to get an advantage over them. Or maybe you're right, this is all a trick to get rid of Garnet."

Moon hadn't said exactly that, but it was certainly a possibility. "If Garnet was away from Ocean Winter when Jade arrived, she might not know what happened. Or that anything happened." Then the reigning queen had sent Garnet off on this supposed trading trip, hoping that

Indigo Cloud would take revenge on her. Except that meant a large part of the Ocean Winter court had taken part in the conspiracy. That was a little much for even Moon's suspicious nature. "That doesn't sound likely."

"No, it wouldn't be a big plot, it would be a small one." Bramble straightened her blanket. "Say Ocean Winter is innocent. But when Garnet arrives at Indigo Cloud, Venture realizes this is a chance to get rid of her. So she gets herself sent along with us, then she does something to you. Pearl assumes it really is war, and she kills Garnet in revenge for you and Jade."

Moon lay down, head pillowed on one arm. The problem with that was that Venture would have to be willing to die to make it happen. And there would have to be a queen in Ocean Winter who would be willing to risk outright war with another court just to dispose of a rival. Even Halcyon hadn't included a war in her plot against Tempest. "Is that what the Arbora think?"

"Not really," Bramble admitted. "We talked about a lot of possibilities, but most of them are pretty unlikely."

It was true. The most likely possibility was still the one that they could do nothing about, that Jade and the others had been attacked during the night at one of their camps, and that none of them had escaped. Moon tried to push those thoughts away, knowing they would accomplish nothing except to make him even more crazy.

From outside the shelter, Stone growled, "Shut up and go to sleep," and that put an end to speculation for the night.

☾

Moon woke before dawn with Bramble's head pillowed on his hip and Strike curled up against his side. When Moon had first met Strike he had been an adolescent, one of the small group of Arbora hunters who had escaped the Fell attack on the old colony in the east. Now he was a little taller and broader, though still obviously young.

He shook them awake and sent them to get the others up. By the time the light changed from pre-dawn dark to gray morning, they were on their way.

The next two days went much the same as the first. Moon and the warriors flew through the day and made camp in the early evening. Then Stone arrived by sunset, having found another one of Jade's camps, but no traces of anything happening to the Raksura who had camped there.

That was the most nerve-racking part of the day, waiting for Stone to return, knowing the word he might bring could end all hope. Moon spent it pacing, trying not to pace, keeping an eye on the warriors' hunting efforts, and watching Merit scry. Merit was vague about his results, mostly because his results were vague. At least Moon knew he was trying hard, maybe too hard; all he did was scry, staying up most of the night to do so and sleeping during the day when he was being carried by a warrior. He staggered around blearily before they left camp every morning and had to be reminded to eat and wash. Moon worried that he would push himself too hard, but Merit insisted he was fine. "I know you're thinking about how Flower died," Merit said on the second morning. "But this is different. I'm a tenth her age." Moon just hoped Merit wasn't overestimating his stamina.

Venture was less trouble than Moon had expected; she mostly stayed with the younger warriors, who seemed overawed by her.

"Seemed" was the important point. On the third evening, when Venture was out hunting with Serene and Sand, Aura came to Moon's hearth to report to Floret.

"She asks a lot of questions." Aura wrapped her arms around her long legs. She was young, with dark copper skin and red-brown hair. Moon didn't know much about her, except that she had Arbora clutchmates. She looked from Floret to Moon. "Mostly about Jade, and the consort, and the court. I think she doesn't believe we're telling the truth, that Jade was still at Indigo Cloud, hiding somewhere. That this is all a trick to make Ocean Winter look bad."

Bramble, Merit, and Plum sat nearby, and River had crept close enough to listen. Floret frowned and glanced at Moon. "Can she really believe that?"

"It could be a trick," Bramble said, and shooed away a flying frog that had landed on her pack. "She knew you'd tell us."

Moon suspected Bramble didn't want to hear evidence to contradict her own theories. As of last night, the Arbora had arrived at a consensus that this was an elaborate plot by Ocean Winter to take over Indigo Cloud's territory. Moon had stopped listening at that point, so had no idea how this was supposed to be accomplished. He knew the Arbora were only doing it to occupy themselves on the long flights, coming up with complicated plots to argue the merits of over the hearth in the evening to keep from thinking about what might have happened to their lost queen and warriors. But it was too much for his already tense nerves.

Aura didn't agree. She said, "No. Venture thinks Band and I are idiots. She thinks we're so overawed by a reigning queen's clutchmate showing us attention that we can't think straight."

River made a skeptical noise. Moon ignored him and said, "You can think straight. What about Band?"

Aura twitched a little uneasily. "I know he's been rude to you," she admitted. "But he'd never go against anything Pearl wanted."

Everyone muttered agreement. Moon caught River's eye, and River gave him a cynical shrug. To Aura, Moon said, "Make sure he's not alone with her. I don't want her to take advantage of him." Band might not intentionally betray Pearl, but he might be talked into something stupid that would amount to the same thing.

Aura's brow furrowed and she nodded seriously.

Aura went to rejoin the others and the Arbora huddled up to discuss this new information. Floret sat down and planted her chin in her hand. "That's not good."

River said, grimly, "Did you really think this was an Ocean Winter plot?"

"I wanted to." Floret's answer was bleak.

Moon rubbed the bridge of his nose, partly to conceal his expression. He had wanted to, as well.

At midmorning on the fourth day, their route took them near the camp Stone had located the day before. On impulse, Moon called a halt at it, to give the warriors a chance to switch out who was carrying an Arbora, and to give the Arbora a chance to stretch and rest. The place was just as Stone had described, a large platform hanging on the outer branches of the left hand cluster of a gnarled twinned mountain-thorn.

Standing in the sparse grass near the small stream, Moon looked up at the twisted thorn branches arching overhead. They were huge, each one supporting its own little forest of small spiral and fern trees, of bushes and puffblossoms and every other kind of foliage that called the Reaches home. The second half of the thorn hung to one side, blocking off the view of the other platforms and sheltering this one. It didn't look so much like a tree as it did a giant carved puzzle, festooned with greenery. He wondered why Jade had chosen this spot; the lack of visibility was worrying, though it also meant that predators on the platforms of the other mountain-trees couldn't see the camp. *Maybe there was a storm and they needed the extra shelter.*

There was little sign left of Jade's camp, just the remains of the small firepit, the latrine spot, and a place where what had been a neat pile of fruit peels and other food debris had been turned into a nest by scavenging insects.

Moon paced absently around while the others explored or drank from the pond. *They were here*, he thought, *days ago*. Just days. But standing here he had the same feeling that he got in ancient groundling ruins: that an unbridgeable gulf of time separated him from the people who were once here.

A tiny spark of blue near the firepit caught his eye, and he dove for it as if he expected it to be the answer to something. But it was just a bead, stained with dirt. He dug around a little and found a few more and a frayed piece of thread. It hadn't been torn off in a struggle, but looked as though the loose thread had finally given way under the weight of the beads.

He should just drop them. He knew they weren't Jade's, and he couldn't remember if he had ever seen Chime or any of the others wear blue beads like this on their clothing. But he closed his hand around them and held them tightly, and after a moment dropped them into the bottom of his own pack.

(

That evening they made camp as usual, on a smaller platform in a young mountain-tree that had been crowded into a narrow column by more robust neighbors. It was the first platform Moon spotted in the area with a pond and no obvious signs of predators, and he couldn't be bothered to find one that was more comfortable. Seeing Jade's deserted camp had affected him more than he had expected, and his mood was so obviously dark that no one complained.

They set up camp, hunted and ate, and waited for Stone. Moon paced almost continuously, his nerves drawn tighter than ever. They were only two days from Ocean Winter at most. *We have to be close*. It was hard not to imagine scenarios where Stone discovered a camp with them all alive but the warriors too injured or sick to fly, and Jade guarding them and waiting for help to arrive.

But evening passed into dusk and then night fell, and Stone didn't arrive.

Everyone except the lookouts huddled in worried groups; no one went to sleep. Floret, Bramble, Merit, and Strike sat at the hearth with Moon, not speaking. It was so late, Moon was starting to wonder desperately what they would do if Stone was lost too. *Where is he?* If Stone had found Jade and the others, if he had fallen into the same trap, whatever it was . . . Moon knew vaguely the area where they should search for him, but the suspended forest seemed so unbelievably vast at the moment.

Of everyone here, Moon knew he was the one most used to being miserable for long periods of time, and even he felt like he couldn't take a moment more of this. He didn't know how well the others could cope.

Then from the branch above Drift called out excitedly, "I hear him!"

No one needed to ask who he meant. His skin flushed hot with relief, Moon was on his feet in an instant and reached the edge of the platform just as Stone landed. He winced away from the rush of air from Stone's wings, then Stone shifted down to groundling.

Moon demanded, "Well?"

Stone said, "I couldn't find a camp."

Merit had spelled some moss and clumps of flowers to light the camp, but Stone's expression was hard to read. "What—" This was a setback, but not an insurmountable one. "We'll just have to help you search tomorrow."

"Moon." Stone shook his head, weary, his shoulders hunched as if his back ached. "I couldn't find a camp, because there isn't one."

Moon just stood there. For a long moment, he couldn't understand what Stone was saying.

Stone stepped forward and put his hands on Moon's shoulders. "The camp yesterday was the last one."

Moon pulled away. Now he understood, but he didn't want to. "But . . . That camp wasn't disturbed. There was no sign of anything . . . "

"Whatever happened to them, it happened sometime after they left there."

Moon turned away, taking a few steps into the dark at the edge of the platform. He wanted to shift and throw himself into the night; he wanted it so badly his blood burned with the need to change. But he knew if he did it would be a sign of failure and weakness, and he would lose the confidence of the warriors and Arbora. *You can't afford to break down, even for a moment. You need to keep searching.* Jade, Chime, Balm, Song, Root, and Coil were depending on him.

He took a deep breath, forced down the sick disappointment. He turned back to Stone.

Stone hadn't moved, and it occurred to Moon that he must be exhausted. Moon took his wrist and tugged, pulling him over to the hearth. The warriors and Arbora had been staring in dismay; now they moved, the warriors hurrying to bring Stone a portion of the meat left from their last kill, Strike and Plum putting a kettle on for fresh tea.

Stone didn't groan, but he eased down to sit beside the hearth like he was in pain. Moon sat beside him. Stone put an arm around him, pulled him close, and gently bit his ear. He whispered, "This isn't over."

Moon nodded as he sat up, swallowing down the lump in his throat.

They sat there while Stone ate, the warriors and Arbora making occasional quiet comments to each other. No one asked what they were going to do now, a small mercy which Moon would be grateful for forever. When Floret asked Moon to approve her choice of who would stand watch for the rest of the night, Moon saw Venture watching them with a thoughtful expression. He wondered if she still thought they were acting all this out just to fool her. If she did, she must be a complete idiot.

When Stone was drinking tea, Merit cleared his throat.

Moon looked up, and Merit said, "I have an idea. I don't know that it will work."

Everyone stared at him and Moon's heart thumped. He felt a little like a drowning groundling who had been tossed a lifeline. "Tell us."

Merit took a deep breath and admitted, "I've tried scrying on Jade and Balm and Chime, trying to see where they are, and that's not working. I want to try something else."

Moon suppressed the urge to panic about the fact that Merit couldn't see where they were. He managed, "What else is there?"

"I want to try to scry the last camp Stone found. Maybe I can see what they did, what they talked about, to give us some idea of what to do next, where to search." He spread his hands. "I mean, we assume they just flew on in the direction of Ocean Winter. But if they didn't, if they went hunting, or if someone was hurt that night at the camp."

Stone had been listening intently. "Do it," he told Merit.

Moon couldn't tell if it sounded like a good idea or it sounded like grasping at the last fast-disappearing hope.

Merit nodded, both relieved and unnerved. "I need something from that camp first. If we can go back there tomorrow morning—"

"Wait." Moon turned for his pack, and rummaged in it for the beads he had found. "These were near the fire pit, buried in the dirt. I think they came off a shirt or a pack."

Merit held out his hand. "Is there still dirt on them?"

"A little." Moon was just glad no one had asked him why he had picked them up.

He handed the beads over and Merit carefully rolled them on his palm. Merit muttered, "I think this will work." He stumbled to his feet, still engrossed in the beads, and headed off toward the shelters. Plum and Salt got up and followed him without being asked. While Merit was auguring, he had no attention for anything else and needed to be guarded. The rest of the time he was so exhausted from the augury and the travel, he had no attention for anything else, and still needed to be guarded. The other Arbora were taking turns at it.

Moon blinked and rubbed his eyes, realizing he had drifted for a moment. He told Stone, "You need to get some sleep."

Stone sighed, packed his cup away, and got up. "Come on."

Moon shook his head. "I'm going to wait and see if Merit gets anything."

"You don't know how long it'll take him." Stone leaned down, caught Moon's arm, and hauled him to his feet. "Merit can sleep tomorrow, and you have to be able to fly."

Moon lay down in the shelter with Stone, not that he expected to sleep much. His thoughts chased in circles, and he slept for only moments at a time, until he woke in the deep gray-green light of early dawn to find Merit crouched just outside the shelter. Merit whispered, "I think I saw something."

☾

They flew back to the twinned mountain-thorn and reached it in the late afternoon. Moon chose the same landing spot as before, on the large platform where Jade's deserted campsite lay. Tree frogs, each nearly as large as an Arbora, leapt away at their arrival, a good sign that the platform was still clear of predators. The light was murky, making the spot look subtly different. Somewhere above the mountain-trees' multi-layered canopies, the sky had gone gray, threatening rain and throwing deep green-gray shadows across the suspended forest.

Despite its size and the complexity of the entwined branches, the mountain-thorn didn't have nearly as many platforms as a mountain-tree and they were much smaller. Most of them were above this one, dripping curtains of vines and other vegetation. Moon thought their quarry, whatever it was, would be in the branches and the canopy, not on the exposed platforms. He turned to Merit. "Which way?"

Serene had been carrying Merit, who staggered a bit as he recovered from the flight. He yawned, looked up and around at the branches arching over them. "I'm not sure."

Merit wasn't exactly sure what he had seen in his vision, either, but his scrying had shown that someone, maybe Chime, had seen something astonishing. Merit had explained, "And I think Jade spoke to someone – something—in the mountain-thorn near their camp. I feel like there's something there, some clue, and we just didn't see it because we weren't looking in the right place."

Something astonishing. Moon didn't like the sound of that. Astonishing things hidden in the bowels of mountain-thorns and other cave-like places were more likely to be dangerous than awe-inspiring. Merit had added, "But I don't see death. I mean . . . " He ran a hand through his hair. He was hollow-eyed with exhaustion. "I don't want to give false hope or anything. But I just don't get any sense of death, or pain, or fear . . . I get surprise."

"Surprise?" Stone repeated, his tone making it clear this was not the good news Merit seemed to think it was.

"Yes." Merit had nodded. "I keep getting the feeling that they saw something that surprised them."

Moon didn't like the sound of that, either.

Now Moon told the hunters, "Find a way into the canopy. They would have had some reason to leave camp." He turned to River. "You stay here with Drift and Briar and Venture." As River opened his mouth to protest, he added, "If we walk into the same trap the others did, somebody's got to get us out."

River's protest caught in his throat. "All right," he said instead.

Turning to follow the hunters, Moon wasn't sure why he had chosen River to guard his back. Maybe because he wasn't sure what River would do if they didn't return, whether he would come after them or go back to the court for help, but he knew River would do something. And because River was the one least likely to be influenced by anything Venture said. He had chosen Drift mostly to be company for River, and chosen Briar in case they needed a female warrior to do the thinking.

Venture didn't protest being left behind. She looked disinterested in the whole process, as if certain now that the whole thing was an elaborate sham for her benefit.

Looking for food was the obvious reason to leave the platform, and the mountain-thorn's enormous branches held whole forests of other trees, some of which probably bore fruit or berries. This platform was cradled in several branches, but the largest was the easiest and most obvious way into the canopy.

The hunters started up it, climbing to find a path along the branch through the thick clusters of symbiotic trees and plants. Moon, Stone, and the warriors followed, hanging back to give the hunters room to look for tracks.

Moon used his foot claws for purchase on the branch's uneven surface as it sloped upward. Within moments the relatively open platform turned into a tunnel formed by the thick foliage. The scents grew thick, too, with the mountain-thorn's own faintly sweet musk heavy in the air. Behind Moon, Stone hissed in annoyance and shifted to his groundling form; the passage was too narrow for his winged shape.

The constant birdsong, hum of insects and lizards, click and clink and call of treelings and frogs and everything else that lived here was louder in the closed-in space. The foliage cut off the breeze, and the humid air clung to Moon's scales. The branch curved upward and they passed under a thorn vine, the first of the outer layer. This one was as big around as Moon's wingspan, a good twenty paces, the thorns tall and curving with tips as sharp as his claws. This mountain-thorn had obviously never been tamed by a colony tree seed, and the big thorn vines grew all around the outer layer of the tree's canopy, making almost impenetrable knots.

Bramble hesitated, then motioned Braid, Plum, and Strike to split off to climb along the thorn vine to the next large branch. "Make sure they didn't go that way," she told them.

Salt said, "Why would they go that way?"

"I don't even know why they'd go this way," Bramble retorted.

Moon said, "Sage, Sand, Aura, go with them."

Wings rustled behind him as the three warriors swung up to the thorn vine after the hunters.

Moon and Stone continued down the branch after Bramble and Salt, with Floret, Serene, and Band spreading out behind them. Moon wanted to growl in frustration at their slow pace; Bramble was right, there was no way to tell if they were on the right path. They might have to explore the entire mountain-thorn.

Then Bramble said, "There's a patch of ground fruit through here. Melons and redflower. If they came this way, they couldn't have missed it."

Moon pushed past a bush to catch up with her. She crouched above an area of flowering vines that had taken over a relatively flat part of the branch, and the dirt was lumpy with the belowground fruit. Salt moved through the patch and pulled at the vines, looking for signs that some of the fruit had been collected. Salt muttered, "If they were looking for food, they would have taken some of these and turned back."

Moon looked around and tasted the air. Salt was right, if Jade's group had come in this way and found this ground fruit, there would have been no need to go any further into the canopy. But he didn't see anything that could be interpreted as surprising or astonishing, just multiple levels of tree-lined branches and hanging foliage, and colorful streaks as a swarm of tiny flying lizards fled. Disturbed by Salt's efforts, a clump of the small creatures that Moon thought of as walking mushrooms pulled their roots from the ground and ambled away. He could hear the other warriors and Arbora searching around the foliage, moving cautiously. Thinking aloud, he said, "But Chime was with them."

"So?" Stone said.

"So he'd never been on a mountain-thorn before, except for Emerald Twilight. He's never seen a wild one like this. Maybe he wanted to explore further."

Merit, who had been sticking close to Stone, said, "There are all kinds of rumors about mountain-thorns. That herbs and other things grow on them that don't grow on mountain-trees."

Stone stepped past Moon and motioned the Arbora to keep moving. "We know they left the camp and came in here. The why doesn't really matter."

Maybe it doesn't, Moon thought, following. Maybe he had been infected by Bramble and the other Arbora, trying to create complicated theories about everyone's behavior.

They pushed on, the two hunters keeping in contact with Plum's group with clicks and whistles. From what Moon could hear, Plum had followed the thorn vine down to another branch, and they were working their way along it now. Another giant thorn-vine loomed low overhead, then another. For a stretch it was nothing but thorns, and all of them crept carefully, avoiding the sharp points.

Then the branch curved around to run beside a platform, an open flat space in the green cavern. It held a glade of trees, with tall slender green trunks like thick grass stalks stretching up, topped with brushy caps of tiny gray-green leaves.

Salt hesitated. "Go across?" he asked Bramble.

Her eyes narrowed. "Stay on the branch."

The branch grew narrow, and it was awkward to make their way along it, but Moon could see why Bramble wanted to avoid the platform. The ground was soft and lumpy, covered with a white moss with a texture like bread dough. Six broad pathways formed by branches snaked away from the far end, all weaving away into the canopy in different directions. Moon's throat went tight. *And no way to tell which one they might have taken, if they even came this way at all.* They could be searching this mountain-thorn for a long time.

Moon spotted movement on an upper branch that curved around behind the platform, but it was only the second search group. Plum waved. *We should have brought more people*, Moon thought.

Then Stone hissed at the hunters to stop. They froze, and he said quietly, "You see it?"

Moon didn't see it, though he could sense faint motion somewhere ahead, a slight displacement of the air. Then his spines rippled. Something had moved.

Thirty or so paces ahead, a tree in the center of the platform shivered and unfolded its trunk.

Moon hissed a warning to the warriors behind him as the creature unfurled itself, tendrils lifted and expanded out as it turned toward them. It was at least fifty paces tall and even now looked like an animate tree, the central trunk supporting dozens of branches, all in fluid motion, sprays of tiny gray-green leaves fountaining up like a Raksura's spines.

One of the warriors growled, and Bramble said, "Moon—"

"Get back," he told her. Bramble made a sharp gesture to Salt and they both slipped back behind Moon. There wasn't much room to retreat on the narrow branch and he tried to watch the animate tree while looking for a gap in the thorns behind them.

Then Stone stepped forward. Moon said, "Stone—"

Stone said, "I don't think it's a predator."

Floret eased up beside Moon. "Stone, why do you think that?" she whispered.

Moon tasted the air. "The scent isn't rank." All he could smell was plant, that intense mixture of earth and green, the subtle odor that came from broken grass stalks.

Merit peered around Moon's elbow. "It's not just a moving plant, it knows we're here."

"It can't talk to us," Bramble said, her voice a whisper too. "It doesn't have a mouth."

"How do plants talk?" Salt wondered.

Stone took another cautious step forward, moving along the branch, closer to the tree. "I don't know, but all the Arbora need to shut up now."

Moon stepped with him, ignoring Floret, who was tugging on his spines to pull him back. "Stone—"

Stone kept moving. "If they wanted to kill us, they would have attacked us already."

A chill shivered straight down Moon's spine. He motioned the warriors to drop back, ignoring Floret's hiss of protest. Every slender tree on the platform was one of these creatures, the others just hadn't shown themselves yet. If Chime or one of the other warriors had walked into this . . . Except Stone was right, the tree-beings weren't doing anything except watching and waiting. He said, "This . . . is different and a little creepy, but it's not surprising or astonishing." He didn't think this was what had sparked Merit's vision. Plant people just weren't that odd.

Stone grimaced in agreement. "But maybe it—they—saw Jade and the others."

They picked their way forward along the branch. Plum's group watched anxiously from their overhanging vantage point, their spines twitching nervously. Stone stopped directly across from the tree. Its vines or tendrils or whatever they were waved gently, drifting on a current of air Moon couldn't feel. This close he could see dark gleaming spots on each of the leaves. *Those are eyes*, he thought, finding an uncomfortable resemblance to the multiple eyes of branch spiders and other similar predators. Then Stone said, "We're looking for people like us. Did they come through here?"

All around them, on the other tree-stalks, hundreds of leaf-eyes swiveled to regard them but none of them unfurled their limbs. The tree swayed toward them and it took everything Moon had not to leap backward. But its vines formed patterns in the air, shaping figures, spreading stalks from each vine to make more complex designs.

From behind them, Merit said softly, "Maybe that's how plants talk."

Moon watched the show until it ceased, then threw a despairing glance at Stone. Stone's jaw was set. Hoping against hope it was some sort of sign language he wasn't familiar with, Moon said, "Did that make any sense to you?"

Stone growled low in frustration, then made his voice even and soft again. "We can't understand you."

One of its tendrils, drifting near the ground, flicked up and brushed Moon's tail. He flinched away, his fight or flight reflex almost sending him right off the branch. The only thing that stopped him was that the vines jerked back too, as if the tree was just as startled as he was.

Stone tensed, but didn't flinch. He said, "See, I don't think it's dangerous."

"Just because it doesn't eat people doesn't mean it's safe . . ." Moon began, but the tree's tendrils stirred into motion again, making more complicated gestures. He gave up. The creature seemed more interested in talking than attacking.

Floret muttered, "It probably wants us to leave."

Merit eased forward cautiously, staring intently at the tree. "Let me try. It might understand this."

Merit stepped away from Moon and Stone, and the tree's leaf-eyes turned to follow him. He started to act out a pantomime of someone crossing the platform, and others searching for him.

Floret groaned under her breath, but Moon thought this was better than nothing. The tree seemed to be studying Merit closely, though it was hard to tell. Then it suddenly stretched out a tendril and brushed Merit's arm.

Merit froze, then shook his head, frills flying. He sat down abruptly and Moon lunged for him.

Moon got there a heartbeat before Floret, grabbed Merit's arm and hauled him to his feet. Merit blurted, "One came first, and went up the wind-curved branch toward the trunk. Others followed, and tried to speak to it. It didn't understand but it thought they must be after the first one, and pointed the way for them. And can we hurry up and go, our voices make it itch and we're keeping the children awake."

Above them the tree's vines waved in silent agitation.

Moon handed Merit to Floret and waved to the other Arbora and warriors to follow. "Thank you," Stone said to the tree, and they made for the branches on the far end of the platform.

They had to step down onto the spongy ground, but Moon was careful not to use his claws. *They were here.* Until now, he hadn't really believed it. He looked back to see the tree folding itself into its stalk again, some of its leaf-eyes still watching them.

"Wind-curved . . . which one is that?" Stone demanded.

Merit, tucked under Floret's arm, pointed to the third branch from the left. "That one!"

The branch arched up away from the platform before dropping down to wind away through the heavy greenery. Bramble hurried past them to lead the way.

As they climbed further away from the platform, Stone asked Merit, "You all right?"

"I think so, yes," Merit said, though he thumped himself in the side of the head as if trying to shake something loose. "Floret, you can put me down."

Floret did, but kept a hand on his arm to steady him. Merit said, "It doesn't see things the way we do. It touched Moon's tail because it looked like a vine. Our tails were the only things on our bodies that made any sense to it."

They were past the arch in the branch now and at the point where it turned away into the canopy, out of sight of the platform. Floret looked warily back, as if checking to make sure the trees weren't following them. "So that was who Jade spoke to in your vision? That tree person?"

Merit nodded. "I think so."

Moon hissed under his breath. This didn't make sense. "Why did one of them go into the canopy alone?" Jade had been here to go to Ocean Winter, not to explore, and she wouldn't have let the others get so distracted.

Stone shook his head, his intense frown suggesting that he found this behavior just as unlikely as Moon did. "Did it say if it saw them come back?"

Merit said, "No. But then, they didn't have to go back the way they came in."

Bramble echoed his thought. "Maybe that's what they did. The firepit in the camp was covered, so they must have come through here in the morning, after they had gotten ready to leave." Her attention was on the terrain ahead, as the branch wove down through the layers of the canopy. More thorn vines crossed above and below them.

Plum's group climbed down an intersecting branch and Moon signaled them to fall in at the back. Now that they knew Jade's group had taken this branch, there was no reason to split up.

The canopy grew more shadowy as they made their way further in. The Arbora found more patches of ground fruit and roots, and a whole grove of bevel nut trees clustered on a branch that crossed above them. Multicolored treelings fled shrieking as they passed, and tree frogs bigger than Moon hung from the thorn vines and stared unblinking at them. Thick clouds of insects swarmed around them, then departed, frustrated by their scales and by Stone's strange scent. Moon still didn't see any reason for Jade or Chime or any of the others to want to come this far into the canopy. There were lots of interesting things here, but only if you liked somewhat creepy plant life.

After they passed a place where giant blue globules of what might be mold or some sort of spore hung from the bottom of another branch, Band said, "Maybe the tree lied. It could be sending us into a trap."

Moon hissed in pure irritation. "We know that." It was a possibility, but Merit's moment of contact with the tree-person had given Moon the impression that it wasn't much interested in the strange creatures who had walked past it. It spoke like something that just wanted to get back to its own concerns.

Bramble said, "Maybe—"

Just ahead of her, Salt stopped abruptly and said, "Or maybe they saw this."

Moon pushed forward and stepped past Stone. Below their vantage point, the branch they stood on curved down into a giant open space in the center of the enclosing green foliage of the canopy. At first Moon thought they were looking at a jumble of fallen platforms, overgrown with vines and small trees. Then he saw shapes among the foliage that were too regular, straight lines, spirals, elegant curves. He thought, *It's a city.*

Something had built a city inside the mountain-thorn, an enormous city.

There were hisses of awe from the Arbora and warriors. It filled the entire center of the canopy, a space big enough to comfortably fit Indigo Cloud's colony tree. It must have been built on a series of branch platforms, but Moon could see fragments of weathered white and gray stone through the vines and creeping greenery. Even buried by plant growth, the structures were huge, monumental buildings. There were round towers, so covered with moss they looked like trees. The city must have been too heavy for the platforms, because the supports had clearly collapsed at some point, sending buildings sliding into each other, crushing the platforms below. Structures had crashed into branches, held up only by the heavy entangling vines. There were broken bridges, toppled columns.

"This isn't anything Raksura would build," Plum said, in a hushed voice. "Is it groundling? Or Kek?"

"Kek couldn't move those stones, not without help," Bramble muttered, sounding confused.

"Maybe the tree-people built it," Sage said. "Before they were trees."

Then Floret said, "Moon, is it like the city under the island? The fore-runners' city?"

Floret had waited for them on the surface, and hadn't seen the under-water city for herself. Moon said, "No. I don't think so." He hoped not. "I'd have to see the inside."

Then Stone said, "It's a flying island. It fell here. That's what twinned this mountain-thorn. It hit the trunk and split it in two."

Moon shook his head, about to say that it was impossible, that it was too big for a flying island city. But the longer he looked at it, the more sense that made. The high arch of the canopy overhead had long grown back, so there was no sign of the damage it must have done to the upper part of the tree. But it would explain the stone construction, and the way it had collapsed.

He took a step forward, and Stone caught his wrist. His voice low, Stone said, "If Chime saw this, he would have wanted to get closer."

"But he would have known that might be dangerous." Chime, having stumbled on this place, might have been hard put to pass it by, but he would have been too wary to linger. Moon didn't know about Coil, but even though Jade, Balm, Song, and Root didn't exactly suffer from any lack of curiosity, they all knew better. "Merit, is this what you saw in your vision?"

Merit boosted himself up on his foot-claws to see past Serene, and she pulled him forward to give him a better view. "It must be. It's a huge surprise."

Stone was giving Moon a look, and Moon didn't need to ask what he meant by it. While this city was bizarre, it wasn't nearly as astonishing as some of the other strange things he knew Jade and Chime had seen. *They went inside*, Moon thought, *and that's where it happened.*

☾

Chime should have known better, Moon thought. Somehow he knew it was Chime who had gone into this place and that Jade and the others had followed. Chime should have known better, which made him think that Chime must have had a reason to come here. Maybe not a good reason, but a reason nonetheless. *Or something forced him to come here.* Something or someone the tree-person hadn't seen.

Like the creature imprisoned in the underwater city.

The thought made Moon so cold it locked his joints for an instant and he slipped while climbing over a knot in the branch. That Band was the one who caught his arm to steady him didn't make the moment any less awkward. Fortunately Band looked more confused than anything else and said nothing to call attention to the incident.

Chime would have known to resist a mental voice like the one that had drawn the Fell to the coastal island. And the other warriors all knew enough about that voice to be frightened by it and tell Jade. *So maybe it didn't just ask Chime to come to it, maybe it forced him somehow.*

He reminded himself they didn't know anything yet, that just because the city was old was no reason to suspect that it was a prison for some horrible creature. There were stories all across the Three Worlds about the flying islands and their former inhabitants, all vague, all contradictory, probably because the flying island people hadn't been one species, but many, all very different from each other. Moon had never heard a story about monstrous creatures imprisoned on islands, either. But that didn't set his mind at ease.

By the time they made their way down to a branch near the city's fringe, the gray-green light was deepening into heavy gloom. It was only the edge of evening, but there must still be clouds overhead and the mountain-thorn's canopy blocked so much light that night would always fall early inside it.

Moon burned with frustration but there was no way they could start the search now. The city was already in deep shadow, and even with Merit spelling light for them, it would just be too dangerous. Walking into the same trap that Jade and the others had sprung wouldn't help anyone.

Trying to distract himself, Moon told Stone, "If they're in there somewhere and just . . . stuck, we might be able to see firelight once it's full dark."

Stone didn't say any of the things he might have said about the unlikelihood of a trap that provided access to food and water and firewood but no way out. He just grunted thoughtfully. "There's no telling if they're inside. They might have found something here that led them somewhere else."

Moon had thought of that. It was one of those possibilities that meant they were alive, but just not acting in any way that made sense.

Moon didn't want to split the group overnight, so he sent Aura and Sage to take the alternate route along the thorn vine and to lead River and the others back here.

They made a camp on the intersection of two broad branches, about a hundred paces above the edge of the nearest crumbled stone terrace. The building it still supported was a mostly featureless lump under the vines and moss, but Moon could make out three large domed towers, linked by a bridge at least three stories tall. This close, they could see there were openings into the lowest level, big circular portals into blackness, each one three times Moon's height. With most of the city cloaked in shadows and the canopy going dark around them, it wasn't a reassuring sight.

It was already too late to hunt, but they had eaten last night and the Arbora collected some melons and other ground fruit and roots from the scattered patches on the surrounding branches. With all the forage available, if any of the inhabitants of the city had survived the fall, they might have been able to live for a time here.

He said that to Bramble, as they sat beside the pile of thorn chunks Merit had spelled for heat, so the Arbora could make tea and bake some of the roots. Bramble said, "That would make sense."

But Merit, sitting nearby and spelling clumps of moss for light, said, "I don't know. I feel like this place is old."

"Of course it's old," Bramble said. "But whoever lived here still had to eat." She glanced at Moon. "And if it is a forerunners' city, like the underwater one you found, then the people who lived here probably ate the same kind of things we do."

"I mean very old," Merit explained. "So old it didn't fall into the mountain-thorn. That it fell, and the mountain-thorn just grew up around it."

Bramble frowned at the city, considering it. Moon wasn't sure why it should be startling. He had seen the underwater city, grown out of the base of the coastal island, older than the Raksura and the Fell. And the Opal Night mountain-tree had grown through the ruins at its base.

But this just seemed wrong, here in the heart of the Reaches.

In a little voice, Strike said, "If it's a forerunners' city, does that mean it has a monster trapped in it too?"

Everyone went quiet and still. So quiet and still, Moon knew the question had already occurred to all of them; Strike had just been the only one to dare speak it aloud.

Bramble gave Moon an apologetic grimace, aware that bringing up the possibility repeatedly probably hadn't helped. Stone, apparently agreeing, flicked a fruit stone at her and bounced it off her head. As Bramble shook her frills and rubbed her temple, Moon said, "It doesn't mean that. Even if it is a forerunners' city, and there's nothing to say it is, it would be a wild coincidence if it had something that dangerous locked up somewhere in it."

Everyone rustled and settled their spines, at least pretending to be reassured. Then Venture, who had been staring at them in incomprehension, said, "What's a forerunner?"

Aura looked at Moon, he nodded, and she said to Venture, "I'll tell you the story," and took her aside.

The conversation went off into tangents then, and Moon stopped listening. He had to fight the urge to shift and fly into the city. They needed light to search, he told himself. They might not be looking for trapped Raksura but for a sign that something had lured or taken them away to somewhere else.

Merit collected his pack. "I'm going to try scrying again. Now that we're here, maybe I can get a better vision."

Moon glanced at him, then hesitated. Merit was hollow-eyed with exhaustion, and it brought back a vivid memory of how Flower had looked, scrying their path to the leviathan and the stolen seed. He reminded himself that Merit was young, and had seemed confident about being able to take the strain. He hoped Merit was right. No one had ever mentioned anything about young mentors dying from too much use of their powers. He said, "Band, Serene, keep an eye on him."

☾

It was late at night when Moon twitched awake to quiet footsteps on the moss and dead leaves. He had fallen asleep sitting up beside the hearth, and the quiet footsteps were Merit's.

Four warriors were on guard on the branches above, but the others were scattered around close to the hearth, drowsing or just sitting up, too nervous to sleep. The Arbora had put up one shelter, but no one was using it. Stone had stretched out beside Moon, in his groundling form. He was breathing deeply, but Moon didn't think he was asleep.

Merit made his way unsteadily around the hearth, followed by Band and Serene. Stone sat up, soundlessly. Merit knelt in front of Moon, wavered, and Moon gripped his shoulder to keep him upright. Merit was small for an Arbora and had always looked a little fragile, at least to Moon; it was reassuring to feel the solid muscle under his hand. Merit said, "I'm sorry, I just saw the same vision again," and folded forward into Moon's lap.

Moon caught and cradled him, felt his chest to make sure he was breathing well. As the other Arbora gathered around, Serene said, "He tried very hard."

"I know." Moon handed Merit off to Plum, who carried him to the shelter.

Moon looked toward the city, holding back a groan of despair. The place was huge, and after so long they could easily miss the subtle traces of tracks. Some idea of where to start the search would have been . . .

Moon blinked, then squeezed his eyes shut and opened them again. It was a faint glow, in the center of the darkness where the city lay. It was partially obscured, so he must be seeing it through a window or door. He nudged Stone and pointed.

After a moment, Stone made a thoughtful noise in his throat. "Not fire. Not a mentor's light, either."

The color was wrong for a mentor's light, too white. Not that Jade had had a mentor with her to make one. "We didn't see that in daylight." Even the murky green light inside the canopy hadn't revealed it, and if it had been lit, they should have seen some sign of it when twilight fell. "I don't think it was lit until some time after dark." He raised his voice a little to say, "Sage, did you see that light?"

Sage was on watch, on a branch about thirty paces up, where the dim moss-lights wouldn't hinder his night vision. He answered, "What light?" The other warriors on guard muttered a puzzled agreement. A slight rustle of wings sounded as Sage dropped down beside Moon. "Where— Oh." He told Moon, "The angle is wrong, we can't see it from up there."

Moon tried to visualize where the light was, from his memory of the city, but he hadn't looked at it long enough to have a strong recollection of detail. He said, "Jade and the others would never have seen this." They would have approached the city in daylight.

Stone grunted an acknowledgement. "They could have walked up on whatever is making that light, with no warning."

The Arbora had all drawn closer to listen. Moon heard slight, edgy movement from the warriors. Strike whispered, "But why did they go in at all?"

"Good question," Stone said, not patiently. "Still don't have an answer, no matter how many times someone asks it."

Moon hissed in frustration. "One of them got lured in somehow, and the others followed."

There was a murmur of agreement from Bramble and Plum and the others. Salt added softly, "Chime likes to learn new things, but he doesn't want to die, either."

"Or," Floret pointed out, "they didn't go in at all. We don't know that they did."

Unexpectedly, Venture said, "Do you really think that? Isn't it too much of a coincidence that in the last place we know they were, we find this?"

Everyone turned to stare incredulously at her, where she sat beside the hearth with Band and Aura. She drew back in confusion and affront, then said, "Am I wrong?"

Exasperated, Floret said, "You've made it clear you thought this whole search was some kind of trick to start a war with Ocean Winter."

Venture half-sighed, half-hissed. "I'm not a fool."

Moon supposed that was all the apology they were going to get for Venture's skepticism over the past days. He got to his feet, and shifted to his winged form. "I'm going in there. If the light goes out by morning, we'll never find where it was."

There was an immediate chorus of protest. "Moon, you can't—" Floret began at the same time as Venture said, "Consort, that's madness—"

River stood and shifted. "I'll go with you."

Drift caught River's wrist and hissed in alarm. "No! You don't have to prove anything." River might be bent on getting back into a higher position among the warriors by risking his life, but Drift clearly wasn't happy about it. "You don't have to take such risks when you don't—"

"I do." River's expression was such a mix of impatience and anguish that Moon had to look away.

Stone's low growl of annoyance cut off the protests. He stood up. "Moon and I will go. The rest of you stay here."

Venture said, "But consorts shouldn't—"

Stone turned, stepped across the hearth, and stood over her. Venture shrank back. He had ignored her until now, and he had been mostly asleep during the short times he had been at their camps, and maybe she had made some incorrect assumptions about his temperament. Stone said, "Do I need to repeat myself? Because I don't like to do that."

"No, line-grandfather," Venture said quietly.

Stone looked around at the others. Nobody argued.

Moon walked to the edge of the branch and climbed out on a knoll. Facing away from Merit's moss-lights, his eyes adjusted rapidly and he could make out more of the city, the elegantly curved outlines of the towers in what dim moonlight filtered through the mountain-thorn's canopy. He spread his wings and dropped. There was little air movement this far inside the canopy, and he had to flap rapidly to reach the top of the nearest structure. He landed lightly on the sloping surface of a roof, the mossy stone cool under the scales of his feet. Stone's silent shadow passed over him.

Moon couldn't see the light anymore, but he had marked the location. It was above his current position, several hundred paces further in. He crouched and leapt into flight again.

Long hops and short flights took him up across the city, an occasional ray of moonlight revealing a roofed terrace with the columns formed into the shape of willowy trees, a sculpted hollow in a plaza that might have been a pool or a fountain, curved bridges between towers still miraculously intact. He landed at the base of a large structure and looked for the light again. It was shining from a jaggedly round opening a short distance down the side of the domed wall of the next tower, throwing a white glow on the heavy coating of greenery below it. He tasted the air deeply, but could scent nothing but mountain-thorn and treelings.

Stone landed beside him with a soft whoosh of air and scrape of scales. He shifted down to his groundling form and tugged on Moon's frills, telling him to follow. Moon stepped after him, not sure why Stone wanted to be a groundling in this place.

It was too dark to see the shape of the opening against the wall, but Moon felt the change in the air as they passed through it. The slight sounds of their footsteps bouncing off the walls told him the room was cavernously large. Listening hard, he thought it was empty.

Then suddenly it wasn't. He heard running water and felt a cool breeze. The scents carried on the air were intense and dry and floral, as if it had swept into the chamber over fields of tall grasses filled with flowers, not through the branches of the mountain-thorn. There was movement around him, brushing past him, close enough to detect acrid sweat on skin and sun-warmed fabric and the sensation of falling–

It was gone. The room was dark, silent, filled with the smell of dirt and stagnant water and the mountain-thorn, the air still and heavy and damp. The breath had stopped in Moon's throat and he had to gasp to get his lungs working again. His arm hurt and it took him a heartbeat to realize it was because Stone was gripping it, so hard even in his groundling form that Moon's scales were grinding together. Moon managed to whisper, "You saw that?" Except "saw" was the wrong word. It hadn't happened in front of his eyes, it had all happened in his head.

"Yes." Stone let go of Moon's arm, and rustled in his pack. After a moment he pulled out a small rock spelled for light. Its glow lit a floor stained with moss and broad treesnail tracks, strewn with beetles and windblown dirt, but still showing patterns of blues and grays flecked with metallic silver.

"It was the past," Moon said. "I think." Those scents came from somewhere else, somewhere far across the Three Worlds from the Reaches. Either that or the city was capable of suddenly shifting to a new location and back in the space of a heartbeat, something he wasn't quite ready to rule out.

Stone's expression was more annoyed than awed. He said, "If that keeps up, it's not going to make searching this place any easier."

Moon had to agree. He wondered if that brief moment of vision was what it felt like to be a mentor. He wondered what Chime had felt when he had stepped in here.

Stone handed the rock to Moon and stepped away, shifting back to his winged form. They crossed the large chamber slowly, the light reflecting off arches overhead. They passed through two more doorways into two more cavernous rooms, and Moon began to feel cautiously optimistic that they had seen the only vision the city had to offer. Then they reached a gap in the floor, a long deep trough bisecting the chamber and disappearing under the curved wall to the left. It was only about twenty paces across, and Moon assumed it had once held water. He crouched and leapt to cross it—

And hit a midair wall like a curtain of air, heavy smoky scent, babble of voices, fear not his own squeezing his heart, and the terrifying sense that something had just rushed past not far below his feet.

The vision vanished when Stone knocked him out of the air and dumped him on the dirty floor past the trough. The light-rock bounced out of his hand and slid across the floor. Moon sat up, shook his spines, and gasped, "That was a bad one."

Stone grunted assent, warily scanning the chamber around them.

Moon pushed to his feet, still unsteady, and found the light-rock. He looked back at the trough, a slice of deeper shadow in the dark floor, and wondered what he would have seen if he had fallen into it. He had the sense that something had traveled in the dark space, and that something had gone terribly wrong with it.

Stone growled low under his breath and moved on. Moon followed.

They crossed the chamber, slowly and cautiously, then went through a passage that connected several smaller chambers, all silent except for the occasional hum of insects. From the curve of the walls, they were inside one of the larger towers. Then Stone hissed sharply at Moon.

Moon shifted to groundling, tied the light rock up in the tail of his shirt, then shifted back. In the renewed darkness ahead, he saw the shaft of dim light, a white glow shining from below.

They crept forward, until Moon saw that the light shone up from a hole in the floor, a good fifty paces across. From the cracks and crumbling pavement around it, the shaft wasn't meant to be there. He looked up to see it mirrored the jagged hole in the curved roof he had spotted from outside.

Then Stone whispered, "There." A moment later, Moon saw it too.

Something small lay crumbled on the floor, its shadow etched by the glow from the opening. *Not a body,* was Moon's only thought as he started forward.

Stone caught his arm and jerked him back. Moon realized Stone was right and hissed at his own stupidity. The thin layer of moss and dirt on the floor might show tracks, though Moon couldn't see any in this strange light. Stone shifted to his winged form, stretched out one long arm, and hooked the object with his claw. As he lifted it, Moon saw it was a bag with painted designs on the tough fabric, the kind with the tie-down flap that most of the Raksura in Indigo Cloud used.

Stone brought the bag toward them and dropped it into Moon's hands. The flap was already open, and Moon dug through the contents. There was some food, dried fruit and berries, and a cake of tea, all of which bugs had gotten into. But there were also a couple of copper and leather bracelets, a roll of pressed paper, a wooden pen, and a cake of ink wrapped in leaves.

"It's Chime's," Moon said. None of the other warriors would have brought writing materials to give them something to do during a visit to another court, and he knew Chime had planned to try to get access to the Ocean Winter libraries.

Stone, just a dark shadow against the light, stretched further, extending his wings slightly to balance himself, and craned his neck to look down the opening.

The light went out. Stone flinched back with a startled growl. Moon shifted to groundling just long enough to untie the light-rock from his shirt tail. He held it up, heart pounding, but nothing leapt at them out of the opening.

After a moment, Stone hissed, and held out his hand. Moon put the rock into his palm. Cautiously, Stone stretched forward again and dropped the rock into the opening. Moon couldn't stand it a moment more. He jumped up, caught hold of the scales under Stone's right wing and climbed up to his collar flanges. Hooking his claws on them, he twisted around to look.

The light-rock fell, its glow giving Moon heartbeat-long glimpses of shattered tile and crumbled stone floors and walls, some covered with encroaching vines. It was impossible to tell if something had burst up through the ruined island or had tunneled down. Then the rock tumbled into overhanging leaves, broad and deep green, and vanished.

Stone grunted thoughtfully, and Moon climbed down his back and dropped to the floor. Stone eased away from the edge, then shifted to groundling. In the now complete darkness, he said, "Should have brought more of those rocks."

"We can go back, get Merit to make more," Moon said, then remembered that Merit was probably still unconscious. He thought of the vines and foliage half-glimpsed below, and said, "This is old. I mean, nothing tunneled up here from below just to come after them."

Stone said, "We have to wait for daylight."

Moon felt a growl build in his chest, and suppressed it. There was no other choice.

☾

Moon and Stone retreated back to the camp, told the others what they had found, and then withdrew to talk over what they meant to do once dawn broke. The others seemed determined to sit up through the night talking. At least they were quiet, mostly because Moon told them if anybody woke Merit, he would personally beat them into unconsciousness. He was hoping Merit would be recovered enough in the morning to use the bag in his scrying.

Sitting near the hearth with Stone, Moon went through the contents of it again, feeling the corners carefully to make sure they hadn't missed anything. He doubted Chime had had time to leave any clues about where he had disappeared to, but he unrolled the paper anyway.

He was expecting to find the sheets blank. Chime shouldn't have had much time to write anything down during the journey; Moon had been assuming he had brought it along to give him something to do at Ocean Winter. But the pages were covered with notes.

It was all in Raksuran, of course, in the red-brown ink the Arbora made. The oiled skin wrapped around the roll had protected the pages from the insects that had attacked the food. Moon thumbed through it all, frowning, trying to pick out something he recognized. He could read Altanic and Kedaic and bits and pieces of other groundling trade languages, but his knowledge of Raksuran was rudimentary at best. It didn't help that it was insanely complicated compared to the symbols of a trade language. He knew all the letters now, and could read the names of most of the people he knew, and pick out a number of simple words and sentences. But nothing Chime had written here looked simple.

He glanced up to see Stone watching him with an ironically lifted brow. Moon hissed in frustration and shoved the papers at him. "Fine, you read it." No one knew Moon couldn't read Raksuran, except maybe Thorn. But perhaps Stone had guessed. Or if he had ever had a suspicion, this had confirmed it.

Stone took the sheaf of papers. "You should have that little scrap that Pearl took teach you. At least then he'd be good for something."

"Leave Ember alone," Moon said, by habit.

"Quiet." A line of concentration between his brows, Stone sorted through the papers, turning so the light from the nearest moss bundle fell on the pages, reading sections here and there. "Most of this isn't recent. He's been writing down everything he's found out about changing from an Arbora to a warrior." He looked more closely at one page. "Looks like he's been copying things out of court histories, but I don't recognize these names."

That made sense. "I know he spent some time in the libraries at Opal Night while we were there. He's been looking for stories about other Arbora who turned into warriors."

"Hmm," Stone commented, and kept reading. After a while, he handed the papers back to Moon. "I can't see anything there about this city, or even this whole trip." Stone sighed. "He thought he could talk his way into the Ocean Winter libraries?"

"Yes." Moon rolled the papers up again and carefully tied the protective skin back around them. Going through the motions, as if he was certain Chime would eventually get these back.

Stone glanced at the shelter, then across the hearth where the nearest Arbora and warriors were talking quietly. He lowered his voice. "You've thought about why they might have gone into that place."

It was an oblique reference to the creature at the forerunners' city, and the way it had drawn groundlings and Fell to it. "Yes. But . . . if there was something here that could trick, or force, Raksura to come to it, why hasn't it done it before? And why can't we hear it?"

"Because no Raksura ever camped close enough before. Or no Arbora-turned-Aeriat who's been able to hear and see things others can't for the past turn."

Moon growled under his breath, because he wanted to argue and couldn't. "You think a creature made that light? And if it did, why did it stop making it?"

"Stop asking questions that start with why." Stone looked toward the dark shape of the city again. "I don't know. If it called Chime to it and the others followed . . . "

"Why is the light still lit? Why didn't we find the creature, or find their bodies, or—" Moon ducked Stone's slap at his head.

Stone growled, "Go to sleep."

Moon retreated away from the hearth, knowing that Stone had reached the limit of his patience for speculation. But Moon was too jumpy to even try to sleep, and ended up going to sit with the others and rehashing all their theories with Bramble and Salt. If he got any sleep that night, it was purely by accident.

As soon as dawn started to lighten the gloom under the canopy, Moon sent the Arbora to gather hanging moss and make bundles of it using the cords from the shelter tarps. They also needed to eat, so he sent Drift, Sand, and Aura off to hunt on the platforms of the nearby mountain-trees. It took all his patience to wait, but by the time the light had brightened into full morning, they had four grasseaters to share, several bundles of hanging moss, and Merit had stumbled out of the shelter. Moon explained the situation while Merit was eating his share of the meat, and Merit spelled the moss bundles into light for them.

Moon divided the group, leaving two of the Arbora, Salt and Strike, and two warriors, Sage and Aura, to guard Merit while he scryed over Chime's bag. The others he and Stone took to the city.

They landed on the balcony Moon and Stone had found last night. In daylight, they could see worn carving under the coating of moss and greenery, but the encroaching vines had bitten into the stone and obscured most of it.

They had warned the others about the voices and images that had seemed to pervade the place last night, but as they crept through the doorway, there was nothing. It was just an empty ruin. Moon wasn't sure if that was a good thing or not, if the visions only came at night, or if he and Stone had changed something in the ruin just by entering it.

As they moved through the chambers, the spelled light-bundles shed a warm yellow glow onto the walls, revealing reliefs that were partially covered by furry green or white mosses and creeping vines. They were all complicated designs of circles crossed by lines, with square intricately detailed glyphs that must be writing or symbols of some kind. It looked intriguingly like navigational charts that Moon had seen ships use off the coast of Kish, but far stranger and more complex. In a low voice, Braid said, "Merit might be able to make some sense of this."

"Maybe," Plum said doubtfully.

They made their way through the other chambers. In dim light, the trench was just an empty channel running through the floor, no more than thirty or so paces deep. The bottom held stagnant water, a variety of encroaching water plants, and some white and gray swimming things that had too many limbs to be fish, but without the hard carapaces of shellfish. The Raksura all leapt across it without incident.

When they reached the big chamber, it was dimly lit by the large hole in the arch of the ceiling. In daylight Moon could see it was cracked and crumbled around the edges, and had clearly been caused by whatever had crashed through the floor.

At Moon's direction, the warriors held the light bundles at various angles, until they could see the faint marks in the moss around the hole. Bramble, Plum, and Braid examined them closely.

Avoiding the scuffed tracks on the floor, Moon stepped as close as he could to the opening, Stone moving to stand beside him. The crumbling edges of the ceilings and floors of the level below this one were visible, all the way down to what should be the lowest part of the city, where it was obscured by a small jungle of greenery. There was no sign that anyone had climbed, or been dragged, either up or down it. But Moon thought he, or any Raksura, could probably do it without causing much, if any, disturbance.

Keeping his voice low, Moon said, "We couldn't see our light once it fell past those trees. How could the light from below shine up through them? Our light wasn't that bright, but still . . ."

Stone said, "Maybe it wasn't a light."

Then from the other side of the hole, Bramble said, "There's no scent left, but these are foot tracks. I can't tell if they're Raksura, but—"

"But Chime's bag was here," River interrupted, moving his moss bundle onto his other shoulder. "So they must be—"

"I know that," Bramble growled. "I'm trying not to make any assumptions. And don't move the light."

"There were at least five of them," Plum said. She had nearly flattened herself to the floor, studying the faint scuff marks. "That fits, too."

Bramble added, "They came from across the room, that way, from the same direction we did."

Plum stood and moved around the hole in the opposite direction. "And they didn't leave. But something did. This whole side shows scrapes and scuffles. Whatever it was, it didn't cross the floor to leave." She frowned and looked up at the hole in the ceiling. "It's as if it went up and out that way."

Moon's breath caught in his throat. *No bodies*, he reminded himself.

The others just stared. Sand made a noise of distress, and Briar said, "So . . . they went down there, and then something big came out? And we don't know if they came out?"

Plum looked around to see the reaction she had caused and said hastily, "As far as I can tell. The tracks are confused, I can't really . . ." She made a helpless gesture.

Bramble and Braid circled around to Plum, and Bramble crouched to look more closely at the floor. She said, "That's what I'm seeing, too."

"We could get into this shaft from below, couldn't we?" Plum said. She scraped her claws against the tiles. "What's under this floor?"

Moon shook his head. Stone had tried that earlier, climbing around the outside of the structure and into the tangled greenery and jumbled rock below it. Stone said, "As far as I could tell, the levels under this one are collapsed, like this part of the city fell first and the rest got pulled down around it. It's too much to tunnel through, and I couldn't see any openings."

"Pulled down?" Plum said, and exchanged frowns with Bramble and Braid. Arbora in general knew far more about building things than Aeriat, and Plum had been a teacher before she had decided to turn hunter. "That's odd, isn't it?"

Bramble's spines flicked thoughtfully. "I'm trying to imagine something falling like this, and . . . wouldn't it more likely break into pieces in the air and come down in sections?"

"Yes, but a flying island wouldn't necessarily do that," Braid said, warming to the subject. "It's the mineral chunks inside the rock that keep them aloft, right? So if the mineral pieces stopped working at different times—"

They continued the debate and Moon hissed impatiently under his breath, and said to Stone, "We have to go down there."

"Not we." Stone folded his arms. "I'll go. I'm waiting to hear if Merit got anything off the bag."

"You're not going without me." Moon had had this argument before, and always won it. "What if there's a passage too narrow for you to get through? Are you going to have to come all the way back up and get me?"

Stone gave him a look that would have turned poor Ember's bones to water. Moon got that look a lot, so he was used to it.

River said, "I'm going too. You can't stop me."

Drift groaned in dismay, and Floret said wearily, "Pearl is not sleeping with you again, so just get over it."

River dropped his light bundle and rounded on her, snarling. Stone's sharp growl cut across the chorus of outrage on River's behalf and agreement with Floret.

Fortunately, before Stone took more precipitous action, someone called out from above. "Hey, Merit needs to speak to you. Should we come down there?"

Moon looked up to see Aura and Merit peering over the edge of the hole in the dome. He flicked his spines in assent, his heart beginning to pound.

Aura took Merit under her arm and dropped down to the floor. As she set Merit on his feet, the others reached them and gathered around. Merit looked past them toward the hole in the floor. "That's it, then." He turned to Moon and Stone. "Chime—I think it was Chime—went down there because he thought he was helping someone. I think the others followed him."

That was what they had expected, but it was still nerve-racking to hear it confirmed. Moon said, "So something lured him down there." It might be another creature that the forerunners had imprisoned, but it could also be some kind of predator, using this place as a trap.

"Maybe," Merit said. He looked around the big chamber again, narrowing his eyes as if to see past the shadows. "This place . . . feels dead and alive at the same time. Those things you saw last night . . . That has to be a part of it. I don't understand how Chime's visions work since he's changed, and neither does he, but I can't believe he wouldn't have seen those too."

"Are you seeing them?" Moon asked.

Merit grimaced, as if he had hoped to see them and regretted the missed opportunity. "No. I don't know why any of us would see them last night but not today."

Stone said again, "The light's not on."

They all turned to look at the opening. Under the dim daylight and the glowing moss, it was just a hole in an ancient ruin, nothing more. Moon said, "We have to do it."

Merit let out a breath and settled his spines. "I'll go with you. I don't want to, but . . . I think I'd better."

River had moved close to listen. Stubborn as a rock, he said, "And me. I went through the gullet of that leviathan with you, you know I won't panic."

Drift said, "River . . . "

River rounded on him. "I'm not going to do anything stupid and get myself killed. But I've got experience the rest of you haven't."

Drift subsided reluctantly.

That was what Moon had been thinking, so he didn't argue. Whatever River's reasons were—and Moon was fairly sure the motive was to get himself a place in Jade's faction—he could be depended on in a situation like this.

Stone stared at nothing for a moment. It would have been impossible to tell for anyone who didn't know him well, but Moon could see he was clearly having some internal debate. Then Stone growled in a way that made everyone except Moon flinch back a little and said, "Get the packs together."

☾

Stone went first, taking his winged form to flow down over the edge of the opening like a dark cloud. Moon went next, with River and Merit behind him.

The walls were crushed and crumbled, lined with broken tiles and broken shards of paving stone, coated with streaks of moss and dripping with water. The climbing was easy, with plenty of claw-holds. These were the levels below the tower floor, crushed down by the weight of the structures above them. Whatever had fallen through here had cut through the thick slabs like a claw slicing through fruit. Moon climbed around a pillar wedged into the wall, forming a gap that allowed a glimpse into the darkness between the compacted floors.

It wasn't like Jade not to leave anybody outside the ruin if she had had to go in after Chime. She might have left one or two warriors behind to get help if the rescue went wrong, but then something had happened to them as well. Moon could easily imagine her taking Balm and Song with her, leaving Root and Coil outside. He didn't want to imagine what had happened next.

The light from above began to fail, but Merit was spelling chunks of rock and broken tile as he climbed, leaving a trail of faint light behind them, just enough to see what was ahead. Vines curled out of the gaps in the broken stone, with parasite bulbs and feather spikes and other plants that could thrive just on the air studding the ruined walls. Snails bigger than Moon's head were tucked under the leaves and multi-colored miniature versions of tree crabs skittered away from his claws.

Below, the foliage was getting thicker as they drew closer to the lowest depths of the city. The lights Merit created shone down on layers and layers of big air ferns that had grown out across the width of the opening, blocking any view of what they were climbing into.

Then from above Merit whispered, "Stop! Do you hear that?"

Moon froze in place. Below him, Stone stopped, the end of his tail curled inquiringly. Listening hard, all Moon heard was dripping water, a buzz of insects somewhere nearby, and the faint sound of the others' breathing. He looked up at Merit, who balanced easily on the collapsed wall, next to River. Moon said, "Hear what?"

Merit frowned slowly, and started to climb again. "A rushing sound, like something falling . . . I think we're getting close. That must have been something like the visions you had last night."

Below, Stone turned one baleful eye to glare up at them, then started to climb again, the foliage barely rustling as he passed.

Then Stone's tail twitched and he halted abruptly. Moon hissed to warn Merit and River, then crept slowly down toward Stone, past the thick growth of ferns and vines. He climbed down alongside Stone's dark shape, staying close to the wall.

He could see just enough to tell the foliage abruptly stopped here, leaving most of the passage open, just a big dark empty space. Then Moon narrowed his eyes. Not quite empty.

Near the center of the space there was a shape, an unmoving shape, just hanging in midair. Moon's heart squeezed tight with dread. He turned and slipped back up the wall, past the barrier of ferns, to where River and Merit clung to the narrow ledge. River flattened his spines, reading something off Moon's expression. Moon said, "I need a light."

Wide-eyed, Merit handed him the bulb of a parasite plant, spelled to glow. Moon tucked it in between his side and his wing and climbed back down.

Beside Stone again, Moon hung with one hand and his foot-claws, and held out the light.

The figure was Coil, the fifth warrior Jade had taken with her. He hung suspended in the air as if he had just leapt into flight, wings partially extended, hands out ready to brace for a landing. When Moon had realized the shape hanging in mid-air was a Raksura, he had expected to see it caught in some net, or impaled on a piece of debris. But Coil was just suspended there, like a fish suspended in water, like a bug caught in amber. Not coherently, Moon said, "But . . . What?"

Stone's body rumbled with a nearly soundless growl, then he adjusted his position on the wall. A heartbeat later he shifted to his groundling form. His feet were balanced on a ledge barely a hand-span wide and he had one hand jammed into a gap between the crushed floor levels. Moon braced to grab him if he fell, but Stone balanced easily. He said, "He's trapped in something, we just can't see it."

"But what . . . " Moon let that go, as there was obviously no point in asking what Coil could possibly be trapped in. He tilted his head, trying to see Coil's face in the dim light. He could see a gleam on Coil's eyes, as if they were open. He couldn't make out his expression. Moon took a deep taste of the air, but he didn't scent death. "Could he still be alive?"

There was a rustle above them as River and Merit climbed closer. Stone leaned back and told them, "Careful. Stay close to the wall."

River eased down beside Moon and hissed in astonishment. Merit gasped, his spines flicking in agitation. Groping for an explanation, any explanation, Moon said, "Merit, do you know what this is?"

"It's . . . " Merit's expression was baffled and frightened. "No, but . . . there's something here. I mean, I can't feel it, I can't see it, but I hear voices. I don't know what they're saying . . . "

"Can we get to him?" River craned his neck, trying to see better. "There's nothing to perch on, but if we got a rope—"

"No." Stone jerked his chin. "Look up."

Moon twisted to look. The jumble of intertwined creeping vines, the air ferns, the parasite bulbs and other plants stopped about twenty paces up. Stopped as if a knife had cleanly sliced them off. Moon looked around at the walls. There was still moss and some small plants growing out of the gaps between the floor levels and the cracks in the stone. But nothing extended out into the center of the shaft. He felt the wall behind them and found a loose fragment of tile. Gently, he tossed it toward Coil.

The tile flew for about ten paces then started to slow, as if it had fallen into honey. It slowed to a gradual stop still several paces from the tip of Coil's wing.

Like a bug caught in amber, Moon thought again. "A rope would never reach him, and he's . . . too stuck for us to pull out."

Stone studied the scene again. His expression was opaque, a sure sign he was deeply disturbed. He shook his head slowly. "If this is what it looks like . . . "

"The others are lower down." Moon swallowed back bile. "Merit, can you tell if Coil is alive?"

"No. But—" Merit leaned forward a little, narrowing his eyes. "Look at his right foot, fourth claw."

Moon squinted. Hooked on Coil's claw was a sprig of greenery, that must have caught there from his last perch on the wall. After a heartbeat, Moon realized what was wrong with that. "It's still green. It's not even wilted." The fragment of vine was frozen, just like Coil.

River sucked in a breath. "Even if they've only been here a day, and we know they were here longer, the vine should have wilted—"

"There's a chance he's alive. They're alive," Moon said. He didn't want to speculate any further than that.

"Stay near the walls, and only climb where the plants grow," Stone said. He leaned away and shifted back to his winged form, then started down the wall again. Moon ducked to avoid his tail, then followed with River and Merit.

Every nerve itched now, both with renewed fear of what they might find and terror that whatever this effect was would catch them too. *How are we going to get them out? What if we can't get them out?* The thought was agonizing. They didn't even know what they were dealing with.

Forty paces down they found Root, suspended in the air, posed as if he had just leapt off the wall and was aiming for a perch on the opposite side of the shaft. They all paused for a moment, then Stone rumbled in his throat again and kept climbing.

The shaft grew wider, and the lights Merit spelled didn't reach far across it. But when he looked down, Moon could see shapes in the dimness.

The shaft ended in a large space. Not a cavern; a pocket formed in the bottom of the city.

Stone hesitated, and Moon tasted the air again. There was still no scent that didn't belong, no hint of movement in the deep shadow. And there should be movement. This section of the city must be resting on part of the mountain-thorn's trunk. It should be alive with insects, and teeming with the things that fed on them.

Merit plucked some moss off the wall, held it until it began to glow, then dropped it. It fell, scattering fragments, about sixty paces or so to land on a cracked pavement. Stone made a low noise in his throat. Moon said, "More, Merit. As many as you can."

Merit spelled more moss and parasite plants to glow, dropping them down into the chamber. When he had almost denuded this whole side of the shaft, the light gradually revealed the figures standing below.

Moon had been expecting this, but it still squeezed his heart and stopped his breath.

Chime was near the center of the chamber, in groundling form, standing frozen in place. Merit started to spell and toss shards of tile and fragments of paving stone toward the still figure, illuminating more of the space as the glowing fragments gradually slowed and came to a halt in midair. Jade, Balm, and Song were about twenty paces away from Chime, toward the other side of the shaft, perched on a triangular wedge of fallen wall. Jade and Balm faced Chime, looking down on him. Song stood behind them and half-turned away, as if she had just heard something. All three were in their winged forms.

Stone pushed off from the edge of the shaft and dropped to the pavement below. The faint sounds as he moved around were almost imperceptible, but Moon could tell he was carefully exploring the chamber. If Stone walked into something and was trapped as well . . . Moon asked, "Merit, are you having any more visions?"

"I can still hear voices, off and on." Merit stirred uneasily, and a little dislodged moss and dust drifted down. "Not any words I can understand. They're like echoes, as if the people speaking are a long distance away."

Then Stone came back into view, settled his wings and shifted to groundling. Moon strangled the urge to tell him to be careful, and dropped down beside him. Merit's spell-lights had marked the whole side of the danger area, but it still made his spines twitch to land so close to it. River followed, with Merit tucked under one arm.

Stone paced along the perimeter, then sat on his heels near the edge, studying Chime.

River set Merit on his feet and flicked his spines in agitation. "How did they get all the way down here? This magic, or whatever it is that freezes things in place– why did it stop Coil and Root up there, but let the four of them get here?"

"Whatever is doing this let Chime come down here." Moon's voice came out low and harsh. "It lured him down. Then when Jade and Balm and Song came after him, it . . . did this. Jade must have left Root and Coil up at the top, and they heard something that made them follow, and they fell right into it."

River twitched and settled his spines. "So where is it?"

Then Stone said, "I think it's still there."

Moon stepped to his side, crouching down so he could see what Stone was seeing. Merit scooted over in beside him. From here, Moon had a better view of Chime's face. With Chime in his groundling form, it was easier to read his expression. His lips were parted, and Moon thought his eyes were focused on some point only a few paces away from him, his chin tilted up . . . Moon let out his breath in a hiss. "He was—is—talking to someone."

Stone nodded. "And Jade and Balm. They're looking at it too."

"So it's hiding itself from us." Moon sat back. "It knows we're here."

"Or . . ." Merit eased back from the edge. He shook his head. "I think there are a lot of things in here we can't see."

Moon felt a chill pass through the skin under his scales, an aborted flight reflex. He took a deep breath, making himself think. "It didn't happen just because they were here. This thing has been here a long time."

Long enough to keep the jungle from growing down through this part of the shaft. "And that light. The one we saw last night. What does that have to do with it?"

Stone growled under his breath. "We'll have to wait for tonight, to see if it comes again, and find out."

☾

It was still some time until dusk, and they knew the light might not appear until much later. Moon sent River up the shaft to tell the others what they had found, while he waited with Stone. Merit withdrew a short distance away and tried to scry.

Hoping for some clue, Moon explored the shadowy corners of the chamber, taking one of Merit's spelled rocks for light and tossing broken tile pieces ahead of him to make sure he didn't walk into a trap. The walls were covered with faded paint and inlay, too stained by turns of dripping water and mold to make out anything but the occasional elegant curve. They had been crushed along the top and tilted sideways at an angle that didn't look at all stable, and Moon found several broken supporting columns strewn around. But a huge single slab of stone had come through the ceiling at the back; braced against the floor, it seemed to have kept the big chamber from collapsing. Now it was supported by a wayward branch of the mountain-thorn that had grown up through a crack. Vines had worked their way in as well, and small colonies of parasite plants. They crept across the floor, stopping well short of the frozen area.

Moon gave up and returned to the others. Merit had found a spot further back in the chamber, cleared off a space on the floor and spelled all the plants around him to glow with light. The paper and ink from his bag was spread out and he huddled over it, writing rapidly. Stone still sat near the edge of the frozen area and Moon sat down beside him. After a time, Stone cocked his head, and a few moments later Moon heard the faint sounds of more than one Raksura climbing down the shaft. Moon sighed, but he had expected this. "Who do you think is with him?"

"I'm betting on Floret, and probably Bramble," Stone said. He added thoughtfully, "Bramble bit me in the head when she was barely three days old. It was an omen."

Moon was exasperated enough to growl. "I left Floret in charge up there."

Stone snorted at this example of naiveté. "Warriors obey queens. Us they obey as long as we're standing there staring at them."

"I noticed." Moon pushed to his feet.

River, Floret, and yes, Bramble appeared on the wall of the shaft and one by one carefully dropped down to the chamber floor. Only a little sulky, River said, "I told them not to come."

"We know," Moon said. Floret and Bramble stared at the tableau, Bramble sidling cautiously to the right and craning her neck to try to see better. He could tell from their expressions that they were in shock, so he didn't say anything.

After a time, Floret turned to him. "But when the light comes back, it could do this to you."

Moon said, "Believe me, there is no horrible possibility that I haven't thought of already." And it was very much a possibility. The light had to have something to do with whatever had happened here. It might be a trap, a lure. But whatever it was, they had to find out, and the only way to do that was to stay down here and watch for it.

Floret shook her head. "I just . . . I don't know."

Bramble said, "Can't we try to get a rope in there and haul them out?"

From behind them, Merit said, "You can try. It won't work."

Bramble hissed in frustration. "I want to try it anyway."

Floret looked at Moon. He pressed his hands to his eyes. "Go ahead."

They tried. It involved bringing down almost all the rope the Arbora had with them, searching for the right size of rocks, and an attempt to build a sling to hurl them. For a stretch of time it seemed it might work, which made it all the more painful when it finally failed. The frozen area was more solid toward the center where the four Raksura were trapped; none of their attempts made it any closer than the spell lights Merit and Moon and Stone and River had already thrown into it. Bitter disappointment made Moon finally break down and shout, "Get out of here or I'll kill all of you!"

Stone, who hadn't moved or spoken during any of the preceding efforts, stirred. "Moon, go sit down. The rest of you—" He turned to survey the group of abashed warriors and Arbora. "Go back up there and wait."

Moon went and flung himself down on a patch of vines, fuming. The others left reluctantly.

☾

Moon hadn't thought he would ever sleep again, but he woke with a start, some internal sense telling him that the sun had just set. He sat up, bleary and confused for a moment. He didn't even remember shifting to groundling. He scrubbed at his ear, wiping moss away.

Nearby, Stone sat up and stretched. "We need to move back further."

He meant move further into the vegetation line. Moon got to his feet and helped Merit gather up his spell-lights and notes and drawings. It gave him a chance to look at what Merit had been making diagrams of, not that any of it made sense to him. Even if Moon had been able to read any of the Raksuran script, the drawings looked more like calculations. It gave Moon a little spark of hope, that Merit was apparently working on something. But he was afraid to ask what it was; if Merit was just passing the time, Moon didn't want to know it right now.

They settled again some thirty or so paces back, among a soft patch of air ferns. Moon shifted to his winged form, just because he felt safer that way.

And they waited. Moon was wide awake now, and settled into the patient trance acquired by turns and turns of hunting through various parts of the Three Worlds. The chamber was quiet but not completely silent; he could hear the soft distant calls of nightbirds and treelings and other creatures that lived in the lower depths of the mountain-thorn, a creak as wind stirred the outer branches and vibrated through the trunk. Merit leaned against his shoulder and sighed.

Moon wasn't sure how much time had passed, when Stone tensed. Then Merit sat up straight and whispered, "This is it."

Moon couldn't see it at first, then he realized the shadows were no longer black but gradually lightening to gray. At first it was easier to see Chime, then slowly the air around Jade, Balm, and Song grew brighter. *As if whatever was causing the light, was closest to Chime.* The glowing tiles and clumps of moss Merit had dropped into the area grew dimmer, not because they were fading, but because the air around them was growing lighter.

Then out of that light more shapes formed, shadows at first that grew gradually more solid. Like the Raksura, they were frozen in place. They were groundlings of some kind Moon had never seen before. Their skin was a slick blue hide, their heads smooth and almost fish-like, with lipless downturned mouths and only a small bump with a single nostril for a nose. Except unlike fish and other amphibians, the expressions in their wide eyes were easily read. There was terror there, and shock, and confusion.

Not unlike what Moon was feeling right now. *What happened here? What did Chime find?*

They were dressed in loose drapes of different fabrics, filmy and light or heavy with brocade. Their appendages were willowy and their hands long-fingered and delicate. Moon couldn't tell how many limbs they had; it seemed to vary from individual to individual. They stood all around the frozen area, some huddled in groups, others apart, some half-crouched, all staring upward. Except the one who stood a few paces from Chime. He—she—it stood with one arm uplifted, hand extended and slender fingers spread as if to catch something that was falling towards its head. And it stared directly at Chime's face.

Moon pushed to his feet slowly. He stepped forward and hit a wall of sound and motion, voices crying out, the sour tang of fear heavy in the air, choking dust, smoke, figures ran, turned, clung to each other—

Stone grabbed his arm and Moon hissed out a breath, dazed. The chamber was silent, empty except for the still figures, but the silence was like the echo after a great crash of sound. Stone stood to one side, and Merit to the other. Merit's expression was rapt, the light pulling glints out of his scales. Moon managed to say, "Did everybody see that?"

"Yes." Stone's voice rumbled in his chest. "So what do we think about this?"

Moon gathered scattered wits. "When the light's glowing we can see the past. They have to be the people who lived here, and this was the moment the city was destroyed."

"It's not the past, it's not a static image. It's a moment, happening over and over again." His voice almost dreamy, Merit said, "It has to do with that one in the middle. The one Chime was talking to. I was hoping . . . I was hoping the light would show us more."

With forced patience, Stone said, "Merit, you need to explain that for us."

"This is . . . I think Chime is talking to a groundling sorcerer. I think he's the one who did this." Merit leaned forward and waved a hand to indicate the whole frozen area.

It didn't make sense. Moon said, "If he did this, he trapped himself too. And no one's looking at him except Chime. The other groundlings are all looking up."

"Whatever they were afraid of, it was up there, coming toward them," Stone agreed. He eased forward, trying to see up the shaft without getting too close to the spell area. "There it is," he said grimly.

Moon stepped up beside him and craned his neck to see. Not far up the shaft was the ghost image of a boulder. It filled most of the shaft and the light seemed to be coming from it.

"Yes," Merit said, twitching with excitement. "The rock we find on the forest floor. We've always thought it was there and then the forest grew up around it. What if it fell from the sky, long before the mountain-trees grew here? If this city was passing over this area when the rock started to rain down, and it was hit—I think the working or spell the groundling sorcerer did was meant to save the city, or at least try to save the groundlings who were down here."

Moon sorted through that and it made him see the whole scene in a different light. "So a big rock fell from the sky and hit the city, smashed it down out of the air, and he was trying to stop it. And instead he . . . froze everyone here." If that was the case then it wasn't a trap, it was a terrible mistake, made in a desperate moment.

Merit frowned, twitching his spines. "It didn't freeze them, it preserved them, but not the way he meant it too. It's like he created a temporary world where they all lived, but he wasn't strong enough to actually make it happen. So it's stuck here, always on the verge of happening. The visions, the things I heard, they're echoes of the event, all coming from what he did."

Moon understood some of what he was saying, but not all. "Then why can't we see them when the light isn't showing?"

Merit's expression went bleak. "Because it's been too long. Time is passing in the moment, but slowly, so slowly. It might have taken hundreds and hundreds of turns, but they died. Their bodies aren't there anymore. They rotted away."

Moon blinked. The pavement the groundlings stood on wasn't bare, it was littered with debris. He had seen it as just the same broken tiles and stone rubble that covered the rest of the floor, but were there bones there, rotted wisps of fabric . . .

Stone narrowed his eyes. "So how did Chime get stuck in the middle of it? And the others."

"Maybe it has to do with the light. Maybe . . . " Maybe the light made the frozen area, or the moment, or whatever it was, more permeable. Moon bent and picked up a tile fragment and tossed it into the area. But like the others, it just fell more and more slowly until it finally stopped.

Merit said, "It does have to do with the light. It's all that's left of the falling rock that struck the city, the moment of impact, the moment this sorcerer tried to stop. Every day it repeats, the moment almost happens but not quite happens, and the light is visible. That must mean the wall between the moment and the real world is very thin during this time." He turned to them. "Since Chime changed, he's been able to hear and see things that he shouldn't be able to. It's like his mentor abilities changed too, and we just can't understand how. I think the magic left here drew him in, and when he saw the light he followed it. He saw a vision, but instead of just seeing it for an instant, he was able to walk into it, into the moment, and doing that opened it up long enough for the others to follow him."

Moon's throat was dry. "The groundling sorcerer saw him, and Chime spoke to him."

"But the opening didn't last." Merit lifted his hands, claws sheathed, and made a gesture of dropping something. "It all went back to the way it was."

Stone said, "Do they know what's happened? Any of them?"

Merit's spines shivered. "I don't think so. If anyone knows . . . it would be the groundling sorcerer."

"So what do we do?" Moon was glad his voice came out mostly even. It sounded hopeless. It sounded like they were trapped inside this moment of death suspended forever.

But Merit said, "My lights went in there, and they're still glowing. Which means a mentor can get their power inside the moment." He looked at Stone. "We need more mentors. How far away is Ocean Winter?"

☾

After some experiments to make sure the light hadn't made the danger area any wider, they climbed up the shaft to tell the others about the plan, such as it was.

While Stone and Merit returned to the camp outside the city to get ready to leave, Moon had River lead Venture down the shaft so she could see the situation with her own eyes. It was Floret's idea, who said, "She believes us now, but it'll just be easier for them if she can tell her queen that she saw it herself. And it'll help her be able to describe it. I mean, I couldn't describe this to anyone if I hadn't seen it myself."

Moon would be staying here, mostly because he felt his lack of experience with Raksuran courts was a real disadvantage now. A normal consort would know exactly how to navigate this situation without a queen's protection; Moon had no idea. It seemed simpler to send a line-grandfather and a mentor, since the usual rules of court etiquette tended not to apply to them, and Venture to attest that they were telling the truth. He was mostly worried that Ocean Winter would take violent exception to Garnet being held in Indigo Cloud as a hostage, and insist she be released before they agreed to help.

He asked Floret, "Do you think the Ocean Winter queen will be angry about Garnet?" He was debating the idea of sending two warriors back to Indigo Cloud to tell Pearl the situation, but he could only spare two and it just wasn't safe for so few to travel through the suspended forest.

Floret thought about it, frowning, and finally shook her head. "Yes, but by helping us she'll get such a big advantage over us that it'll benefit her court in the long run. And it isn't like Garnet or her warriors will be hurt or uncomfortable. Just very bored and anxious."

"It's not like anyone at Indigo Cloud will do anything rash," Bramble added. "We brought most of the rash people with us."

By dawn, Stone, Merit, and Venture were ready to leave. At the camp outside the city, Stone told Moon, "Keep an eye out. Don't let them get too comfortable here."

He meant, *don't get so distracted worrying about Jade and Chime and the others that you let everybody else get eaten.* Moon just said, "I won't."

Stone shoved him in the head and walked toward the path through the mountain-thorn. Merit shouldered his pack, nodded to Moon and hurried to catch up. Venture hesitated, but just nodded and followed. She was treating Moon like a real consort now, like an important member of a foreign court; in other words, not someone she should be speaking casually to without a pressing reason.

Watching them go, the humid breeze ruffled through Moon's spines. The calls of birds, treelings, and insects were a continuous din. The scents were heavy and so intertwined with that of the mountain-thorn itself, it would have been hard to pick out a predator's rank odor until it was almost on top of you. The other thing Stone had probably wanted him to think about was the fact that Stone's presence tended to drive off large predators. With him gone, maintaining two separate camps with people going back and forth between them was a bad idea.

Moon had left two Arbora, Salt and Strike, and two warriors, Sage and Aura, stationed at this camp. They were all watching him, alert and a little worried. Moon said, "Pack up. We're all going to make a camp in the city."

Strike jumped to his feet, excited to see the inside of the city, and Salt and Aura hurried to start taking down the shelters. Sage, the oldest warrior here, looked distinctly relieved.

It would take one day, maybe less, for Stone to reach Ocean Winter carrying Merit and Venture, one day to get back, plus whatever time it took to talk the Ocean Winter queen into allowing her mentors to help. If she agreed; the others seemed to think it wouldn't be an issue, but Moon couldn't let himself have that much confidence.

The waiting was going to be painful. But at this moment, Moon couldn't remember what it felt like not to be waiting in terrible suspense.

☾

They made their camp in the big chamber with the shaft opening. Moon found out that some of the others had experienced several visions in the chamber while the light was shining, but the sensations seemed confined to specific spots. So Bramble and Braid had carefully mapped them out, marking off the danger areas with piles of pebbles and broken tiles.

After working out a roster of lookouts for the top of the dome and the chamber where Jade and Chime and the others were trapped, Moon sent a group of the warriors hunting. The Arbora already had the lumps of wood Merit had spelled for heat, flown over in the water kettles, and more clumps of moss, wood, and other things spelled for light than they could possibly need. The Arbora just spread the treated cloth on the floor so they wouldn't have to sleep on the muck covering the pavement and they were done.

The rest of the day passed uneventfully. Moon wanted to stay below in the chamber to keep watch over the trapped group himself, but realized quickly that was impractical. Any threat was more likely to come from outside the city, and he needed to be at the top of the shaft to deal with it.

That evening, Bramble, Plum, and Braid took turns telling stories. Band kept reminding them of his favorites that Blossom and Rill had always told until, frustrated, they forced him to tell the stories. He wasn't bad, though he tended to make up details when he forgot the actual plot. If it failed to really distract Moon, at least it distracted some of the others and gave them something else to talk about.

Moon either fell asleep or passed out from exhaustion at some point, but woke suddenly sometime well into the night when Bramble nudged him. He sat up abruptly, dislodging Salt who had had his head pillowed on Moon's hip.

Moon had been sleeping in a sweaty and uncomfortable pile with the rest of the Arbora. The light was shining up from the shaft, throwing a soft illumination over most of the room. River and Drift were sleeping curled together a short distance away, with Aura and Band just past them. Bramble and Serene were wide awake and standing over Moon, which meant it was the second shift of guards, and that Floret and Sand were down at the bottom of the shaft, and that Sage and Briar were on top of the dome. When he managed to focus his eyes on her, Bramble said, "Briar says something's wrong outside."

"Should I wake the others?" Serene added.

"Not yet." Moon carefully detached himself from the pile of Arbora, and stepped over Strike. His left leg had gone partially numb and he limped over to stand under the opening in the dome. One of the warriors leaned over the edge, waving at him. Moon shifted, braced himself, and leapt upward.

He caught the crumbling edge with his claws and hauled himself up. For a moment he couldn't see anything except the surface of the dome itself, curving away toward a lower tower. Then Briar's shape moved in the dark and she whispered, "This way. Sage is down here, so the light doesn't ruin his vision."

Moon followed her down, seeing that they had sensibly stationed Briar up near the opening so she could use the light to make sure nothing approached over the dome and Sage further down the curve, so he could keep an eye on the surrounding canopy.

They reached Sage and Moon crouched beside him, while Briar returned to her post. After a moment, Sage said, "There. Do you see it?"

Moon blinked hard. His eyes were still bleary from sleep, and dazzled by the light. But after a moment he made out the shapes and textures of the mountain-thorn's branches and the heavy growth along them, coiling just past the city's platform. Then the leaves and other foliage moved, rolled like a wave, as something undulated through the growth about two hundred paces into the canopy.

If they could see it from here . . . it's big, Moon thought, the skin under his spines itching with nerves. *Oh, that's all we need.* "They took the offal from the hunt out to another tree's platform like I told them to, right?" *They better have.*

"Yes, Floret made certain. All we have near the camp is fruit," Sage said. "It's not been drawn here by that."

There were, conceivably, large creatures in the suspended forest that were plant-eaters, but Moon wasn't willing to bet that this was one. "Then it's after us."

"Probably," Sage agreed.

Moon considered several ideas, all of them bad. He said, "Let me know if it gets any closer." It felt like a stupid thing to say, as if Sage, having managed to see the thing, would take his eyes off it for a moment now. But Sage just gave him a serious nod.

Moon climbed back up the dome and dropped down through the opening to the floor of the chamber. Bramble and Serene watched him anxiously. Moon had a number of conflicting impulses. Wake everyone up now or let them get more of the sleep they needed while he waited to find out just how bad the situation was. Go down to the bottom of the shaft and take over guarding Jade and Balm and Chime or trust Floret to do the job he had given her while he worried about the rest of the group. It was a reminder how nice it was to have queens in charge of the hard decisions. He took a deep breath, and said quietly, "There's something nearby, in the mountain-thorn's branches, something big. It's probably hunting."

Serene looked up at the opening above their heads, her spines twitching. Bramble said, "Uh oh."

"Right." Moon hesitated again. "Bramble, go down the shaft and tell Floret. Tell her we'll hold tight here until we see what this thing is going to do."

Bramble hurried toward the shaft. Moon told Serene, "Don't wake the others until it's time to switch the lookouts. I'm going to check around down here."

Serene twitched a spine in assent.

Moon circled around the sleeping piles of Raksura and did a quick but thorough walk through the surrounding chambers, making sure they were empty of anything dangerous and that the routes to the outside were still clear. He had two brief visions, just flashes of sunlight and the sensation of falling and overwhelming doom. Though the overwhelming doom lingered long enough to where he couldn't tell if it had come from the vision or was just a natural product of their situation. Then he went back up to the top of the dome.

Sage whispered, "It's getting closer."

Moon hissed. He told Briar, "Tell Serene to wake the others." He couldn't leave the lower chamber unprotected, but if the predator got any closer he would have to move the Arbora.

The movement drew closer to the platform, then they could make out a shadow, a big shadow, blotting out the lighter colored stone as it climbed up onto the city's platform. Moon's eyes tracked it more by the change in the darkness' texture, the void where what little light there was should be gleaming off the city's stones. It moved forward, disappearing between structures, winding around towers. It was headed right for them. It was still nearly five hundred paces away, but there was no mistaking its intention. Moon drew breath to order Briar to go and tell Floret to flee with the Arbora to the other edge of the city, when it stopped abruptly. Sage whispered, "It's seen us."

From behind them, Briar asked, "Didn't it already know we were here?"

"I thought so, but . . . " Sage let the words trail off as the upper part of the predator lifted up, as it tried to get a better look at them.

On impulse, Moon stood up.

There was a long moment when no one moved. He thought, *It is surprised. It didn't know we were here, but it was heading for this building.* He thought about the tracks the Arbora had found around the edge of the shaft, the scrapes that looked as if something large had climbed out of it. Did this thing hunt the lower chamber on some sort of schedule, searching for prey who were trapped in the spell area? But then how did it get in and out of the spell area without being trapped itself?

And was he looking at an animal, or something else?

After a long moment, the shadow turned away. Sage and Briar hissed out in relief. Watching it move toward the edge of the city, Moon felt the tightness in his chest ease. But he felt this was just a temporary reprieve.

Sage said, "Well, maybe it won't come back."

Briar snorted. "Optimist."

☾

They watched all night and through the morning. The movement in the canopy stopped long before dawn, and Moon found not knowing where the creature was actually far more nerve-racking than being able to track its progress.

By early afternoon, he decided he had to go over and see if it was there. It felt like a bad idea, but everyone agreed that they should do it. Which didn't make it less of a bad idea.

Moon made Floret stay behind but agreed to take Serene and River with him. All the Arbora wanted to go, but Moon only took Bramble.

As they flew across the short distance to the canopy, he carried her himself. From the uncomfortable glance Serene gave him, it was probably one of those things consorts weren't supposed to do, but if Moon was going to take an Arbora into this situation, he wanted to keep her as close as possible.

The canopy was so thick on this side they had to land on one of the big branches supporting the platform. The bark was cracked from the weight of the platform's stone, but the wood was as solid as bedrock as they climbed up along it. It led upward into the forest of small trees, ferns, and vines that grew along the wide branches. Bramble slipped a pace ahead or two of Moon, tasting the air deeply. Moon couldn't detect anything but mountain-thorn, but he noticed the treelings and birds were suspiciously quiet; there was nothing but the hum of insects in the air.

They had moved some distance into the canopy when Bramble froze and twitched her spines, signaling them to halt. A moment later Moon caught it too: an odd odor, blended with the mountain-thorn's scent and hard to define.

Bramble glanced back to make sure they had all detected it, then crept forward again.

A little further on, she slipped through a thick stand of grassbrush and hissed in dismay. Moon motioned Serene and River to stay back and stepped up beside Bramble.

Ahead a whole section of the winding branches of the mountain-thorn had been scraped raw, bark, thorns, trees, and plant life scoured away by the rough skin of whatever had climbed across them. The bare area formed a pathway extending back into the mountain-thorn. Moon guessed whatever it was, it was about thirty paces wide. Bramble said, low-voiced, "It's not that big."

As an attempt to be optimistic, it wasn't successful. Moon told her, "We don't know how long it is. This thing could be huge."

From behind Moon, River hissed, "What is it?"

"Tracks," Moon hissed back.

Serene leaned around him to look, made a worried noise in her throat, and retreated back to describe it to River.

Bramble glanced at Moon, spines cocked inquiringly. He told her, "We follow it." In his own attempt to be optimistic, he added, "Maybe it left."

Bramble's expression suggested this was a fond hope. He picked her up and leapt to a branch above the clearing that still had its coating of brush and small trees. Serene and River followed, and they made their way above the cleared area, leaping from branch to branch. The pathway wound back through the mountain-thorn, deeper into the green-tinted shadows.

Bramble proved her hunter's eyes were better than Moon's when she suddenly squeezed his arm, denting his scales with her claws. "There!" she hissed.

Moon signaled the others to halt with a flick of his spines. He narrowed his eyes, scanned the clearing below. A moment later he spotted it.

It was hard to see, blending in with the gray bark, and at first it looked like one of the huge thorn branches curled in on itself. But it was a living creature, wound up into a giant knot and resting on the wood it had scraped raw. Moon couldn't tell much about it, couldn't see its head or even if it had one. Its hide was mottled gray-black, and its scales were large, ridged, and spade-shaped.

Moon twisted around and motioned for the others to go back. Serene and River turned and fled, and he followed with Bramble.

☾

They waited through the day and into the evening. Moon had decided not to send the warriors out to hunt, hoping the creature would lose interest in them. Raksura didn't need nearly as much meat when they weren't doing anything other than sitting around and waiting, and the dried travel rations and fruit they still had was enough to keep everyone mostly content.

As the green twilight began to deepen, Moon went up on top of the dome with the warriors on watch, Floret, Serene, Sage, Briar, and River. There had been no movement in the canopy yet, except for the small flickers of birds and other creatures. Moon was certain there were other predators in the canopy watching them, but nothing else seemed eager to venture up to the city and try its luck.

River kept saying, "What do we do about it?" Moon didn't answer, currently spending most of his energy not hitting River in the head. He had been thinking about it all day, coming up with various unworkable plans.

Floret said, "I just wonder why this thing came here now. If it just wants to eat, there's lots of grasseaters on the platforms of the other mountain-trees around here. Is it attracted to us because we're moving around so much?"

Serene shook her head. "We haven't been moving that much, except to go hunting."

"That's all it takes," River said. "Obviously."

All the female warriors flicked their spines in annoyance and Serene eyed him as if considering slapping him sideways.

Moon said, "I don't think it was after us. I don't think it knew we were here."

Floret settled her wings uneasily. "So nothing we do will help. It'll either come back, or it won't."

She was right, but Moon wished she hadn't put it quite that way.

The night wore on and there was no movement in the canopy. When nothing had happened by the time the light started to shine up from the shaft, Moon was cautiously optimistic and even thinking he might be able to afford to take a shift guarding the lower chamber. It might not do Jade and Chime and the others any good for him to be there, but it would at least make him feel like he was doing something for them.

Then Serene muttered, "Oh, no."

Moon saw it too. Sinuous movement in the canopy, right in the spot where they had last seen the predator. He snarled under his breath. "It's the light. That's what's drawing it here."

Just as it had last night, the predator advanced up onto the city's platform and worked its way further in. Moon turned to Aura. "Go get me one of the moss light bundles. A big one. And wrap it in a blanket before you bring it up here."

Aura sprang toward the dome's opening while the others stared at him. Floret said, "Moon, what are you going to do?"

He didn't answer. He didn't want to give her the chance to talk him out of it. Aura jumped back up to the edge of the opening clutching a blanket-wrapped bundle. Moon took it and leapt into the air, snapped his wings out and shot toward the predator.

He tore open the blanket at the last moment and dropped the glowing moss, then circled away to land on a balcony and half-furl his wings.

The moss fell where he meant it to, about ten paces in front of the predator as it crossed an open plaza. It stopped and reared back, lifted its front section the way it had before. The moss provided enough light to get a better view of it.

Away from the mountain-thorn's canopy, its scent was easier to detect. It was metallic and heavy, like earth, like rock. There was no rankness of predator to it. Moon heard Floret and Serene land on the roof of the tower above him, their claws scraping as they clung to the stone. He twitched his spines, warning them to stay back.

He couldn't see anything on its front that was recognizable as eyes, but there were four irregular lighter patches that might serve that function. The scales in those areas were tiny and delicate, like flower petals, very different from the big rough plates the rest of it was covered with. Moon took deliberate steps along the edge of the balcony and the head twisted

slightly to follow him. He thought if this thing was just a mindless predator it would have attacked him by now. Maybe it made its lair in the
ruin, and had been gone when they arrived. But that didn't explain why
it seemed to be drawn to the light. He said, "We don't want this place.
We'll leave as soon as we can."

It drew back a little, rough scales scraping along the pavement. Then
it surged forward.

Moon snapped his wings in and leapt up and back, landed on the curve
of roof near Floret. She and Serene hissed in chorus.

The predator hadn't come forward any further, making no attempt to
come after them. But that had definitely been a warning. Moon's heart
was pounding in reaction, his pulse beating in his ears.

Floret whispered, "Did it understand you?"

"I don't know. Probably not." If it had, they might have been able to come
to some sort of agreement or bargain, but as it was, they still had no idea
what this thing wanted. He shook out his spines, trying unsuccessfully
to shed some tension. "Let's get back."

☾

The light from the lower chamber winked out as usual, but the moss-
light on the plaza showed the patient creature was still there, waiting.

As the canopy began to lighten with dawn, it made no attempt to
leave. *So it's a stand-off, and you can stop waiting for it to give up,* Moon
thought. Midway through the night, he had changed out the look-outs
so the warriors could stay rested, but he had remained up on top of the
dome. He was too edgy to rest anyway, but had shifted to groundling for
a short time just to take the weight off his back.

Now Moon rubbed his face wearily. His eyes felt like they were full of
sand and his head ached. He had to face the fact that it wasn't safe for the
Arbora. As soon as it was light enough, he was going to tell the warriors
to take them back through the canopy to the outer platform, and to be
ready to carry them away if the predator attacked. He was trying to decide
which warriors to keep with him when Band said, "Moon! Look!"

Moon shifted back to his winged form and looked first at the creature,
which still hadn't moved from its position on the lower plaza. So he missed
Stone's approach and had to scramble back as Stone landed on the dome.

Two Arbora had been huddling up near Stone's collar flange and now
jumped down. It was Merit and an older female Arbora Moon didn't

recognize. Merit said, "This is Violet, the chief mentor of Ocean Winter. Their sister queen Flame is on the way too, with some warriors."

Violet had a heavy pack slung over her shoulder. "Hello, Consort. I see we need to move even faster than Merit thought."

Stone twisted off the dome and fell into flight, one hard flap taking him to the edge of the plaza. The waiting creature lashed its body like a tail, banged against the tower walls surrounding it, but didn't retreat. Moon picked up Merit and told River, "You take Violet."

They dropped down to the floor of the chamber, near the startled Arbora gathered anxiously in the camp. Salt spotted Merit and shouted, "Stone's back!"

Moon took them straight into the shaft, dropping from hand hold to hand hold, down through the foliage and past it to where the spell area started. He asked Merit, "Do you have a plan?"

"She does," Merit said, breathlessly enough that Moon adjusted his hold so he wasn't squeezing Merit around the chest. "She thinks that I'm right about the way to reach Chime."

"Stop!" Violet called out when they reached Coil. River scrabbled, missed a handhold but caught the next and hung there. Moon stopped with Merit, waiting impatiently. A moment later, Violet said, "All right, let's go on."

Moon stopped when they reached Root, but Violet waved at him to continue, and he dropped on down to the floor of the lower chamber. He set Merit on his feet, as River landed with Violet. Merit hurried to the cleared spot in the moss and Violet followed, unslinging her pack.

She stepped close to the edge of the spell area and stared hard at Chime. Then she turned to Moon and said, "We're going to do something similar to the way we look into someone's mind, to test for sickness or foreign influences. But we want to try to actually communicate with Chime. We're going to try to—" She waved her hands. "Nudge him awake. He was able to defeat this groundling's spell before, when he walked into it and stopped it long enough for the others to follow him. We think he can do it again, if he is made to realize what has happened to him."

"I couldn't do it alone," Merit said, "But Violet is much stronger. We're going to try to do it together."

"All right." Moon just hoped they knew what they were talking about. He had had mentors look into his thoughts before, to check for Fell influence. He had never been aware that anything was happening. He turned to River, "Go tell Floret that if the creature comes any closer, she needs to get the Arbora out of there and back to the outer platform."

River nodded sharply and leapt for the wall of the shaft.

Merit settled on the floor, drank from a water skin, and took a deep breath. Violet sat beside him and they joined hands.

Moon watched them for a while, heart pounding, until he finally realized this was not going to be the quick process he had thought it would. He stayed where he was, not pacing or moving around for fear of disturbing them.

He couldn't hear anything from above, and wished he had thought to tell River to come back down afterward, at least so he could send him back up to find out what was happening.

Moon looked at Chime, hoping for some sign of consciousness. After a time he realized he had been staring so long he almost thought he could see Chime's eyes move . . .

Moon's breath stopped in his throat. "He's moving. Chime's moving."

His gaze went to Jade, but she and Balm and Song still stood like statues. The light began to glow softly and the groundlings materialized. For a moment that was all, but then a little motion caught Moon's eye and he saw the lifted edge of the groundling sorcerer's robe was falling. The motion was terribly slow, but it wasn't his imagination.

As Moon watched he saw Chime's expression change slowly to consternation, his head start to turn. The sorcerer's stiff body became fluid, its gaze leaving Chime, slowly lifting up. The motion was gradually getting faster. Moon waved his arms and yelled, "Chime, can you hear me?"

Chime moved a little faster all the time, but his gaze passed Moon as if he couldn't see him. And maybe he couldn't, maybe he was only seeing what the groundling sorcerer saw, what the other groundlings trapped in this moment saw.

Moon turned back to the mentors. They had both shifted to groundling, as if the effort of what they were doing had left them with no power to keep their scales. Merit's face was drawn with effort and Violet's dark bronze skin had gone ashy. They had woken Chime, but they couldn't keep this up for long. And Chime didn't seem to be reacting to them, he wasn't looking for them, he was still facing the sorcerer.

No, I'm thinking about this wrong, Moon realized. Chime was the one who had walked into the spell, who had temporarily stopped it by getting the sorcerer's attention. If Chime walked out of the spell, Jade and the others would still be trapped inside. The only solution was to tell Chime what had happened.

Before he could stop himself, Moon surged forward. He hit a wall of air that was like slamming into mud. He pressed forward, each step a little easier, and pushed toward Chime.

To his relief, Chime's head turned toward him and his eyes widened. "Moon! What—"

"You're trapped in a spell!" Moon said, having to force the words out. It felt like something was squeezing his throat. "You've been here for days and days. Merit and a mentor from Ocean Winter woke you but you have to keep doing whatever it is you're doing or we'll all be stuck here."

"A spell?" Chime's body moved more fluidly, almost at normal speed, as he turned to stare at the groundling sorcerer. "I knew that, I knew the groundlings were trapped here, but—"

"The groundling froze time, trying to save the city. It didn't work, and it trapped you too. Just don't let it freeze us again."

The groundling's head turned toward Moon. Chime's expression was aghast. "I don't know what I did! I just—I tried to tell it that it must have been here for thousands of turns. It didn't believe me—"

"Keep trying, keep talking to it, I have to get the others!" Moon headed toward Jade, still standing on the broken chunk of debris. She and Balm moved now too, their spines lifting, their heads turning slightly, but so slowly. Song turned to stare down at the groundlings below her, who still reacted to the invisible threat overhead.

As Moon drew closer to them, it was like walking into mud again, deeper and thicker mud the further he got from Chime and the sorcerer. His muscles burned from the effort and it was grindingly hard to draw breath. He managed to inflate his lungs enough to shout, "Jade!"

Jade's head tilted and her eyes focused on him, widened in shock. From her perspective he must have just appeared in front of her. He said, "This is a spell-trap! You've been here for days! You have to get out, now!"

For a moment she didn't move and his heart sunk. She must think it was a trick, a hallucination. But he had forgotten about the difference in time between them. All at once, Jade grabbed for Balm's and Song's wrists, and lunged forward off the rock, dragging them with her.

"That way!" Moon pointed past the groundling sorcerer to the edge of the frozen area. He couldn't see anything outside it but a blur. He didn't think that was a good sign.

Jade pressed toward him, Balm and Song both obviously badly confused but following her. Moon sensed movement above and looked up to see Root falling toward him, gaining speed the closer he got, Coil some distance above him.

Moon braced himself and as Root came within reach, he grabbed his ankle, turned and slung him toward the edge of the frozen area. Moon staggered, the effort nearly enough to knock him flat. Root yelped, the sound distorted as he flew faster and faster the closer he got to Chime and the sorcerer. He sailed over their heads and vanished into the blur that marked the spell's boundary. Chime gestured and shouted at the sorcerer, still moving almost at a normal speed, and as Root passed overhead Chime pointed up at him and yelled, "See? I'm telling the truth!"

Coil saw what Moon had done and brought his wings down in a flap that propelled him forward enough to accelerate and vanish through the blur after Root. The groundlings were all jerking into motion too, fleeing in slow confusion toward the edges of the chamber. Moon turned as Jade reached him. She shoved Balm and Song forward and ordered, "Keep moving! Follow Root and Coil."

Balm grabbed Song's arm and pressed forward grimly. Song bent forward, and together they started to move faster. Moon caught Jade's arm to keep himself upright and gasped, "Chime's keeping the—" It really took too long to explain and he had no idea how. "He has to go last, or we'll get stuck here."

"Right." Jade slid an arm around his waist and pulled him toward Chime.

Moon leaned his weight forward, his legs trembling with the effort. The pressure eased as they approached Chime, and Moon could hear him arguing with the sorcerer, though he couldn't hear the sorcerer's answers. "I'm not lying, it's not a trick," Chime said, his voice harsh and urgent.

Moon couldn't hear the response, but as if the sorcerer had spoken, Chime replied, "No, the other survivors left, more turns ago than I can count. It's over, it's long over. There's nothing more you can do!"

As they reached him, Jade said, "Chime, follow us."

Chime turned to her, his expression bewildered. "But I have to convince him— There's— It's attacked the city, he has to save them—"

"He's falling under the spell again," Moon gasped. It was even harder to breathe, pressure crushing in on him from all directions. "The mentors, they must have lost him—"

Jade growled, grabbed Chime by the shoulder, and flung herself forward.

Moon hit the ground a moment later, and Jade and Chime landed beside him. He got a lungful of air, enough to clear his head. A few paces in front of him Violet had collapsed and Merit leaned anxiously over her. Blood trickled out of her nose. Coil and Root stood nearby, staring in wild confusion, and Balm and Song were just staggering to their feet. Moon shoved himself up on his arms and turned to look back at the sorcerer.

The groundlings who ran toward the edge of the spell area faded out of sight as they reached the boundary, but the sorcerer had turned his head toward Moon. From the look of shock and disbelief in his eyes, he could see them.

From somewhere above, Stone roared, and Floret yelled, "Moon! Merit! Are you there? Did it work yet? That predator is trying to get in!"

"We need to get out of here," Moon told Jade, "There's something up there—"

"Of course there is." Jade stood and dragged him upright. She ordered the warriors, "Grab the mentors and get back up that shaft." She nudged Chime with her foot. "Can you stand?"

Chime waved helplessly and tried to push himself up. Moon felt light as air now that the weight of time wasn't pressing in on him. He pulled Chime to his feet. "I'll take him."

"Good, now go!" Jade gave Root a shove to get him moving.

Balm had picked up Violet and flattened her spines so she could sling the Arbora over her shoulder. Song grabbed Merit, who wrapped his arms around her neck. Both leapt up to the wall of the shaft. Root and Coil followed, and Moon asked Chime, "Can you hold onto me?"

Chime slung one arm around Moon's neck and hooked the other hand around Moon's collar flange. He gasped, "Just go."

Moon leapt, caught the edge of the shaft and hauled himself up. He paused to make sure Jade was right behind him, and then put all that was left of his strength into climbing.

Above them he heard Floret call for him again and Balm answer, "We're here, we're coming up!"

Chime said, plaintively, "What happened? I thought there were ground-lings trapped down here. And what are you doing here?"

"There were," Moon told him, breathless with the effort of dragging them both up the shaft. He no longer felt lighter than air. He felt like an exhausted Raksura climbing up a very tall rock wall hauling another exhausted Raksura. "It's a long story, and it got complicated."

Behind him, Jade said, "How long were we trapped?"

"At least twenty-five days? I lost count." Moon heard Jade hiss with relief. *Yes, it could have been so much worse.* "The others are up in the city."

"The others?" Jade asked. "How many did you bring?"

"Uh, a lot," Moon admitted.

They had just reached the ghost image of the boulder when Balm snarled in alarm. Song, Coil, and Root suddenly stopped and scrambled back down the shaft. Looking past them, Moon saw why.

The predator climbed down toward them, flattening the parasite plants and vines against the walls. It filled most of the shaft, and somewhere above it, Stone roared in rage. Moon frantically skittered down the wall, realizing they couldn't just drop down; there was too much danger of falling back into the spell area. And they couldn't let the creature trap them in the chamber below; in the shaft there was at least a chance for some of them to get past it.

Jade swung up around him and put her body between Moon and Chime and the creature. Song managed to scramble away with Merit and Coil swung after her. But the creature ignored them, its clawed feelers missing Balm and Violet, huddled against the wall, and brushing past a trembling Root.

From only a few paces away its hide was still more like rock than flesh, big scales like slabs of mottled gray stone, the edges lifting to show little glimpses of the white flesh beneath. Right above Moon, it stretched out from the wall and extended its big head toward the center of the shaft. Moon shrank back against the rock, trying to become part of it, and Jade's spines flattened. Chime whispered, "Oh, that's what he meant."

Moon didn't have wits to ask for an explanation. The predator was climbing into the spell area, into the faded image of the boulder. Or what Moon had thought was a boulder. Moving slower and slower as the spell took it, it curled its body around, its shape fitting perfectly into the ghost image of the rock. As if it was the rock.

With most of the creature in the center of the shaft, Moon saw Stone clinging to the wall above it, his winged form braced for battle but something about the tension in his body conveying complete consternation. That was pretty much how Moon felt, too.

As the creature's long tail slid off the wall and slowly wrapped around its coiled body, the light in the shaft started to fade. The predator faded with it, just like the groundlings on the chamber floor. It was entering the moment preserved in the spell, disappearing into it.

It vanished completely, the shaft shadowed without the light source. For a long moment they all just hung from the wall, staring. Then Chime nudged Moon and said, "Can we go?"

Jade twitched into motion and said, "Balm, keep climbing. Root, Song, Coil, follow her. Go."

The others flinched and jolted into motion again, continuing the climb up the shaft wall. Jade slipped away from Moon and he managed to unclench his claws enough to reach for the next handhold. Jade asked quietly, "Do you know what that was?"

Moon said, "It's been hanging around the city, but . . . What just happened?"

"I know," Chime said, sounding weary but less confused. "I'll explain later."

☾

They ended up on a platform off another mountain-tree some distance away, one that was used as a regular camping point by warriors on their way to and from Ocean Winter. The sister queen Flame had arrived with a party of ten warriors and another two mentors, and led them to it. The Arbora had managed to pack the camp before the rock creature had crashed through it, so Indigo Cloud had withdrawn in good order, and when they landed on what was formally considered Ocean Winter territory, the whole group looked much less scattered and desperate than Moon was afraid it would.

The platform had a large shelter built onto it, the pitched roof made of bundled saplings and the walls open. It had started to rain in the late afternoon just before they arrived, so the warriors scrambled to attach the water-resistant tent canvases to the sides. The Ocean Winter mentors heated some stones left there to warm the space and hurried to tend to Violet, who was conscious but groggy, and Merit, who just curled up on the nearest blanket and went to sleep. Salt and Braid filled the kettles and got tea started.

Fortunately, Flame was the sister queen who had originally come to Indigo Cloud to initiate a trade alliance, so she and Jade had already formally met. Moon could tell that it also helped that he and Stone were here, along with Arbora from both courts. It made both sets of warriors disinclined to be impolite and there was none of the maneuvering for dominance that was usual between two strange courts. And everyone knew Indigo Cloud was going to owe Ocean Winter a big favor for sending Violet to help, so there was not much point in even the structured rudeness Raksuran courts enjoyed so much.

With a few unlucky Ocean Winter warriors posted as sentries, everyone else settled in around the hearth, queens in the front, then Moon and Stone and the mentors, with Arbora and warriors gathered around them. Between the rain and the fresh air on the way here, Chime had revived somewhat, and now sat between Moon and Balm, huddled down and trying to be unobtrusive. Everyone except the two queens had shifted to groundling, another gesture to show that this was a friendly gathering.

Moon was caught between trying to be unobtrusive too and trying to look as much like a real consort as possible. With Flame and her warriors here, he had been extremely conscious that he was again doing something that consorts weren't supposed to do. He had had Pearl's permission, but she wasn't here to take the blame. Fortunately Flame seemed to be too polite to refer to Moon's part in the whole expedition, whatever she thought it was. The Ocean Winter warriors were staring at him like he had three heads, but that was nothing new.

Once tea had been handed around, Jade said to Flame, "Thank you for sending Violet. I understand if not for her, my warriors and I would still be trapped."

Flame nodded, with the air of a Raksuran queen who could well afford to be gracious. Stone had told Moon that Flame already knew about Garnet being held hostage from Venture, and Moon was waiting tensely to see if she would mention it. But she only said, "Our warrior Venture, and your line-grandfather and your mentor, had told us some of what happened, but as to the rest . . . ?"

Jade didn't betray any relief, though when Moon had told her privately about what had happened back at Indigo Cloud, she had covered her eyes and growled. She sipped her tea and said to Flame, "They told you about Chime's unique situation?"

Chime, leaning wearily on Moon's shoulder, said, "It was my fault."

Well aware that Jade needed to be the one to handle this, Moon hissed at him, and Balm poked him in the ribs. "Ow," Chime muttered.

Everyone politely ignored him, and Flame said, "Merit explained."

Jade said, "On our way to Ocean Winter, we camped overnight on an outer platform of the mountain-thorn. In the morning, Chime said he had been having strange dreams all during the night, and when we made ready to leave, we realized he was gone. We followed him through the canopy and to the ruin, where he had been drawn by the groundling sorcerer's spell. I and two of my warriors went down the shaft after him, and I left two in the chamber above to go for help if necessary." She turned to eye Root and Coil. "But apparently they chose to follow us down."

Root sunk down a little, embarrassed, and Coil moved a little to take cover behind River.

Jade continued, "The rest Chime will have to explain."

Moon elbowed Chime and he sat up a little. He said, "It was my fault."

"We know," Stone told him. "Now tell us what it was all about."

Chime took a deep breath. "I didn't really know, until Merit told me what he had seen and figured out. When I went down there . . . I thought I was seeing living groundlings, who were trapped. Part of the time, I thought the city was still occupied. I could see other groundlings, but none of them seemed to care that the city was being attacked, that these others were stuck down in this chamber . . . " He lifted a hand helplessly. "None of it made sense, I can see now."

Violet, seated behind Flame and wrapped in a blanket, leaned forward. "It was an illusion, caused by the spell. You were seeing what the groundling sorcerer saw, in the moment when he made the spell and died."

Chime nodded, an expression of relief crossing his face. With Merit still sleeping off the experience, it must be reassuring to have the understanding of the other mentor. "I was trying to convince the groundling sorcerer to let me help him, I thought I was talking to him. Maybe I was, I don't know. Jade and Balm and Song came then, and really, the next thing I know I heard Merit in my head telling me to wake up and then Moon just appeared in front of me."

Flame's head was cocked with interest. "But what was the creature? We saw it enter the chamber as we arrived."

Moon, along with everyone else, listened intently.

"It was a sorcerer too." Chime frowned, as if trying to sort it out in his own mind. "I saw it, in the groundling sorcerer's head. There was some sort of battle, and it attacked the city. It used its own body to crash down into that tower, rolled up like a boulder . . . The sorcerer was trying to stop it when he made the spell. It must have been caught in it too."

Jade watched him, frowning a little as she thought. "We didn't see it when we went down there after you."

"When you walked into the spell, and opened it temporarily," Violet told Chime, "it must have escaped. But it was so powerful, it was able to survive." She lifted her brows. "Unlike the poor groundlings."

Jade asked her, "Then why did it come back?"

Violet shrugged one shoulder. "It must have realized what had happened. That it was out of its time."

Moon thought about what that must have been like, to one moment be waging war and the next to find yourself what must be thousands of turns out of your time. It must have spent all the days since Chime had accidentally released it exploring, trying to find out what had happened to it. Stone had seen it lift up and move through the air when it had returned to the shaft; perhaps it had been using its magic to travel over the Reaches, finding nothing of what it remembered of its own world.

Everyone was quiet, absorbing that thought.

Then Flame set her cup aside and smiled at Jade. "While you're here, let's speak about trade."

☾

Later, Moon sat with Jade, Chime, Stone, and Balm on Indigo Cloud's side of the shelter. Some of the Arbora and warriors had already curled up to sleep, others were talking quietly. Floret had fallen asleep with her head on Briar's shoulder; she must be as relieved as Moon to have this over with. Merit had woken just long enough for Bramble to make him eat something, and to prove he was still coherent, just exhausted, then had gone back to sleep. The rain was pattering softly against the roof, a damp breeze making its way between the gaps in the cloth walls. The Ocean Winter group was politely leaving them alone, though Violet had gone back to sleep near Merit.

Keeping his voice low, Moon told Jade, "We owe Merit a lot." Doubting Merit at all had been a huge error in judgment; Moon felt he should have remembered that both Heart and Merit had been singled out by Flower as the best mentors in the court. "We owe Floret and Bramble, too." Moon glanced over to make sure River and Drift were further down the length of the shelter, both asleep, before he added, almost not reluctantly, "And River." He was going to have to make sure Pearl knew just how brave, and more importantly cooperative, all the warriors and Arbora had been.

Jade squeezed his wrist. "I owe you and Stone a lot."

Stone shrugged and poured another cup of tea.

Chime still looked unhappy. He said, "So what are we going to do about me?"

Jade eyed him. "What about you?"

Chime waved his hands. "I almost got us . . . not killed, something much worse, as far as we can tell."

"Chime . . ." Jade sighed. "It was like being attacked by a predator. It just happened."

"But whatever has happened to me caused this—"

Stone snorted. "It also caused us to find the seed, remember that? Not directly, but it helped."

"And to figure out what the Fell wanted with Shade," Moon added.

"That's twice it's been so helpful it's saved lives." Jade ticked the incidents off on her fingers. "Plus more times than anyone has bothered to keep track of that it's been useless but didn't hurt anything, and only once that it was a liability."

Stone said, "I wish Moon's record was that good."

It was Moon's turn to sigh. Jade glared at Stone. "If you're not going to help—"

Chime persisted, "It's only been a liability once so far! What about the next time?"

Moon hissed at him. "Don't wake Merit."

Chime subsided. Balm propped her chin on her hand and asked, "What exactly do you want us to do to you?"

Chime grimaced at her, but Moon could tell he was losing the urge to be a martyr. Chime said, stubbornly, "This can't go on."

Moon said, patiently, "Chime, some day you're going to find a book, or a mentor, or even a groundling like Delin, who knows what this is and why it happens and what you can do about it. Until then, you're just going to have to put up with it." He added, "You should talk to Violet. After all this, she might want to help you get into the mentors' libraries at Ocean Winter."

Chime perked up a little. "So you think I should keep looking?"

"Yes. I didn't before, but—that was stupid. Obviously." It seemed obvious now, anyway. Chime's situation was unique, and just accepting it wasn't going to be enough. Chime might never find the kind of answers he was looking for, but not looking for them didn't mean the problem was going to go away.

Chime said, "No, I knew what you meant, but . . . " He reached over and squeezed Moon's wrist. "I was just always afraid something like this would happen, that I'd have a vision and get some of you into trouble somehow. When it did happen—I didn't know how to explain what I was experiencing, or what was happening . . . "

Balm pointed out, "If you had tried to tell us, we wouldn't have understood."

"Exactly," Jade said, with an air of finality. "So in the future, Chime, when you tell us you've had strange dreams, or strange anything else, we'll listen better."

Later in the night, when everyone except the Ocean Winter warriors who were on watch had settled in to sleep, Moon was curled up with Jade on a blanket pallet. The others were gathered close around them, their mingled scents a reassuring counterpoint to the damp forest air. Keeping his voice low, he said, "So you don't think that I—"

"No, I don't think you should have stayed at home and left me and the others to die like a normal consort," Jade said into his ear. "I doubt Flame thinks so either. Ocean Winter knows Pearl had no one else to send, and they know our situation is unique. Not many courts have a consort so experienced at travel, fighting, and strange circumstances." She let her breath out. "I just don't know what your mother is going to say about this."

Moon frowned. "Malachite won't find out."

Jade obviously thought this was just wishful thinking. "Please. Ocean Winter may be understanding, but they will spread this story to every court they have contact with. It's bound to get back to Opal Night."

Moon turned that thought over. He wasn't afraid of Malachite, though he didn't entirely trust her. "So what would she do?"

Jade considered for a moment, giving the impression she was sorting through several awful possibilities. "I have no idea. That's what worries me."

On Moon's other side, Stone made a noise that was half-groan and half-growl. "Quiet, you're scaring the kids."

Moon became aware that the others were listening intently. Jade retorted to Stone, "You be quiet," but tugged Moon closer and subsided.

The prospect of gossiping courts getting Malachite's attention was something to worry about in the future; for now, everything was as right as it could be. Moon settled his head on Jade's shoulder and slept deeply for the first time in what felt like forever.

THE TALE OF
INDIGO AND
CLOUD

Cerise was on her way back from the colony's lower levels and a visit to the nurseries when Streak stopped her. They were near the waterfall pool in the greeting hall, the heart of the colony tree, and so were guaranteed an audience.

"Are you busy?" Streak demanded.

It wasn't the best way to speak to the reigning queen, but Streak was the chief of the Arbora soldiers' caste, and had been old since Cerise was a fledgling. So Cerise said, "No, I'm about to go to my bower, where I'll lounge around in idle dissipation. What do you want?"

Streak sighed to acknowledge the sarcasm, and gestured toward a group of male warriors standing with the Arbora soldiers who guarded the entrance to the colony. The greeting hall lay at the base of the massive central spiral of the colony tree's trunk, where a tunnel through to the knothole allowed access to the outside. It was an important defensive point, though the hall itself was meant to impress visitors and was lined with stairways, balconies, and delicate pillars, all carved into intricate shapes by the Arbora artisans.

The warriors had obviously Done Something. As Cerise looked at them they all shifted to their groundling forms and guiltily avoided her gaze. Streak said, "I know the warriors think it's a joke, but snatching the soldiers' patrol off the outer terrace and—"

Cerise flicked her spines in annoyance, already contemplating possible punishments. Young male warriors were inclined to be boisterous and weren't exactly experts at applying good judgment; keeping them from becoming so unruly they disturbed the rest of the court, especially when they were bored, was a constant occupation. And the court had been fairly boring lately, which was exactly how Cerise liked it. She drew breath to ask who the ringleader was, just as Wake slammed in through the entrance passage and dramatically skidded to a halt across the floor.

Cerise and Streak both stared at Wake, who stared back, wide-eyed and also guilty, like a fledgling caught stealing bread dough. *What is wrong with the warriors today?* Cerise wondered. Then she remembered that Wake was on patrol duty this afternoon, charged with guarding the outer perimeter of the colony tree's canopy. Her voice level, Cerise said, "I take it it's not good news?"

Wake took a deep breath. Her green scales were speckled with rain-drops, or possibly spray from the outer waterfall near the entrance, and she had brought with her the strong green scent of the outdoor air. She settled her spines and folded her wings, obviously trying to regain her composure. "Indigo is back, they're just coming into the clearing. Lapis told me to fly ahead and warn—tell you."

Cerise exchanged a look with Streak, whose brow furrowed in consternation. Reigning queens didn't normally need warnings that the youngest sister queen was returning from a perfectly ordinary trading trip to an ally. Cerise hissed to herself. If Indigo had somehow managed offend the touchy Emerald Twilight court . . .

The soldiers and guilty warriors had drawn closer to listen, along with other Arbora who had been passing through the hall. Someone said anxiously, "Is anyone hurt?"

"No." Wake's spines flicked uneasily. "No one's hurt."

Cerise felt her spines lifting, no matter how hard she tried to appear calm. She said, "What did Indigo do?"

Wake said, "She has a consort with her," and winced in anticipation.

Cerise flicked her spines, baffled. They had been trying to get Indigo to take a consort for the past five turns, since her status had been lifted from daughter queen to sister queen, and Emerald Twilight's bloodlines were well known to be excellent. But Indigo had only been there for seven days, her first long visit, so it must have been a short courtship. . . . but the expression on Wake's face . . .

Streak said, confused, "But that's good news. A consort offered by Emerald Twilight . . . " Her voice trailed off.

Cerise felt her spines flare and her gut clench. *She can't have. She can't. She wouldn't.* Not Indigo. She said, "He was offered?"

Wake shook her head. "Lapis said Indigo stole him."

There was a collective gasp from all the Arbora and warriors in earshot. That was when Indigo and her warriors entered the hall, coming out of the entrance passage in a jumbled rush of wings and spines.

Cerise was vaguely conscious of Streak turning to the nearest Arbora and saying quietly, "Get the first consort down here. Now, get him now."

Indigo was the first and so far only queen Cerise had given birth to. Her first few clutches had been all male warriors and a few consorts, and Cerise had been worried that she might not have any queens at all. Then Indigo and her warrior sisters had come, and they were strong and intelligent and sensible, when they weren't being rash, silly, and brave to the point of blind idiocy. The warriors had all grown out of it; Indigo almost had, and she had become Cerise's favorite child in the process. They even shared the same colors, both having dark blue scales overlaid with silver.

It was really too bad Cerise was going to have kill her.

Indigo landed on the floor of the greeting hall, the five warriors who had traveled with her settling some distance behind her. All stared at the ground except for Lapis, one of Indigo's warrior clutchmates. She gazed at Cerise in mute appeal, either on her behalf or Indigo's, or probably both. Indigo carried the consort, who was in his groundling form.

The trepidation in Indigo's expression saved her. Her spines were flat and she looked like someone who was clearly not certain of her welcome. If she had seemed proud or defiant, Cerise might have lost the tattered shreds of what was left of her self-control.

Indigo said, "Cerise, I, uh . . . " and her voice came out a little uneven. She set the consort on his feet and he stepped away from her. She finished awkwardly, "I can explain."

The consort was young and pretty in his groundling form, but certainly not pretty enough to destroy Umber Shadow's reputation in the Reaches and possibly ignite a war among all their and Emerald Twilight's allies. He was tall, not quite Indigo's shifted height, with dark hair, dark eyes, and skin of a warm, dark shade of bronze. The dark colored pants and shirt he wore were a little mud stained around the hems, and his only jewelry was a gold armband and a few earrings. His sharp features and lean jawline didn't immediately set off any sparks in Cerise's memory, and his scent was unfamiliar. He wasn't from any of the Emerald Twilight bloodlines that she knew well. But none of that mattered; another queen's scent marker overlaid his own. He had been taken, and not by Indigo.

His expression was closed and hard to read, but at least he didn't look terrified.

Cerise became aware that a large percentage of the court was now in the greeting hall, in groundling form or scaled, either on this level, or up on the balconies and overlooks, or hanging from the walls. People entered speaking in normal tones and were quickly hushed by those already here. An appalled silence seemed to be spreading all through the enormous colony tree.

Cerise swallowed back the urge to knock Indigo through the nearest wall, and forced herself to focus on the immediate problem. There would be plenty of time to commit filicide later. She said, "How far behind you are they?"

Indigo's flattened spines twitched. "Not far," she admitted.

Near Cerise's elbow, Streak made a noise somewhere between a groan of dismay and an angry hiss.

Cerise realized her most trusted female warrior, Tranquil, now stood a few paces away. Tranquil was trying to control her expression and her spines, both of which twitched between consternation and disgust. Including Streak in the order, Cerise said, "Get the Arbora inside, and send out extra patrols. But don't let them provoke a fight."

Tranquil nodded and leapt toward the entrance, and other warriors split off from the crowd to follow. Streak turned and bounded toward the stairway down to the lower levels.

Indigo said, "I think—"

"I'm not really interested in what you think." Cerise thought she had done well so far. If only Indigo kept her mouth shut, Cerise might be able to get through this without killing anyone. At least anyone in her direct bloodline.

Indigo's spines flicked again. "If you won't listen to my explanation—"

"Did they give him to you?" Cerise asked, her voice flat.

The consort folded his arms and looked away.

Indigo let her breath out. "No."

"Then I don't need to listen to your explanation."

At that moment, a black blur dropped out of the upper levels, scattered startled warriors and Arbora, and landed on the floor of the greeting hall in a bristle of angry spines. The dark shape drew itself up and became Cerise's consort Paragon, first consort of the court.

All his spines flared in rage and when he shook his wings back the displaced air knocked a couple of warriors sideways. His matte black scales drew the eye of everyone in the big chamber. Any remaining whispers among the Arbora and warriors stopped abruptly. Consorts, at least consorts with any spirit, got angry just as much as any Raksura, but they didn't often display their anger to the court, and Paragon was usually reserved.

Paragon stared at the young consort, who dropped his gaze and hunched his shoulders. Then Paragon stared at Indigo. It might have been hard for anyone who didn't know him well to read his expression, but to Cerise it clearly said, *I raised you from the time you were small enough to fit in my hand, and this is how you repay me.* Then he looked at Cerise. Yes, she could read that expression too. She sighed.

Paragon pounced, caught the young consort with an arm around his waist, then leapt for the upper levels of the greeting hall. Three warriors fell off a balcony trying to scramble out of his way, then he disappeared into the nearest doorway.

Cerise and Indigo were left staring at each other. Indigo, if possible, looked even more miserable, and Lapis seemed ready to sink through the floor. Indigo said, "I haven't touched him. He'll tell you that. And I didn't steal him. He wanted to come with me."

It had the ring of truth. Cerise felt the tension inside her heart unclench, just a little. She realized abruptly that most of her anger was sparked by fear. The Indigo that would steal an unwilling consort was not the Indigo she had given birth to. It was a relief to realize that her Indigo still existed, and was in fact standing in front of her. She let out her breath, her spines settling, and the whole court seemed to relax a little. She said, "What exactly did—"

A warrior bounded in from the entrance passage, calling out, "Cerise! A strange group of Aeriat just entered the clearing."

Indigo glanced at Lapis. "That was close."

Lapis hissed in dismay. "If they'd caught us—" She swallowed the rest and glanced worriedly at Cerise.

"We'll discuss it later," Cerise said. Streak had reappeared with a few dozen more Arbora soldiers, all shifted into their scaled forms and ready to defend the entrance passage. It was the only way into the tree that couldn't be completely sealed off, but the twists and turns in it made it a death trap for attackers. Cerise told the hall in general, "No one follows me out. Understood?"

She waited until there were reluctant assents from everyone nearby, then she turned to go.

Fluff, the chief of the mentors' caste, dropped off a balcony and landed in front of her. Breathing hard, he gasped, "Take me with you."

He was right, it might help. She grabbed him around the waist and flung herself into the entrance passage.

❦

Raksuran life was all about living without killing each other. They were two races of shapeshifters, the winged Aeriat and the wingless Arbora, who had joined together at some point in the distant past of the Three Worlds to make a better whole. The Aeriat knew their past was violent; Cerise had read the mentors' histories and seen the carved images at the older courts like Emerald Twilight, that showed how the Aeriat had once used their shapeshifting to prey on helpless groundling races. Whether the Arbora had once been prey or rivals, whether they had gotten their shifting and scales and claws and tails from the Aeriat like they got their mentors' skills, or whether they had had them all along, no one seemed to know. But the elaborate rules and etiquette among the courts all existed for good reasons. And what Indigo had done was one of the worst violations of etiquette that a queen could commit in another court.

Carrying Fluff under one arm, Cerise paused on the edge of the knothole that formed the tree's entrance. The colony was formed out of a tamed mountain-tree, and its canopy stretched up hundreds of paces above them, multiple layers of leaves dimming the late afternoon light and holding the other giant trees of the suspended forest at bay. The water that was channeled out of the pool in the greeting hall ran out in a fall to one side of the knothole, the tree's way of expelling the extra moisture drawn up through its roots; it dropped all the way down through the clouds of mist back to the forest floor.

All the colony's agriculture was done on the multiple levels of platforms formed by branches that had twined together and collected dirt and plant growth over time. These formed naturally on all mountain-trees, and had created the suspended forest that occupied the understory of the Reaches. Dozens of platforms stood out from the colony tree's trunk, and some were as much as a few hundred paces across, and held gardens, orchards, reservoirs, and channels for ornamental water and irrigation. Normally at this time of day Arbora would still be working out there, but Streak had acted quickly and they had all vanished inside through the door into the trunk that led off one of the larger platforms. "No hunters out today?" Cerise asked Fluff.

"No," he said from under her arm. He was still a little winded from what must have been a frantic climb-and-run through the colony to reach the greeting hall. "Fortunately. They decided it was too likely to rain and stayed in to work on the last batch of hides."

A few warriors were still in flight, from the group whose duty it was to patrol the clearing today. As they swung around in formation and lit on the platform below Cerise, she spotted the strangers.

They had landed on one of the outermost platforms, a small one about two hundred paces above her current position and at the very tip of a branch. It wasn't big enough to grow any substantial crops or fruit trees and was too far from the trunk to make a good pleasure garden. But it was big enough for a resting spot.

From here she could see there were two queens and at least fifteen warriors. If alone, Cerise would have buried her face in her hands and groaned. Obviously, Emerald Twilight was not taking this lightly. And it wasn't as if she could blame them for it. It was also embarrassing that Cerise knew both queens, had met them on a long ago visit to Emerald Twilight when she was still a sister queen. The elder was Beryl, now a sister queen herself, and the younger was Silver, still a daughter queen.

Tranquil flapped up to land nearby, four warriors following her. She said, "Are we in as much trouble as it seems?"

Cerise said, "In a word, yes." Fluff made a noise between a chuckle and a groan.

She flicked her spines to tell Tranquil and the other warriors to follow, and leapt into flight.

Cerise lighted on the platform and set Fluff on his feet. He immediately shifted to his groundling form. He was short and stocky even for an Arbora, old enough that his reddish hair was starting to show glints of gray and his copper skin starting to lighten, both signs of advancing age in Raksura. He smiled at the foreign queens, as if this was a trading trip and Cerise was here to invite them in for tea.

Tranquil said hurriedly, "This is Cerise, reigning queen of Umber Shadow."

Cerise approved; Tranquil was following the formalities of a normal visit, though rightfully it should have been an Emerald Twilight female warrior making the first greeting. But if they were lucky, they would be able to turn this into a conference rather than a battle. Cerise hadn't needed to tell Tranquil that, which was one of the reasons she had sent Tranquil out here.

The two Emerald Twilight queens said nothing, but one of their older female warriors, probably the one who would normally have made the greeting, stirred uneasily and looked at Beryl, obviously wondering if she should answer the introduction. *Good*, Cerise thought. Anything that kept them from thinking about attacking.

The other two queens didn't speak, so she took a calculated risk and said, "And this is Fluff, our chief mentor."

Silver, the younger queen, actually blinked. *Yes, we know it's a terrible name for a mentor*, Cerise thought wryly. The story was that Fluff's skills hadn't presented until he was an adolescent, long out of the nurseries, and it had been too late to change his name by that point. Cerise thought it more likely that the Arbora who named him had just had a bad sense of humor.

Fluff beamed at the hostile Emerald Twilight party. He said, "If there's time later, I want to ask after the health of Muse, one of your older mentors. She said in her last letter that her knees pained her."

For him to speak at this point, before the two foreign queens had introduced themselves, was against the protocol, but still not technically impolite for two courts who were close allies. And mentors, especially older mentors, tended to make their own rules.

Beryl flicked a spine, but Fluff's expression of welcome and genuine delight at seeing them didn't waver. Cerise hoped her expression was as calm as she meant it to be. Then Beryl sighed. She said to Fluff, "Muse's knees always pain her during the rain seasons. There is no cause for worry." To Cerise, she added, "I take it you wish to avoid a battle."

Cerise said, "I sent my sister queen to arrange a trade of a new variety of tea plants for paper plants and to open a negotiation about the new strain of redberry. I didn't send her to steal a consort."

On both sides, several warriors breathed out in relief. Beryl flicked a spine again, and said, "But that is what happened."

Cerise tilted her head in acknowledgement. The important thing now was to keep them talking. She looked at Silver, who hadn't spoken yet, and said, "Who does he belong to?" She made sure not to speak in the past tense.

Silver's spines shivered but more in annoyance than anger. "My clutch-mate, Argent."

Beryl said, "She'll be here before morning, probably. Our reigning queen detained her to speak about the situation."

That was a very good sign, though Cerise kept her reaction off her face and out of her spines. Fluff lifted a brow thoughtfully and Tranquil swayed a little, possibly feeling faint from relief. This showed more than anything that Emerald Twilight's reigning queen wasn't keen on the idea of a war, either. This was a message that said *I sent the two calm ones and held back the hothead. You have until she gets there to think of a way out of this.* Cerise appreciated the respite.

Fluff said, "Will you come inside? The Arbora haven't had our evening meal yet, and you must want tea, after your long journey." He was doing a good job of playing a combination of innocent Arbora who had no idea there was any source of tension and elder mentor used to having his own way.

Beryl looked as though she would very badly like to come inside and have tea. She let out her breath, and said, reluctantly, "We'd better stay out here."

Cerise tilted her head in acknowledgement. If Beryl and Silver accepted the invitation, it would be an implicit approval of Indigo's theft. It wouldn't solve anything since the disputed consort was Argent's property and she was the only one who could forgive the theft, but it would have muddied the situation a little, showing that Argent didn't have the support of other queens of her court, which would have been to Cerise's benefit. Beryl and Silver clearly knew that, as well. Cerise said, "You are welcome to camp here. One of our mentors will oblige with stones for heat and light, if you have none with you."

"We thank you," Beryl said, obviously wearily resigned to an uncomfortable wet night, spent within sight of the entrance to a warm, dry colony.

Cerise collected Fluff and jumped off the platform.

She led the warriors back to the trunk. They landed in the knothole, and she told Tranquil, "Send someone reliable to take them the heat and light stones. Set a watch on them, but tell whoever it is not to get too close."

As Tranquil took the warriors away, Fluff said, "I think that went as well as could be expected."

"Sadly, I think you're right." The wind had risen and carried the spray from the waterfall toward them, the cool mist settling on Cerise's scales, mingling with the first few drops of rain. *Poor Beryl,* she thought. Cerise made no move toward the entrance; she wanted a word with Fluff in private. She suspected that once they stepped back into the greeting hall, there would be no chance. "I don't think this Argent will be inclined to be reasonable." Cerise had never encountered Argent, who must have still been in the nurseries the last time she had visited Emerald Twilight.

"No. The Emerald Twilight queen wouldn't have kept her from going with Beryl and Silver if she was." Fluff scratched his chin thoughtfully. "I suppose much depends on whether the consort was taken away against his will. Or not, as Indigo said."

"Paragon will know by now." Cerise didn't know what was going on up in the consorts' level but she was fairly certain it was going to involve Paragon extracting the entire story out of their young visitor.

Fluff eyed her. "You could just hand him back."

Cerise rubbed her face. "I could." But as angry as she was about this whole mad situation, part of her was certain Indigo wouldn't have done this without a good reason. If Indigo had stolen a consort, it was because he wanted to be stolen. She said, "Did that consort look like he was with Indigo against his will?"

"He looked like he was sizing up the situation," Fluff said. "And if I was a consort, and I had been snatched away from my court and my queen, and was deposited in front of a foreign reigning queen who looked not only horrified but enraged at what appeared to be my situation, I would throw myself at her feet at once and beg for protection until I could be returned to my own court. There was a noticeable absence of any of that."

"That's what I thought too." Cerise sighed. "Let's go find out."

☾

When they got back into the greeting hall, Reef, one of Paragon's favorite warriors, was already there waiting for Cerise. He said, "Paragon says that the consort—his name is Cloud—told him that he did ask Indigo to take him away from Emerald Twilight."

"Good." Cerise had thought it likely, but it was still a relief to hear it confirmed. "Tell Paragon I'll come up and speak to him as soon as I can."

Reef nodded, crouched, and leapt back up the central well toward the upper levels.

Cerise found Indigo and Lapis down in the teachers' hall, just below the greeting hall. It was one of the most comfortable halls in the tree, where many of the Arbora and warriors tended to gather in the evening for food and company. The walls were carved with a whole forest of trees that curved up across the domed ceiling. Their branches entwined overhead, and their roots came down to frame the round doorways that led off toward the nurseries and the rest of the teachers' levels. It was always filled with all the warm familiar scents of the court.

Indigo and Lapis sat on cushions near the big metal bowl of the hearth, which was filled with stones spelled by the mentors to provide heat. They were being given tea and someone had put flatbread on a pan to bake, and a number of Arbora were gathered around sympathetically.

Cerise stood there a moment until all the Arbora got the hint and withdrew to a discreet distance. She was going to need to consult at some point with the other leaders of the Arbora castes, the teachers, hunters, and mentors, and she needed to talk with Ruby, the court's older sister queen.

Cerise and Ruby had never developed the rivalry common to reigning queens and sister queens of different bloodlines. Ruby's birthqueen and her consort had died in a brief spell of sickness that had hit the court some fifty turns ago, and Paragon had taken over raising her. Cerise had come to treat her as a combination of clutchmate and daughter queen, and she wasn't sure if Ruby's good temper had been due to her or if Paragon just had a knack for raising mature, sensible queens.

But Ruby was currently in the stage of her pregnancy where shifting was impossible and was closeted with her consort and a couple of her closest female warriors in her bower. She was cranky at best and not in a position to provide any actual help.

Cerise took a seat on an abandoned cushion. As Fluff settled next to her, she said, "Well?"

Indigo took a deep breath. "I didn't force him to leave. He wanted to go with me. His queen, Argent, didn't care about him."

Cerise had rather been hoping Indigo had somehow witnessed Argent actually abuse her consort. That would have made the whole situation much more clear. "Is that what he told you?"

"He didn't have to tell me, I saw it. In front of us, when we had dinner with her and Beryl and the other sister and daughter queens." Indigo's claws curled in indignation. "She ignored him, and when she didn't ignore him, she was treating him as if . . . she was *contemptuous* of him. If any of us treated a consort like that at all, let alone in front of members of a foreign court, you'd throw us out of the tree." Lapis was nodding in agreement. Indigo added, "They haven't clutched yet, either, and he said she doesn't want him anymore."

Cerise exchanged a lifted brow with Fluff. Fluff asked, "He's not from an Emerald Twilight bloodline?"

Indigo shook her head. "No, he's from Sunset Water. His birthqueen was a sister queen there. She died when he was still a fledgling, and he was offered to Argent a turn ago."

Cerise crooked a claw at the nearest Arbora, and when she hurried over, told her, "Go tell Tranquil we're going to be sending a message to Sunset Water. She should find some warriors willing to take it and tell them they'll leave at dawn." A consort belonged to his queen, but until she clutched his birthcourt still retained some rights over him. If Umber Shadow was going to get out of this mess without a fight, they would need Sunset Water's support. If Sunset Water was willing to give it. For all Cerise knew, the consort Cloud might be a perennial troublemaker whose court had sent him away with a collective glad heart.

As the Arbora hurried away to find Tranquil, Fluff said, "But he accepted her." He didn't make it a question this time.

Indigo shrugged that away as immaterial. "He made a mistake. He was young. He's two turns younger than I am."

"Yes, that makes him nearly an infant," Cerise said, her voice dry. Fluff gave her a look of reproof, and Cerise flicked a spine in apology.

Indigo bared her fangs briefly and then settled into a stubborn grimace. "He said she was good to him at first but then her sister got a consort from Starlight Sun with a much more prestigious bloodline and she just . . . she didn't want him any more." Her spines drooped. "He said she was young too, and there's a lot of competition between queens at Emerald Twilight. It's not like here, not like between you and Ruby and me. They're all pushing to put themselves forward, to get the notice of the reigning queen. He said he thought Argent made her choice too quickly, because she was so anxious to get a consort before her sisters and to look as if she was more fit to have a higher position in the court than them. Then he turned out to be the wrong choice, and she blamed him. He says they've only slept together a few times. She just sleeps with her warriors now."

Cerise frowned. Those words carved a forlorn image. A very young consort in an important and wealthy foreign court, believing he had been swept off his feet by a dashing young queen, only to find out she wanted him for his bloodline and was jealous that her sister had gotten the better of her.

Clearly more frustrated than moved by the sad story, Fluff said, "Why didn't he send a message to Sunset Water and tell them he was unhappy? If his birthqueen is dead, does he have clutchmates living?" Fluff had presided at Indigo's birth, and tended to take a sire's interest whenever she did anything particularly smart or particularly stupid. "If he does, they would want to know he was unhappy; if he doesn't, the court may be depending on him to help continue that bloodline. They may be expecting to try to re-breed his line back into their court."

Indigo said, earnestly, "He didn't want to upset them."

Cerise snorted. She reached out a claw to pull the baking pan off the heat before the bread burned. "As if this isn't going to upset them." If this had happened to Light, a consort from Cerise's first clutch who had been taken by a queen of Vale Horizon and had two clutches of his own now, Cerise would have been screaming for war herself.

"So you feel no inclination towards him," Fluff said, watching Indigo sharply. "You helped him out of kindness only."

Indigo looked away, then turned back to glare at Fluff as if she suspected him of sarcasm. Cerise was fairly certain Fluff was being sarcastic. "We were . . . attracted to each other at once. If his queen will give him up,

I'll take him for my consort. If she won't . . . " Indigo's voice hardened. "I'll fight her, and then take him for my consort."

Cerise wasn't aware she had lifted her arm until Fluff grabbed her wrist. Cerise took a deep breath, sat back, and settled her spines. "And you don't care if your court goes to war because of it."

Indigo hadn't flinched. Her daughter was many things, Cerise knew, and brave to the point of folly was certainly one of them. If Cerise could ever get her past the point of folly, she would make an excellent reigning queen. Indigo said, "There won't be a war. She won't drive her court to war over a consort who doesn't want her. She'll fight me, but that's all."

Cerise hissed. "You wouldn't drive a court to war over a consort that didn't want you. I wouldn't. Ruby wouldn't. Fluff and the other leaders of the Arbora castes would see all three of us dead before they'd countenance it. But the reigning queen of Emerald Twilight thinks Argent means to start a war, that she won't be satisfied with a fight, especially if you win. That's the only reason she's held her back from coming here, to give me a chance to think of a way out of it." Things had changed in the Reaches in the past generation. Large courts like Emerald Twilight were the norm, not the exceptions, and they were edging out smaller courts for territory. Alliances were vital and competition for trade was more tense than ever. "You don't know how serious this is."

Lapis hunched her shoulders, looking away in dismay. Indigo bristled her spines and said, "She can't start a war if her reigning queen won't have it."

That was part naiveté, part overconfidence. Cerise said, "Oh, there are ways." And she thought she had had enough of this conversation, at least for now. She pushed to her feet and Indigo and Lapis both twitched a little, startled and defensive. Cerise sighed. "Get some rest. You'll need it. I'm going to see if Paragon is still speaking to any of us."

Lapis winced and Indigo's expression was momentarily stricken. Cerise didn't wait for either to attempt a reply.

She didn't want to take the direct route through the greeting hall—the entire court would guess she was going up to speak to Paragon about their guest and they had all had enough excitement already. She took a passage through the teachers' level and to a back stair that wound all the way up through the trunk to the royal levels.

The consorts' level was above the queens' bowers, and there was no central hall, but there was a number of small sitting areas suitable for general gatherings. She found Paragon in the one nearest his bower.

There was a kettle on the heating stones of the bowl hearth and Paragon sat on one of the furs, nursing a cup of tea. He was in his groundling form and looked pensive. He was several turns older than she was, because Cerise had found a more mature consort far more attractive than the flighty young ones she had been offered. He had dark hair and eyes, and dark copper skin, and she still thought he was the most beautiful thing she had ever seen. His bloodline came from Rain Mist, which was known for a tendency to produce line-grandfathers.

Line-grandfathers were consorts who lived long past the normal span, outliving their queens and often all their direct descendants. It was not something Cerise was sure she wanted for Paragon, as it could become a lonely existence, but it had apparently skipped the previous generation, so hopefully it would skip Paragon as well.

The only other consorts with him were Cinnabar, her sister-queen Ruby's consort, and a young fledgling who was hiding under a blanket and giggling as Cinnabar tickled him. The temper of the group was much less fraught than Cerise had anticipated.

She took a seat near the hearth. Paragon eyed her grimly. Cinnabar tickled the giggling blanket one more time, then said, "Would you like some tea, Cerise?"

"No, thank you. How is Ruby?" Cinnabar had been closeted with Ruby for the past ten days, waiting for the clutch to arrive, and Cerise supposed he had taken the opportunity for a break to help Paragon deal with the crisis.

"Angry. Impatient." Cinnabar smiled.

Cerise flicked a spine in sympathy. "So no different than usual." She badly wished for Ruby's support right now but her sister queen couldn't even shift in her current condition. Cerise lifted a corner of the blanket. "Shouldn't this one be down in the nurseries?" Normally she didn't care to be too strict with the fledglings, but tonight she wanted them all secure in the teachers' level, being watched over by paranoid hyper-alert Arbora.

The fledgling sat up and pulled the blanket off his head. It was Stone, from Cerise's last clutch. She had been trying for more queens, but had ended up with one consort and four warriors again. And Stone had been born with a bad eye, a cloudy streak cutting across the pupil. It was a pity about the eye, as queens usually preferred physically perfect consorts, but Cerise had decided she preferred to keep his bloodline in Umber Shadow anyway. The defect was not likely to be passed down and she thought his growing bone structure and wing length indicated that the rest of him was unusually strong and healthy. She would just have to find a queen discerning enough for him. Watching her seriously, Stone said, "Are you going to talk about the consort that Indigo stole?"

"They are, and you're going down to the nurseries," Cinnabar said, and stood, scooped Stone up and tossed him over his shoulder.

Paragon waited until Cinnabar had carried away the protesting fledgling, then said, "Well?"

Cerise told him about her encounter with the Emerald Twilight queens, Argent's anticipated arrival, and the gist of the conversation with Indigo and Lapis. There was no need to speak of their mutual relief that their favorite child had not carried away a young and vulnerable consort against his will. When she finished, Paragon said, "And what does Fluff think?"

"Fluff is skeptical of Indigo's motives and Cloud's veracity." Cerise tasted the air but couldn't scent the new consort among all the Raksura who were on or had been on this level in the past hour. "Where is he?"

Paragon grimaced and set his cup down. "In the bower next to mine with Bright and Sunrise and their warriors, being told how brave and put-upon he must be."

"Ah. I suppose we could trade Bright and Sunrise to Emerald Twilight for him." The two were among their more foolish consort offspring. Cerise supposed they would show promise eventually. She hoped.

Paragon snorted. "If only."

"And what do you think?"

"I don't know yet." She waited, and after a moment he admitted, "Let's say I share Fluff's skepticism. I don't think Cloud is as helpless as he pretends. And Indigo has already admitted that she isn't disinterested in him. She's intelligent enough that she could have found other ways of helping him."

"Like taking a letter to Sunset Water on his behalf. Yes, I wondered about that too." Cerise picked up the kettle and poured more water into the pot. The tea was Paragon's favorite, the dark earthy scent of it warming the air between them. The words *I think we should have another clutch* were in her head suddenly. She was getting older, and the court needed more queens. There had been a strange dearth of queen births in the past two generations, which the mentors thought might be related to the growing population of the Reaches. She put it aside; she had other things to worry about. "You think Cloud wants her?"

Paragon frowned into the distance, giving the question serious consideration. Cerise, about to pick up one of the delicate green cups, hesitated. She had expected him to say yes. He said, "I don't know."

That could be a problem. Cerise groaned in frustration. "Children. Why can't they make up their minds?"

Paragon gave her a dark look. "Their actions are decided enough as it is; if they knew what they were doing, it would be worse."

He was probably right.

☾

Cerise spent the evening in the teachers' hall, for the convenience of the Arbora and warriors on guard, so they didn't have to carry messages all the way up to the royal levels. And she was impatient for news, for Argent the Emerald Twilight queen to arrive, to find out just how deep a hole Indigo had dug for them.

Indigo's side of the story had already spread through the court, with the news that the consort had been brought here in an ill-advised rescue attempt and not stolen. This had greatly relieved the Arbora, who gathered in groups around the teachers' hall to talk the problem to death, which was what Arbora generally did. The warriors gathered to gossip and wonder what it would be like to go to war with another court; it wasn't something that had happened very often in the collective memory of the Reaches. Cerise sat alone, nursing a cup of tea.

After a few hours Cerise ordered another set of warriors to take the place of those outside on patrol, knowing Streak would be doing the same with the soldiers. A short time later Tranquil dropped down the stairwell from the greeting hall. She shook a last few raindrops out of her spines and then shifted to groundling. She looked tired. As she approached, Cerise motioned to one of the male warriors to bring her some tea. Tranquil sat down on a cushion with a weary groan, and Cerise said, "I take it the rain hasn't let up."

"No, it's steady. Probably last all night." Tranquil smiled a little.

Cerise flicked a spine in amusement. "Well, it was their decision."

A couple of teachers took the tea pot away from the male warrior and brought it over themselves, with a plate of warmed fruit. Tranquil drank the tea but picked at the fruit with the air of someone who was too worried to eat. "What do you think will happen?"

People had been asking Cerise variations on that question all evening. The only person close by was Fluff, who had his eyes closed and appeared to be sleeping while sitting up. She lowered her voice and for the first time answered honestly. "If this queen, Argent, is so rash and angry that she fights Indigo, Indigo may have to kill her to survive."

Tranquil grimaced.

Cerise continued, "Beryl and Silver will attack Indigo in a rage. I kill them, forcing Emerald Twilight to send more queens and warriors to retaliate and the two courts go to war. Or they injure me badly and because Ruby is incapacitated by her pregnancy and can't intervene, and Indigo is injured, the warriors and Arbora panic and attack Beryl and Silver and kill them."

Tranquil lifted a brow, skeptical. "The Arbora? They have more sense than that."

Fluff, without opening his eyes, said, "Arbora are perfectly capable of swarming when in a collective rage. Not unlike flightless dakti, but considerably stronger and smarter. This is why we spend a great deal of effort on not getting into a collective rage."

Tranquil twitched uncomfortably. Cerise said, "We rely on the Arbora as a calming influence, but we forget that we're related to the Fell, and that our blood now runs through the Arbora's veins." That the Raksura were in some way related to the Fell had been debated by the mentors for a long time; not all courts believed it, and some refused to hear it mentioned. Cerise had never thought there was any point in denying it.

Tranquil said, reluctantly, "What if Argent kills Indigo?"

Cerise moved her spines in resignation. "Then I kill Argent in a rage, and it all starts anyway." She shook her head. "I can't let that fight take place. If I trusted them both to fight until first injury, it would be different." She trusted Indigo to fight until first injury. It would be a relief if Argent arrived and proved to be sensible about the whole thing, but Cerise wasn't holding her breath in anticipation. "It's too great a chance to take."

Tranquil didn't ask anything more, and after a time she lay down beside Cerise to sleep.

About an hour later, one of Streak's soldiers dropped down the stairwell from the greeting hall to say, "Another party from Emerald Twilight just arrived."

☾

Cerise flew out to the platform with Tranquil and four more warriors. This time she left Fluff in the knothole entrance. If Argent wanted to provoke a war, attacking an Arbora was a sure way to force Cerise's hand. Cerise had no intention of letting anyone force her to any course of action. *Just keep telling yourself that*, she thought sourly. Keeping her own temper was going to be as difficult as forcing everyone else to keep theirs.

Rain fell steadily and the clearing under the tree's canopy was dark except for the lights around the little camp. The Emerald Twilight warriors had set up a couple of tents and spread around some of the stones spelled for light that Tranquil had delivered to them. The camp still looked small and makeshift.

As Cerise drew near she saw the new party was composed of ten warriors led by a young queen. That had to be Argent. Cerise felt a little relief. At least the reigning queen hadn't come.

As Cerise landed and furled her wings, the new queen rounded on her, snarling, "Where is Indigo? Tell her to come out and face me!"

It was good to know that Cerise had been right about Argent's temper and intent. She strode forward, stopped a pace from Argent while Beryl and Silver tensed and lifted their spines. Cerise said, evenly, "Indigo will come out when I tell her to, and not a moment before."

Argent tilted her head. Her spines were already flared. "So she's afraid of me."

"No." Cerise held Argent's gaze. "She's afraid of me."

Argent had no immediate reply to that. She fell back a pace by instinct, realized what she had done, and stepped forward again, rattling her spines aggressively. "She stole my consort."

Cerise kept her voice even. "He asked her to take him away from you."

Argent hissed. "He told you that?" Behind her back, Cerise saw Silver and Beryl exchange sour expressions.

"And he told us why." Cerise let that hang in the air a moment. She flicked her spines, shaking the rain off, making it a casual gesture. "Sunset Water made a mistake in sending him to you. He was too young to be taken, too young to make this decision."

Argent's hard gaze flickered. Cerise thought, *Yes, I'm giving you an out, you stupid creature. Take it.* If Argent blamed this on the consort's youth, if she set him aside as inferior, she could get out of it with her pride intact. Cloud's pride would not be intact but that would be something for the queens of his birthcourt to worry about. Cerise added, "He's obviously too inexperienced for a mature queen."

There was a hint of uncertainty as Argent said, "He betrayed me."

Cerise moved a spine in agreement. She could tell Argent was having difficulty resisting her. Cerise was a reigning queen and Argent only an inexperienced daughter queen without much self-control; instinct made Argent want to submit to her, even though they were from different courts, different bloodlines. Cerise made her voice just a touch more persuasive, just a touch more confiding. "He's been very childish. At least he's given you an excuse to be rid of him."

Argent tried to hold on to her righteous anger, but her spines were relaxing. The chance to complain about her consort to an older and apparently understanding queen was too much to resist. "He was very difficult, from the moment I took him. Sunset Water isn't a prestigious court. He should have been grateful to me."

Cerise signaled agreement again, wishing she could have convinced Beryl and Silver to come inside, so that this conversation would have taken place in the greeting hall. With the rest of the court around her, their scents filling the air, it would have been even harder for Argent to resist this persuasion. She said, "It was a mistake on his court's part. They should have known."

Then Beryl, obviously damp, tired, and impatient with the whole situation, said, "Argent, if the little fool doesn't want you, let him go. It's not the end of the Three Worlds."

Argent whipped around and snarled at her. Out of the corner of her eye, Cerise saw Tranquil clap a hand over her eyes in disgust. *Yes,* Cerise agreed, *don't be stupid, Beryl, and stop trying to help.*

Beryl snarled back. Argent said, "He's my consort, she stole him, and I demand she face me!" She swung around to Cerise again. "Stop trying to influence me. I know what I want. If she doesn't come out, I'll come in after her."

Cerise heard a low growl from one of the male warriors. She hissed and he quieted. Tranquil turned to bare her teeth at the whole group, letting them know what she would do to malefactors once they got back inside the colony.

Still facing Argent, Cerise said, "You don't want to go to war over this."

Argent bared her fangs and stepped closer. "I do. And I can make you. You know I can."

Involuntarily, Cerise felt her spines flare. Her claws itched. Yes, Argent could make the court go to war. They couldn't keep the Arbora off the platforms forever. If Argent attacked them while they were out tending the gardens, or if she went after a party of hunters, the court would explode. Or if she tried to force her way into the colony now, and Cerise killed her, Beryl and Silver would have no choice but to retaliate. The thought of it made Cerise want to rip Argent's head off, even though that would bring about all the consequences she was desperately trying to avert. Cerise forced herself to say, "What about Sunset Water, the consort's birthcourt?"

Beryl, who was apparently still trying to be helpful in the clumsiest way possible, said, "Yes, they should be involved in this."

Too quickly, Argent said, "They gave him up. It's none of their concern."

Cerise wasn't so enraged that she didn't register that. Argent didn't want Sunset Water involved. Which meant she knew Sunset Water might be inclined to take the consort's side. What Cerise needed was time to get one of their queens here. On impulse, she said, "If you want to go to war, we should do it right."

Argent eyed her with suspicion and Silver and Beryl both tensed, wary. Argent said, "What do you mean?"

Cerise said, "Call a meeting of queens from the courts of our allies. Tell them your grievance. Let them decide if you're right to attack us. If they decide in your favor, maybe they'll help you."

Argent showed her fangs. "I don't need help."

Cerise showed hers, twice as long as Argent's and the right one chipped where she had once killed an overambitious platform predator. "Yes, you do."

Silver hissed, then said, "We agree. We agree to summon the other courts for a judgment." She glared at Beryl.

Beryl flicked her spines. "We agree. Argent, you know your birthqueen will want it this way. The other courts will say they have to return the consort to you, and that Indigo will have to fight you."

Unfortunately, she was probably right, but waiting for the courts to assemble would buy Cerise the time she needed. Argent rounded on Silver. "You're enjoying this. You're glad the consort humiliated me—"

Silver flared spines and wings, and all the warriors flinched in unison. "I don't want to see you dead, you idiot!"

Beryl said, "The courts will side with us." She tilted her head toward Cerise. "Your sister queen did steal the consort."

The consort no one apparently likes or wants, who asked to be taken away, Cerise thought, but she didn't want to fight that battle again. She just said, "We'll see."

Argent snarled, bitter and as angry at her sisters as she was at Cerise. "Very well. We'll summon the other courts."

☾

Cerise took her warriors and retired inside, leaving the Emerald Twilight party to shiver in the rain for the rest of the night. They had said they would leave at dawn, to return to Emerald Twilight and send messages to their allies. Cerise just hoped that Argent didn't change her mind before then.

Now she sat in the consorts' quarters, in the little junction that Paragon used as a general seating area. Paragon and Cloud were the only consorts there; Cinnabar was fully occupied with Ruby at the moment and Paragon had chased all the younger consorts back to their bowers or the nurseries for the night.

Indigo, Fluff, and Tranquil took seats, while Cerise told Paragon what had been decided. She finished with, "So I'm sending messages to all our allies. Once Argent and the others return to their court, Emerald Twilight will be sending messages to theirs." It gave them an advantage, as it would be at least five days before the queens could reach Emerald Twilight and Cerise could get her messages out by dawn tomorrow.

Paragon tapped his fingers on his knee. He was not pleased. "That seems to you a good idea."

"Not really," Cerise admitted. "But it was the solution that occurred to me first."

"Our allies and their allies are not mutually exclusive groups."

"I know that." Cerise lifted her spines a little to make him back down, but as usual it had no effect. Older, settled consorts who had sired a few clutches were often so different from the young inexperienced ones that they might as well be from another species. "It's a delaying tactic, while I contact Sunset Water." She turned her attention to Cloud. "Is there anything specifically you'd like to tell your birthcourt? It would be better if I can include a note from you." It would be best if Sunset Water knew immediately that Cloud wasn't being held here as a prisoner. If Argent had any sense, she would have sent a message to them before she left Emerald Twilight claiming Cloud had been taken away against his will.

Paragon looked at Cloud, who kept his gaze on his folded hands. Paragon had been wearing a grim expression since this whole thing had started, so Cerise hadn't taken much notice of it. Now she thought there was perhaps another cause. Paragon said, "Cloud has something he would like to tell Indigo."

Everyone's gaze went to the young queen. Indigo's spines twitched in agitation. Her voice soft, she said, "What is it?"

Cloud was silent. Paragon, almost under his breath, growled. Fluff and Tranquil exchanged expressions of weary dismay. Incredulous, Cerise thought, *can this actually get worse?*

Cloud eyed Paragon, then cleared his throat. "Everything I told Indigo was true. Except . . . "

Indigo stared. "Except what?"

He looked up and met her anxious gaze. "I don't want to be taken by you either. I want to go back to Sunset Water."

Ouch, Cerise thought. This . . . wasn't exactly a surprise. Cloud had found himself with a queen who regretted her choice and didn't care who knew it; it wasn't believable that he would want out of that situation only to fly into the arms of another queen he barely knew.

Of course, Indigo hadn't thought of that.

From the way Paragon was looking at Cloud, with a mix of sympathy and serious irritation, he knew that too. This was the first time Indigo had shown anything more than friendly interest in a consort, and whatever Cerise had thought of Cloud's part in this situation, she had hoped . . . she let her breath out.

Indigo's spines twitched, as she fought for control of her expression. "You said you wanted me."

Cloud said, coolly, "I said that so you'd take me away from Argent."

As much as she wanted to slap him in the head, Cerise admired Cloud's self-possession. Paragon's shoulders lifted a little, showing that if he had been in his scaled form his spines would have flared.

"You lied to me." Indigo's voice shook, and Cloud winced. She swallowed and regained her control. She settled her spines and said, "You should have told me the truth. I would have taken you directly to Sunset Water, and not put my court in danger for your sake."

Cloud looked away. Indigo stood, and he flinched, then tried to make it look like a twitch of embarrassment. Cerise thought that told them everything about his relationship with Argent that they needed to know. Carefully not looking at him, Indigo hadn't noticed. She walked out of the chamber toward the stair down to the queens' level.

No one said anything for a long moment. Then Tranquil twitched her spines a little to ease the tension and said to Cerise, "Do you want me to check on the warriors who are taking the messages? They should be ready to leave by dawn."

Cerise flicked her claws in dismissal. "Yes. I'll come down and join you in a moment."

Tranquil left. Cloud was still staring at the floor, shoulders hunched a little as if expecting a blow. Cerise said, "I'd still like you to write a note to your birthcourt. And explain everything. Including what you've just told us."

Cloud drew a sharp breath and said, "Yes. I'll do it."

His tone mild, Fluff said, "Good." He rummaged in the satchel he had brought. "I just happen to have some paper and ink right here."

$$\mathbb{C}$$

Cerise went back down the central well to the teachers' hall, glad to get out of the fraught atmosphere of the consorts' level. She had read Cloud's note and he had indeed explained everything, so that was a relief at least. It was clear from what he had written that his situation was unfortunate and not something one would want for any consort, let alone one of your own bloodline. But it was also clear that he had rather mercilessly manipulated a young and inexperienced queen to get him out of it.

If the relationship between Cloud and Argent was as bad as it sounded, the reigning queen of Emerald Twilight was probably glad to be rid of him. Queens and consorts didn't have to have a great deal of affection towards each other to produce royal clutches, but it was better if they were at least friendly. Both often took warrior lovers, and consorts were also expected to spread their bloodline among the Arbora who were hoping to produce mentors. It was rare for a queen and consort to dislike each other so much that it was obvious to even visitors to the court. And Cloud's behavior had showed that he was anything but timid. If Argent provoked him so badly he attacked her, or if she had so forgotten herself as to physically injure him, the Arbora would have been angry it had been allowed to get to that point, and they would have forced the reigning queen to intervene.

The court was finally beginning to settle down for what was left of the night, though there were still plenty of Arbora and warriors awake. Fluff had told her the mentors had finished writing the messages to the other courts, and Cerise wrote the one to Sunset Water herself, to go along with Cloud's note. The groups of warriors who would take them were all preparing to leave as soon as dawn broke. With all that settled, Cerise went to find Indigo.

It took some time, but Cerise finally tracked her down to the mentors' library, below the teachers' level and near the area of the colony where the Arbora did much of their artisan work. The large chamber was lined with shelves stacked with the hide-wrapped books that contained all the colony's histories, its stories, its collected lore and knowledge. Shells provided light for reading, and a few piles of scattered cushions lay abandoned on the floor, but Indigo was the only one here.

She was in her Arbora form, smaller and softer, without wings. Queens didn't have a groundling form the way the Arbora and other Aeriat had. Shorter claws and less pointed spines was as vulnerable as they got.

Indigo was staring at a shelf of books without seeing them. As soon as Cerise drew near, Indigo said, "I've been stupid."

Cerise wasn't going to argue with that. She did counter, "You've been young." She toed a cushion away from the pile and sat down. She needed to get some sleep soon. The room smelled of the past, of tanned leather, of pounded reed paper and ink. "And this is not a situation any queen expects to encounter."

Indigo shook her head, still facing the wall. "I still want him," she admitted, sounding bleak. "I just don't like him very much right now."

Cerise knew she should just let that go. It would be easier to settle this dispute and prevent a war if Cloud went back to Sunset Water. But instead she found herself saying, "You should try courting him."

Indigo frowned, as if the idea had never occurred to her. Cerise knew she had had these conversations with Indigo before, but apparently Indigo hadn't thought any of it actually applied to her. It had been a concern, but there had always been queens who preferred the company of their female warriors to consorts, and consorts who preferred male warriors or other consorts. Usually if you could get them to have at least one clutch you counted the court lucky. Cerise had never been certain if Indigo was uninterested in consorts in general or had just failed to find one who attracted her. She said, "He was offered to Argent and he agreed, because his court probably needed the alliance. He's never been courted before." She shrugged her spines. "Maybe that will make a difference."

Indigo ran her finger down the rolled hide cover of one of the books. "You think so?"

"I think so. And just talk to him, like you would talk to your clutch-brothers." Indigo was accomplished in everything that didn't involve choosing a mate; Cerise couldn't imagine that a sensible consort wouldn't be intrigued by that. She was certain to pass these traits down to her clutches. "Get to know each other. Maybe you'll find that you don't want him." *Like every other consort we've ever tried to interest you in*, Cerise thought. If Indigo could for once use her uncanny power to be indifferent to beautiful consorts for good, it would be a relief, but Cerise wasn't going to urge her one way or the other. "Just don't be alone with him, not while all this is going on. Take one of the mentors with you when you visit him. Or sit with him down in the teachers' hall." Cerise trusted Indigo, and her gut instinct said that Cloud wouldn't lie to bring more trouble on them, but there was no point in being careless.

Indigo considered it all, flicking her spines in indecision. "But it would be better for the court if we just sent him back to Sunset Water. Even if the other courts settled the dispute in our favor, Emerald Twilight will always hate us now." She leaned her forehead against a shelf. "I really have been very stupid."

"Emerald Twilight was never that fond of us to begin with." Cerise sighed. "For now, you let me worry about everything else. Whatever you and Cloud decide, I can make it work."

She hoped she was right.

☾

To everyone's relief, the Emerald Twilight party left in the morning. Shortly after that, Tranquil dispatched the warriors with the messages to summon their allied courts. The date set for the judgment was thirty days from now, which was plenty of time for the word to spread among the other courts and for the interested parties to travel here. Cerise had stipulated that they weren't feeding any of them, which would probably eliminate some of the interest among non-allied courts. Close allies of Emerald Twilight and Umber Shadow were bound to show up, though. *As long as Sunset Water comes*, Cerise thought. That was the only one she cared about. And the sooner they came, the better.

For ten rainy but thankfully dull days life in the court went back to normal. Cerise spent her time worrying about Ruby's impending clutch and consulting with the Arbora about the best choices for post-cool-rain season planting, forming a plan for the trade that needed to be done for the next season, and discussing how best to acquire the supplies necessary for producing the court's own trade goods. A large predator appeared in the hunters' territory which had to be dealt with, and the teachers presented two warrior fledglings who had misbehaved so badly as to need an audience with the reigning queen.

And as far as Cerise could tell, Indigo and Cloud did not speak or acknowledge each other's existence in any way during the entire time.

Cerise had had plenty of opportunity to observe this because Paragon's favorite rainy season activity was to go down to the teachers' hall and listen to the Arbora read aloud. Cloud often followed him along with the other young consorts and fledglings, and Indigo and Lapis were usually there as well. Indigo and Cloud ignored each other in a way they both probably thought was discreet but that Cerise found as pointed as possible. And when they thought no one was looking, they watched each other.

Indigo watched Cloud lie on the furs listening to whatever story was being read, absently carding his fingers through the frills of whichever fledgling was sitting with him. When he had gone with Paragon to the nurseries, the fledglings and young Arbora had taken to Cloud completely. A young adult consort who wanted to play with them while Cinnabar was occupied with Ruby must have seemed like the best gift of the turn.

And Cloud watched Indigo. Watched her talk and laugh with the Arbora and the warriors, watched the female warrior fledglings hang on her every word. Indigo had always had a good disposition and Cerise had worried a little that she might not be aggressive enough. This worry had vanished when Indigo was a fledgling and they had been out watching the Arbora hunt one day. A giant gutripper had dropped down from above and Indigo had gone for its face without hesitation, clawing at its nearest eye and giving the Arbora a chance to run and Cerise an opening to go for the creature's throat. It had turned out Indigo was plenty aggressive; she just saved it up until it was needed. But Cloud seemed to be admiring her more for her patience with the fledglings and her ease with the Arbora and other members of the court.

In frustration, Cerise asked Paragon, "So what does he have to say for himself? Has he shown any interest in her?"

They were in her bower, sitting on the furs near the hearth, having a last cup of tea for the evening. Paragon said, "No, but he doesn't talk much about anything. He's very cautious."

"Cautious of what?"

"Of us. He listens when the others talk, but doesn't say much himself. Of course, Bright and Sunrise are barely more than fledglings, and Cinnabar doesn't have anything in his head these days except babies and Ruby, so our conversation isn't exactly wide-ranging. Cloud plays with the fledglings and enjoys the Arbora's company, but he's wary of us." Paragon set the teapot aside. It was a dark blue glaze, swirled through with hints of red and gold. "I don't think the other consorts at Emerald Twilight treated him very well. I had a talk with Lapis and the other warriors who were with Indigo, and they said they saw some clear signs of dislike between Cloud and the other queens' consorts."

Cerise clicked her claws on her cup, thinking it over. "Is he a trouble-maker?" She wasn't certain if she wanted that to be the case or not. If Indigo and Cloud had no real interest in each other, if Indigo's attraction had been a passing one caused by the drama of their situation which had now been squelched by Cloud's admission that he didn't want her, this would all be so much easier to resolve. But she had to admit, the idea of Indigo securing such a spirited young consort wasn't unattractive.

"If he is, he's not going to trouble-make here," Paragon said repressively. Cerise's birthqueen had told her that you could always tell which one was going to turn out to be a first consort by how annoyed they were by other consorts and male warriors. Paragon was normally easygoing, but he didn't like to see fighting among consorts or their warrior favorites and he was perfectly capable of putting an immediate stop to it if it occurred. "No, I suspect they just all got off on the wrong wingbeat, probably in part due to his queen's influence. And he's told us a little about his birthcourt; it was small and informal. Rustic compared to Emerald Twilight. And he was the only consort from a mixed clutch, with a queen and three female warriors. He spent a great deal of time tagging along with them as a fledgling and I imagine they toughened him up quite a bit. He's reticent, but not shy or timid."

Cerise sighed wearily. Not shy or timid, and not likely to take slights well, or to know how to respond with anything but a slap to the head, like a female warrior. If Argent had treated him well, the situation in the consorts' quarters would have probably settled down eventually. But with Argent openly showing her displeasure with her consort, it would have just made everything so much worse.

It didn't seem like Cloud was likely to be a bad consort. With a queen who was more understanding, and a court that wasn't so formal and competitive, he would probably be perfectly happy. It was just a coincidence that Indigo and the court of Umber Shadow fit that description so well.

Watching her expression, Paragon said, "The conflict with Emerald Twilight would be more easily resolved if he's handed back to Sunset Water."

Cerise eyed him. "You think Indigo has decided that she doesn't want him?" She had certainly shown little sign of it in the past days.

Paragon snorted and reached for the teapot. "I think Indigo wants him more than she wants to breathe."

☾

Except for Cloud's presence, everything continued on much as usual. Cerise was hoping the five warriors who had carried the message to Sunset Water would return on the eleventh day, and it was a relief that at mid-afternoon they appeared just as expected.

But they returned alone, with no party from Sunset Water, and they carried no return message.

Furl, the female warrior who had led the group, reported, "They were perfectly courteous, but we didn't see any queens. They let us come inside and we stayed in the guest quarters, and they brought us plenty of food. They told us the next morning that the queen was too busy to write a return message now, but she would send warriors with it soon. It's not a big court and I did get the feeling they were upset about something, or stressed, as if there had been some problem recently. So maybe the queens really were too busy."

The lack of an immediate return message was deeply disquieting. Cerise kept her spines in place and didn't show it. "Hopefully their message will arrive soon. Go and get some rest, Furl. You and the others did well."

When Furl had left, Cerise sat alone in her bower, absently flexing her claws. A message might have been difficult to write, if the reigning queen had already heard from Emerald Twilight and thought Cloud had been stolen against his will. Cerise wasn't certain what she would have done in that situation. Well, yes she was, she would have called for her warriors and come in person to see what had happened and to retrieve the consort. It was the only response that made sense.

Perhaps Sunset Water didn't want Cloud back, or was struggling with some difficulty that made the idea of taking a stand against the more powerful Emerald Twilight an unwelcome proposition. Cerise hissed in irritation. *Your clever plan might have been a little too clever,* she told herself wryly. And now she had to tell Paragon he had the unwelcome task of informing Cloud that his birthcourt had not responded to the request to come to his aid.

☾

The next day, it got worse.

In the hanging bed in her bower, Cerise curled around Paragon. She was in her Arbora form, bonelessly relaxed, when she became aware they had an audience. She pushed herself up on an elbow and looked over the edge of the bed. Tranquil, Streak, and Fluff stood there.

Cerise said, "This better be important." She and Paragon hadn't slept together much in the past few turns. They were still comfortable together but they had made their clutches for the court and the passion between them had cooled over time. But with all the unrequited lust in the air between Indigo and Cloud, Cerise had found herself interested again.

Wincing in anticipation of the response, Tranquil said, "Emerald Twilight is back."

Cerise stared. *This . . . is very bad.* "How many?"

Tranquil said, "Three queens, forty warriors."

Beneath Cerise, Paragon growled in dismay. She slung herself out of bed and shifted to her winged form.

Streak was still in her groundling form, probably because she couldn't keep her spines under control otherwise. Her expression was deeply worried. "They landed on an outer platform just as the sun was rising."

Cerise hissed and led the way out of the bower, and up one of the private stairs to the consorts' level. She went through the maze of passages and bower entrances to a round door in the outer trunk. It had been originally put here as one of the secondary escape routes, but it also happened to look down on the garden platforms to the right of the knothole entrance. It was used mostly as a way to let the breeze into the consorts' quarters and to admire the gardens. Cerise slid the heavy bolts back and hauled the door open.

Crystalline wood beetles which had been nesting in the cracks fluttered away as she looked down on the platforms. There they were, as Tranquil had said, three queens and at least forty warriors. They had taken up residence on the same platform they had stayed on before, but this time they had come prepared. They were already setting up a shelter, the cloth shiny and stiff where it had been waterproofed by tree sap. From the colors of their scales, the queens were Argent, Beryl, and Silver again. At least their reigning queen was still back in Emerald Twilight and not directly involving herself.

Cerise felt a snarl build in her chest. *Surely you didn't think they wouldn't see through this summoning of courts nonsense, did you?* she asked herself. Maybe she had thought that. Or maybe she thought Emerald Twilight would have the courtesy and sense to let this go gently. *But letting it go would mean they let you win.* Argent clearly had no intention of that. Beryl and Silver's motives weren't as clear, though Cerise suspected they were mainly concerned with preventing Argent from doing anything to disgrace Emerald Twilight, and also afraid that she would get herself killed. Which didn't mean they wouldn't help Argent damage Umber Shadow.

"But why are they here?" Streak said. She was frustrated, the way Arbora always were when Aeriat stirred trouble for little reason. "It'll be days still before the other courts have a chance to arrive. Do they think they can conquer us with forty warriors?"

Fluff said dryly, "They don't mean to conquer, they mean to threaten. They know whoever acts first loses. They hope to force us to make some foolish gesture. Then all the other courts will side with them. It's the only move they can make, if Sunset Water sides with us." He looked up at Cerise. "Which means—"

"That they don't know yet that Sunset Water didn't answer our message," Cerise finished. She sensed movement behind her and glanced back to see Indigo and Lapis come up through the passage. The others made room so Indigo could look out the doorway. After a moment, Indigo said, "They mean to try to pressure us to give Cloud back before the other courts get here. Or before Sunset Water does." She met Cerise's gaze. "That's all that matters, isn't it?"

If Sunset Water plans to come at all. "Yes." Cerise managed to get the word out without a snarl. It wasn't Indigo she was angry at. She turned away and stalked back down the passage.

Streak stayed to shut the door but the others followed. Indigo said, "You won't—What are you going to do?"

Cerise heard the trepidation in Indigo's voice. "I know what I should do." Give in and hand Cloud over to Argent. It was the sensible thing to do. Though if Sunset Water changed their mind or really had been delayed for some reason, and arrived in a few days ready to take Cloud home, they would see it as a betrayal. It didn't mean that Cloud's birthcourt wouldn't be able to get him back from Emerald Twilight, but Cloud would probably suffer in the meantime. Argent couldn't risk injuring him physically without her reigning queen intervening, but it wasn't a situation Cerise would have cared to send any consort into.

No, sending Cloud back was a poor solution for everyone except Argent's pride.

"He's not afraid of her," Indigo said, as if she had been following Cerise's thoughts. Paragon now stood in the doorway from the stairs that led down to the queens' level. Streak, Fluff, Tranquil, and Lapis all gathered around watching Indigo and Cerise. Apparently oblivious to all the scrutiny, Indigo continued, "He won't let her push him too far. He said Sunset Water is smaller and not formal. He used to fight with the warriors—not seriously, as a game—and the Arbora took him and his clutchmates hunting so they would know how, if they had to."

"So they're likely to kill each other," Cerise said, eyeing Indigo sourly. She had thought of that before, as the worst that could happen when a queen and consort mating went wrong. It wasn't encouraging to hear Indigo thought it likely. "And it's become our job to save Sunset Water from their folly in handing over a difficult consort to an extremely foolish young queen, and Emerald Twilight from their compounded folly in putting their pride before good sense."

Indigo flicked her spines in a shrug. "Yes. Someone has to do it."

Cerise found herself unable to reply, struggling between pride in her daughter and irritation at the whole situation. She said, tiredly, "Indigo..."

Someone said, "I'll go back." It was Cloud, standing in the opposite passage entrance, in his groundling form. He was wearing an old shirt and pants borrowed from one of the other consorts; Cerise recognized the vivid blue dye and its tendency to fade along the hems as being unique to Umber Shadow's Arbora. He didn't lower his gaze or even twitch uneasily as they all stared at him. Cerise thought he must have heard her conclusion that he and Argent would kill each other. He said, "I don't want to cause you any more trouble. I won't fight Argent, I'll think of a way to appease her, until Sunset Water comes for me." He said it without a flinch, even though Cerise knew he had taken the news that Sunset Water had sent no return message with Furl very badly. Paragon had said that Cloud had tried to put on a brave array of spines but had been terribly upset.

The atmosphere in the room changed subtly, as Indigo stiffened her spines and tilted her head. "You'll lie to her, pretend you want her?" Her voice was cool with just a little edge to it.

Cloud flushed dark bronze. "If I have to."

Cerise met Paragon's gaze. His lifted eyebrow said "I told you so" as clearly as if he had spoken it aloud. Cerise hissed to herself in resignation. *You're right*, she thought, *she wants him. Now we just have to get her to admit it to herself. Or to him. Or to someone. Anyone, really.*

Indigo said, "She's not stupid. She won't believe you. You should have pretended you wanted her when she first brought you to Emerald Twilight."

"I did want her then." Cloud lifted his chin. "At least, I thought I did."

Indigo's spines lifted, and after a moment Cloud looked away. Indigo said, "Don't be an idiot. It would be a disaster for Emerald Twilight and your birthcourt if you went back and something happened to you." She tilted her head toward Cerise. "The only solution is for me to fight her."

Lapis hissed in dismay and Cloud snarled, "No! You're the idiot if you think fighting her is going to mean anything but—"

Indigo showed her fangs. "I'll fight her if I feel like it, you—"

"Children, quiet," Cerise snapped. She saw Fluff rub his eyes and shake his head in weary frustration. That echoed her feelings exactly. She flared her spines and drew on her connection with the court, giving her voice extra weight when she said, "Tell me right now. Do you two want each other?"

Indigo said, "No," at the same time as Cloud said, "Yes."

Indigo stared at him. He didn't back down or demur. He said, again, "Yes."

Paragon smiled in approval.

Cloud said, "I mean it, I'll go back—" at the same time Indigo said, "What do you mean you want—"

"That's enough," Cerise said. At least now there was no question of sending Cloud back; Indigo was right about that, they simply couldn't risk it with Argent so angry and so likely to do something rash. "Cloud will not go back." She looked from Indigo to Cloud, making sure she had their full attention. "There's only one Raksura I trust to navigate this disaster, and that's me."

☾

Cerise held her council down in the teachers' hall with the leaders of the Arbora castes and several of the older warriors. A number of other Arbora and warriors gathered at the edges of the room to listen, but she didn't want privacy for this meeting; the more the court knew, the better. Indigo lurked by the stairs down from the greeting hall, her spines twitching uneasily.

Bloom, the chief of the hunters, scratched the scales under her chin thoughtfully and said, "Forty warriors isn't exactly enough to give us a fight. I'm guessing they hope it's enough to provoke us, so we're the ones at fault?"

Cerise flicked her spines in approval at this accurate assessment. "Yes. And if we don't provoke as planned, Argent will take matters into her own hands and attack someone from the court, whether the other two queens agree or not." It wasn't an entirely sensible plan, but perhaps Argent meant to have them embroiled in a war before anybody stopped to ask who had started what, or started dragging warriors out to testify in front of mentors. Perhaps Argent was counting on them giving in before it got to that point.

There was a chorus of hisses from the Arbora. "So if we go out to work, or go out at all, she may attack us," Streak said. She tilted her head, considering it. "But we only have to stay in until the first of the other courts we've summoned arrives. That's what, eighteen days?"

Cerise said, "We can hope that some of them will arrive a day or two early, so make it sixteen or seventeen days. I know we have enough dried supplies for that." The warriors all winced at the idea of subsisting on dried meat for that long. She added, "But I also think we have at least a full day, maybe two, before anything happens."

Streak tapped her claws on the floor thoughtfully. "Argent will think we're talking it over, perhaps deciding to give in and hand her back the consort. She'll give us a little time."

Leaf, the head of the teachers, sat up. "We need to get out there and harvest everything we can. I know there are some fruit trees ready to pick."

Bloom nodded. "And we need to go hunting. We can go out through one of the lower doors, and they may not even notice us. We'll need warriors to carry us away from the tree and into the suspended forest."

Leaf added, "If we get too short of meat, we can also go out through the root entrance and harvest some snails from the pools down there, and maybe hunt a little. And we can trade for extra groundfruit from the Kek."

It was a good notion. The forest floor was so far below the level of the suspended forest platforms, and protected by thick layers of mist, that it might as well be in another part of the Reaches. The Kek who often lived among the roots of colony trees were allies, though the Raksura seldom saw them. The forest floor tended to be either swampy or studded with rock outcrops, and was the home of so much deadly plant life and so many predators that it made the suspended forest look safe; Raksura tended to avoid it. But in an emergency they could hunt near the tree roots; the stick-like Kek were uninterested in meat of any kind, and would not be disturbed by the intrusion, especially if it meant a chance for trade.

Everyone got up to hurry away, the Arbora to organize their precipitate harvest and to prepare to hunt, and the warriors to arrange to escort them. Indigo made her way over to Cerise and asked, "Are you going to greet the Emerald Twilight queens?"

Cerise eyed her. "Am I going out there to beg their indulgence again? No. We made an agreement to meet in thirty days for a judgment by our allied courts. They're early, and they've forgone their right to special consideration. I will send Tranquil to offer them hospitality. They'll refuse, of course, but we want them to think we're naively continuing about our business until the Arbora are done with their preparations."

Indigo still looked uneasy. "Maybe I should—"

"I told you no. Don't make me repeat myself." The last thing Indigo needed to do was go out there. If she did, Cerise wouldn't be able to prevent a battle with Argent and all this would be for nothing. "You were right, we have to protect Argent from her own folly. What you should be doing is making up your mind."

Indigo's spines stiffened. "I have made up my mind. I don't want him."

Cerise was pointedly reminded of the time when Indigo was a fledgling and had had a mild lung fever, and refused to take the remedy from mentors, teachers, or Paragon, and Cerise had had to come down to the nurseries and negotiate with her herself. The memory softened her temper, so instead of growling she said mildly, "He's given up pride to say he wants you, in front of me, Paragon, Fluff, and the warriors. If you're still angry at him for misleading you—"

"I'm not still angry." Indigo's mouth set in a stubborn line. "I'm doing what I know is the right thing."

"For the court?" Cerise said, still mild.

"Yes."

Cerise lifted her spines and hardened her voice. "But you still want to fight Argent, for your pride's sake? When you're the reigning queen, you decide what's right for the court. Until then, I do."

Indigo lowered her stiff spines a little but didn't drop her gaze. "That's not what I mean. And you know it."

"Leave the court to me and do what's right for yourself," Cerise said.

Unable to relax her spines, Indigo stalked away.

☾

Tranquil went out to formally greet the Emerald Twilight party, and to offer them hospitality contingent on their entering the colony tree. They refused, and Tranquil and the two warriors with her returned to the court. In the meantime, the Arbora completed their brief harvest, managing to make their behavior look normal and not at all hurried, mostly by having far more people out working than would have been necessary had all the crops suddenly come in at once. By the evening a group of hunters had replenished the larder with a hunting trip in the lower part of the suspended forest. Once that meat ran out, they would risk the more dangerous territory of the forest floor.

It wasn't until well after mid-morning the next day that the Emerald Twilight contingent realized that no Arbora were coming out to work, despite the clear weather, and that no warriors patrolled the clearing. Cerise, Streak, and Tranquil watched them from the consorts' door high in the tree, and were rewarded with seeing Argent pace and flare her spines and wave her arms in anger and frustration while Beryl and Silver just stood there, radiating annoyance.

"Well, that's one day down." Streak glanced up at Cerise. "I hope we have equal good luck for all the others."

Cerise just hoped their allies arrived early.

☾

The next time Cerise was woken in the middle of the night, it was good news: Ruby was about to clutch.

It had been twelve long, dull days with the court confined to the colony tree and the Emerald Twilight party stewing outside, making the clutching an even more welcome event. The only good thing about the enforced idleness was that the Arbora had turned all their attention to making cloth, metalworking, and carving. By the time the other courts arrived, most of the court would have new clothes or new jewelry, several undecorated walls would have new elaborately carved murals, and several other rooms had new inlay.

And after the clutching was over, hopefully successfully, Cerise would have Ruby back.

When Cerise walked into Ruby's bower, it was clear the moment was almost here. Ruby lay on the furs by the hearth, with Cinnabar and Fluff sitting near her. The only other Raksura in the room were the two female warriors closest to Ruby, her clutchmates. Cinnabar looked nervous but determined, Fluff serene, and the two warriors just nervous. It was Ruby's first clutch, and queens tended to become unreasonably cranky during the period when they were confined to their Arbora form, when the clutch was near term, a condition that just got worse as the time drew closer. Usually only their consort and closest bloodline relatives could be present.

Sometimes things even got tricky for the mentor who assisted with the birth, but Fluff was experienced enough that Cerise wasn't worried. She said to Ruby, "Finally. You took long enough."

Ruby snarled at her. Her frills were drooping from weariness, but her eyes were bright and her breathing clear. There was no sign of any potential difficulty. She said, "I am never doing this again!"

"Everyone says that." All queens said that. Cerise was fairly certain even she had said that. The Arbora were more sensible about it.

Ruby bared her teeth. "Get out!"

Cerise left. She would come back for the birth itself, but there was no point in antagonizing Ruby now.

She came out into the queens' hall and found Paragon, Bright, Sunrise, and Cloud already there, along with a few dozen sleepy Arbora, mostly teachers, and several of the older warriors. Everyone who wasn't on guard at the knothole would be assembling in the teachers' hall and the greeting hall to wait for news.

Cerise took a cushion beside Paragon. Several kettles already sat on the large hearth and someone had put on some bread to warm. Knowing Ruby might want something more substantial after the birth, Cerise sent a warrior down to the teachers' hall to make sure some food would be ready.

With a reminiscent sigh, Paragon said, "This brings back pleasant memories."

Cerise gave him an ironic look. "For you, maybe."

Indigo and Lapis came in from the passage to the interior bowers, and settled nearby. Indigo ignored Cloud, and Cloud didn't glance in her direction, but Cerise sensed they were highly aware of each other. Cerise hissed under her breath. Indigo was still avoiding Cloud for the most part, but their few interactions had been highly interesting.

A few days ago the Arbora had decided to replenish the meat supply and a hunting party had cautiously left the tree through a door down in the roots just above the forest floor. Whole different species of predators stalked the swamps, rock outcroppings, and the wooden ridges of the mountain-tree roots in the perpetual twilight, so the hunters had been accompanied by a number of warriors and Indigo for good measure. Somehow, Cloud had ended up going along, something that Cerise would have forbidden had she gotten any hint that it might happen.

After taking some advice from the Kek, the hunters had advanced out along the tall ridge of one of the roots to the far end of the swamp, and found a herd of large grasseaters feeding on the weeds in the shallows.

They had taken several of them and had been in the process of hauling the carcasses back up onto the slope of the root with the warriors' help, when something unfolded itself up out of the mud at the fringe of the swamp. It had made a leap for two Arbora who had lingered behind the others to wash the blood out of their claws. Cloud, who had been watching from the top of the root, had stooped on the predator with wings and spines flared, startling it long enough for the Arbora to scramble to safety. Indigo and the warriors had driven it away and Cloud had been matter-of-fact about the whole incident.

After Cerise had distributed censure and praise where it was due, and discussed the ramifications of allowing a consort who the court was only the temporary and highly disputed guardian of to risk himself doing a warrior's duty, she spoke in private to Indigo. "I know, and I'm sorry!" Indigo said, "But I didn't think he'd really go with us on the hunting trip. And then he did, and I couldn't back down."

"Back down?" Cerise repeated, too angry to say anything else for the moment.

"He was there when the hunters came into the teachers' hall to tell me about the hunt. He said he had never been below the suspended forest. I dared him to go along, sort of. He dared me to let him, and said I never would, and so I had to." Indigo sighed at Cerise's expression. "I know, we sound like fledglings."

"That's one way to put it." Cerise shook her head helplessly. *You wanted them to get closer, didn't you? You wanted them to take a chance on each other.* "Just don't get him killed while you're making your decision."

Indigo tilted her head. "I have made my decision."

Yes, that was why she so lost her mind around him as to try to antagonize him into either admitting fear or doing something foolhardy. Cloud, more confident in his abilities to defend himself than other consorts his age, had let her, or possibly, knowing him, provoked the entire thing deliberately. Cerise just waited. After a long moment, Indigo visibly steeled herself and said, "I won't take him if it will cause the court trouble. That's my decision."

It was admirable, but Cerise couldn't shake the gut feeling that it would be a very great shame if Indigo didn't take Cloud. Cerise said, finally, "Well, Paragon will be disappointed if you don't."

Indigo looked wistful. "Will he?"

Paragon, far more confident of Cerise's ability to bring about a happy outcome than Cerise was, had already been mulling over names for Indigo and Cloud's first clutch. "Yes."

Indigo's expression had turned bleak and she had gone away.

Now, sitting here, surrounded by the closest members of the court and waiting for the new clutch, Cerise felt uneasy. The future was uncertain at best.

A few hours later, the Arbora and warriors were celebrating the successful birth, while the royal Aeriat visited the new babies in Ruby's bower. Ruby had already stamped off with her clutchmates to devour a couple of grasseater haunches and regain her temper, while Cinnabar and Fluff and the other mentors minded the new babies.

Ruby and Cinnabar had done well, with three potential queens and two potential consorts. Only one of the males was smaller, which meant he had been conceived somewhat later than the others. Fluff had had to clear the tiny throat before he had started to breathe, but now the littlest one was flailing his arms and hissing like the others.

Cinnabar's skin was flushed dark bronze and he was nearly giddy with relief. When one of the potential queens tried to roll off the nest of blankets, Cinnabar handed the smallest male off to Cloud, all the other arms around him being already occupied. Cloud curled around the baby and gently rubbed his tummy with one finger. The baby grabbed for his nose.

Across the room, Cerise saw Indigo staring at Cloud, and she knew that look. *Somehow I am going to have to clear the way for them.* Cerise waited until Indigo felt her gaze and looked up. Cerise lifted a brow and Indigo flicked her spines in embarrassed acknowledgment and looked away.

Later, Cerise found herself sitting near Cloud while the others were occupied on the far side of the hearth.

He was still holding one of the babies, and she watched him stroke its frills. She asked, "Why did you change your mind?"

His sideways glance at her was wary, and he didn't speak. Making it clear she wanted her question answered, she added, "About Indigo."

He looked down at the baby, letting its blunt claws wrap around his fingers. "I don't know."

Cerise wasn't sure if that was true or he just didn't want to tell her. She made her voice ironic. "Perhaps it was the wealth of our court that won you over."

Cloud smiled a little, still focused on the baby. "This may not be a wealthy court compared to Emerald Twilight, but it's much more . . . comfortable."

Cerise waited. After a moment, Cloud said, "Everyone in my court told me that when I met the queen I'd want to be with, I'd know immediately."

Cerise lifted a brow. "That's terrible advice."

He met her gaze for the first time. "I know that now."

Cerise tilted her head in acknowledgement. "If you haven't been raised in the same court, you have to get to know each other. Perhaps that's hard for Raksura, because we're all used to knowing each other from the moment we're born." She moved her spines in a gentle shrug. "We're not accustomed to speaking to strangers. That's one reason our greeting rituals are so elaborate. They tell us how to behave."

Cloud considered that, as the little male tried out its baby teeth on his finger. "I didn't trust Indigo at first."

Cerise thought it must have been frightening for him, trusting himself to an unknown queen, in his bid to escape Emerald Twilight. There were queens who would have taken advantage of the situation; he was lucky he had chosen Indigo. "Well, you didn't have reason to."

"I do now." He looked away. "She's still angry at me."

Cerise held out a hand and he let the baby crawl into it. She could tell this was honest emotion. Cloud really did regret lying to Indigo. "You could try courting her," she found herself saying. Indigo had ignored that advice; maybe Cloud could do better.

A line of confusion appeared between Cloud's brows. "Consorts aren't supposed to court queens."

"Oh, of all the things you've done that consorts aren't supposed to do, you balk at that." Cerise let a little mockery into her voice.

Cloud snorted, unwillingly amused at himself. "I could try, I guess."

Ruby stamped back in at that point, recovered and ready to become acquainted with her clutch, and everyone's attention turned to other things.

☾

Finally, on the twenty-eighth day, the first of the other courts arrived. As the visiting group began to set up a camp on a platform of an adjacent mountain-tree, Umber Shadow breathed a collective sigh of relief and the Arbora went out to collect the ground fruit that had ripened over the past days. Emerald Twilight stayed in their own camp, and Cerise was certain she saw spines drooping dejectedly.

The first court was soon followed by two others, and at first it was exciting. Cerise was still hoping Sunset Water would appear, but as each group flew in and settled for a landing, that hope was disappointed. By the next day, it was clear far more courts were arriving than Cerise had anticipated. This dispute was obviously the most entertaining thing to happen in the Reaches for turns.

The ones who had the least far to travel came with only one or two queens and several warriors, while those who had made longer trips often brought along more warriors and sometimes a mentor or two.

Cerise, Tranquil, and Bloom watched them from the door in the consorts' level. Her spines flicking grimly, Bloom said, "I worry about them hunting in our territory. I hope they have the courtesy to control their appetites."

Usually no one minded a party hunting occasionally while they traveled through another court's reserves. But if this many Raksura stayed for more than a few days, it could be a problem. Cerise told Bloom, "We're going to have to organize a joint hunting party. It's better to keep it under our control than let them do as they want." Letting the Arbora and warriors out wouldn't be a problem now, not with this many curious witnesses to anything Argent did.

At least the groups were all courteous enough to follow the first arrival's example and avoid the garden and agricultural platforms attached to the colony tree. It was courteous, but it didn't give Cerise an excuse to invite any of them in, and it made Emerald Twilight's position even more pointed.

Cerise watched one of the larger groups of recent arrivals construct an elaborate camp on one of the adjacent mountain-tree platforms with the air of people who meant to settle in and enjoy the show. She squinted, trying to get a good look at the larger queen, and decided they were probably from Opal Night. Yes, she could see Beryl staring at them in dismay. The most powerful court in the Reaches was here, and there was simply no way they would fail to assert their opinion on the situation. Cerise knew she hadn't invited them, and she was fairly certain any connection with Emerald Twilight was a distant one. The word of the judgment must have spread far wider than Emerald Twilight had meant it to.

Tranquil leaned further out the door, squinting to see as another group flew into the clearing under the canopy. "There's another one."

Cerise said dryly, "Oh good, just in time. I'd hate for them to miss anything." It was a smaller group, at least, with only one queen and five warriors.

But the new group flew past the other occupied platforms, circling toward the colony tree. Cerise thought for a moment they would join Emerald Twilight's camp, but though they flew close by and certainly seemed to recognize each other, they didn't stop. They came all the way in and landed on the platform to the side of the waterfall just below the knothole, the one where visitors usually chose to announce themselves.

"They want to greet us," Tranquil said, startled.

There was no way it could be a misunderstanding. The new party had all but stooped on Emerald Twilight, and their progress through the other groups had been obviously deliberate.

Cerise leaned down, gripping the edge of the doorway, narrowing her eyes. The leader of the group was a young queen, and something in her body shape and conformation was familiar . . . she was part of Cloud's bloodline. Cerise hissed. "I think that's Sunset Water. Finally!"

☾

Cerise sent Tranquil out to make the greeting though she would have preferred to do it herself. But with the other courts watching, she wanted to make it clear that protocol was being meticulously observed. If she was mistaken about Sunset Water's intent and their queen didn't accept the invitation to come inside, Cerise didn't know what she would do. Well, yes, she did. She would end up fighting Argent and all this effort to prevent violence would be for nothing.

But as she paced the greeting hall, anxiety knotting her gut, Tranquil entered with the whole Sunset Water party.

The hall, crowded with worried warriors and Arbora, went silent. In the only clear spot amid the chaos, Cerise stood while Tranquil and the lead female warrior from Sunset Water exchanged the formal introductions. Then the young queen stepped forward, and said, "I'm Fall, sister queen of Sunset Water." She hesitated and added, "Cloud is my clutchmate."

Cerise concealed her almost giddy relief and managed to say with dignity, "I'm Cerise, reigning queen of Umber Shadow. And you are welcome in our court."

Fall lifted a spine in acknowledgement. "I thank you." She was young for a sister queen but there was none of the aggression or posturing of the immature queens who had come into power but as yet had no responsibility. She looked weary and anxious.

Arranging tea for the warriors wouldn't be a problem at least, with half the Arbora in the court now scrambling to make the newcomers welcome. Cerise thought they might skip the further formalities, since the situation was urgent. She said, "I know Cloud is anxious to see you. Will you come up to our queens' hall and speak with him?"

Fall's expression went from uneasy to relieved. "Yes, thank you."

Cerise took Fall and her female warrior up through the colony's center well to the queens' level. When they reached the hall it was empty and nothing was prepared yet, and she realized she hadn't sent word ahead to Paragon, and none of the Arbora had had time to make it up here to set out cushions and make tea or warn the consorts. Cerise hesitated an instant, then decided to do the unthinkable. She said, "This way," and led them back through the consorts' entrance to the hall and up the private stair.

Fall betrayed herself with an uneasy twitch of her spines, aware she was being taken into what should be forbidden territory. At the top of the stair Cerise heard Fluff's voice, and followed it to the seating area near Paragon's bower.

Fluff sat near the hearth, a book unrolled across his lap, reading aloud from it. It usually took a while for two courts to get through the greeting formalities, so Paragon must have asked Fluff to read to pass the time, and to keep Cloud from fretting. It was a very old story, some tale of a queen and her warriors taking a long trading trip across an ocean filled with sealings the size of mountain-trees, and Cerise hadn't heard it in turns. Paragon sat nearby, and Cinnabar was pouring water into a tea pot. Cloud lay on a fur on the other side of the hearth, several fledglings and young Arbora sprawled around him, all of them listening raptly.

It couldn't have been better if Cerise had staged it. Cloud looked comfortable and unafraid and like exactly what he was; a consort visiting a friendly court, not a consort who had been stolen away against his will.

Paragon glanced up and saw them first, met Cerise's gaze with an incredulous lift of his brows. She said, "I apologize for interrupting."

Fluff looked up, and smiled. Startled, Cloud sat up, staring at his clutchmate. The children chorused disappointment, more distracted by the interruption of the story than by the sudden appearance of a strange queen. Fluff said, "Hush. We'll finish it later."

Cerise said, "We need to speak seriously for a time."

Cinnabar said hurriedly, "I'll take them to the nurseries." He shooed the children out the opposite passage as they stared curiously at Fall and demanded explanations in loud whispers. Once the group was out of earshot, Cerise gestured for Fall and her warrior to sit and said, "This is my first consort, Paragon. And our chief mentor, Fluff."

Fall nodded to Paragon and Fluff, and said, "I'm Fall, sister queen of Sunset Water." She looked at Cloud. "You seem well."

"I am well." His expression was guilty and uncertain. "When you didn't come, I thought . . . "

Fall winced, clearly reading beneath the words and realizing how upsetting Sunset Water's failure to appear had been. Speaking to both Cloud and Cerise, she said, "We were delayed. The reigning queen was ill. It was very . . . tense, for a time. I couldn't leave the court until she was well."

"But she's all right now?" Cloud's brow furrowed in worry.

"Yes, she's much better," Fall assured him. She glanced at Cerise and added, "I thought of sending a message, but I wasn't certain what to say."

"We've been at a loss for words, too," Cerise said, making it wry rather than an accusation. "And Emerald Twilight must have sent you a message as well."

Fall dipped a spine in exasperated acknowledgement. "Yes. I felt it was better to wait until I could see for myself." She turned to Cloud and spread her hands. "Cloud, why did you involve this other young queen, and her whole court? Why not just have her send a message to us?"

Cloud hesitated a long moment. "I should have, I know that now. At first I didn't know why I didn't, but I think it was because . . . she was interested in me. Really interested. I wanted to see her again."

Cerise caught Paragon's gaze. It was interesting to hear Cloud admit this, though she wasn't sure if he had really felt like that at the time or was coloring the past with his current feelings. He and Indigo were both so confused, either seemed possible.

Fall's expression went blank. Carefully, she said, "And have you . . . seen her again?"

"Not like you mean." For a moment, Cloud was unguarded and miserable. "She's angry."

Fall stared at him, then shook her head. "Cloud . . . you used to be so sensible. What happened?"

Cloud waved a hand in frustration. "I've been living in a court with a queen who hates me, that's what happened!"

Fall said, "You said you wanted her. Our reigning queen warned you—"

"I thought I did want her!"

"Perhaps that's a conversation for another time—" Fluff began, when Indigo charged into the room.

"Indigo!" Cerise snapped. "What—"

Indigo stopped, dropped her spines, and said, "It was my fault. I talked him into it."

"You did not," Cloud said, angry. "I tricked you. I lied to you. I betrayed—"

Indigo bared her fangs. "Shut up, you idiot!"

Cerise held up her hand to the baffled Fall. "This is Indigo, sister queen of Umber Shadow. Since she arrived with Cloud we've been over this whole situation at exhausting length. We're willing to stipulate that they were both equally at fault, and Umber Shadow has no dispute to settle with Sunset Water."

"Agreed," Fall said in relief, before Cloud or Indigo could interrupt. "Sunset Water has no dispute with Umber Shadow."

Fluff said quickly, "Witnessed by a mentor! Me, that is."

Cerise had been fairly certain that would be the case as soon as Sunset Water had accepted their hospitality, but it was still a relief to have it done. She said, "Well, now we could all have a meal and relax, except for Emerald Twilight and all the other courts waiting outside."

Fall's spines dipped, an agreement that the situation was still fraught. "I'll confront Argent and tell her I'm formally removing Cloud from her care." She cocked her head at Cerise. "I assume she'll have to relinquish any right to a dispute with your court after that."

"If she's sensible," Cerise said. That was still a big "if" but perhaps Argent would see this as the way out of the increasingly awkward and untenable situation that it was. "I'll have to go with you. I'm the one who called for the judgment of the courts." And if Argent didn't see this as a handy way out, Cerise wanted to be there to make sure Fall didn't end up in a fight to the death either. It seemed clear that Sunset Water couldn't afford to lose her, and Cerise still felt they were one violent outburst away from igniting a war with half the Reaches.

Fall nodded. "I welcome your company."

Then Indigo said, "I'm going too."

Cerise looked at her, cocking her spines at an ironic angle. "We have had this conversation before."

"She's going to demand to see me. You know she is. Maybe it'll satisfy her pride to berate me and call me names in front of all the other courts." Indigo sounded more resigned than anything else. "I've thought about what you said. I've thought about it a lot. About how this could start a war, and I know you're right. I won't do anything to cause that."

Cerise found herself hesitating. She suspected Indigo was right, and that Argent would demand to have her present. The other courts might require it for the judgment, as well, if Argent forced that issue. She said, reluctantly, "Very well. But I'm trusting you to keep your temper."

Indigo said, "Of course."

☾

On the principle that they might as well get it over with, Cerise led the way back down to the queens' hall. Ruby had come out, so Cerise stopped to introduce her to Fall, then sent the others on ahead. As they disappeared over the edge into the tree's central well, Indigo carrying Fluff, Ruby said, "I'm coming with you."

Cerise didn't argue. "Hang back with the warriors. I want them to focus on Fall, but know that I'm not alone out there." Emerald Twilight must know that Umber Shadow had another older sister queen, but Ruby hadn't visited there since before she had taken Cinnabar, and Cerise wanted them to get a look at her. Ruby's conformation was stronger and broader than Indigo's, and she was almost Cerise's height already.

Ruby didn't look happy, but she didn't argue either. "All right. Just be careful. Don't let this little idiot trap you into fighting."

"Which little idiot?" Cerise asked, in exasperation. "There are so many of them!"

Ruby snorted and slapped her on the arm. "Argent, the one little idiot who isn't related to us."

As Cerise and Ruby dropped down into the greeting hall, Cerise saw the Arbora had set out tea and food for the Sunset Water warriors near the pool, and were somewhat abandoning etiquette by sitting around chatting with them. New allies were supposed to be more reticent with each other, but with Cloud having spent so much time here, the Sunset Water group's arrival must seem like a visit from an old friend.

As Cerise landed on the floor, Leaf hurried over. Cerise told him, "Tell the Arbora to prepare a meal for tonight, to greet Sunset Water as an ally."

"So you think everything will be all right, then?" Leaf asked, his brow still furrowed with worry.

Cerise didn't want to tempt fate with reassurances that she wasn't certain she believed herself. She said, "I think if everything is all right, we're going to need to properly entertain Sunset Water tonight."

Leaf acknowledged the sense in this and went away to make preparations. Fall, Indigo, Cloud, Fluff, and Paragon waited near the passage through the knothole, and Cerise could see there was already an argument in progress. As she and Ruby reached them, Cloud was saying, "I should go with you. It's about me; I should be there."

Fall shook her head, and said, "Absolutely not." She glanced at Cerise. "I've never had to do this before. Is there a proper form for it?"

Cerise had had a mentor look for the answer to just that question in the libraries some days ago. She said, "It's normally done in private, from what our records say. There's no precedent for this."

Cloud persisted, "I'll apologize to her and take all the blame. That should make it easier for her to give in."

Fall hissed. "Nothing will make it easy for her to give in. If you were a queen, you'd know that."

Indigo told him, "Your clutchmate is right."

Cloud glared at both of them. "Then it won't matter if I go or not. And the courts should see me. There must be all kinds of rumors flying around out there, half of them started by Emerald Twilight. If the other courts see me, at least they'll know I'm not dead, or held hostage."

Cerise lashed her tail in exasperation. He had a point about the rumors. She said, "He's right, it may help our case if the other courts see Cloud in the company of his clutchmate." She couldn't think of any way to make the situation between Sunset Water and Umber Shadow more clear.

Fall grimaced in agreement. "Yes, I see the necessity." She looked at Cloud and sighed. "Everyone is going to stare at you."

Cloud folded his arms stubbornly. "That's going to happen anyway, every time I leave the court."

Paragon squeezed his shoulder in silent sympathy. Indigo's face set in a grim wince. Fluff just lifted a brow, possibly in approval at more evidence that Cloud and Indigo had realized the consequences of their actions.

Cerise growled to herself, "Let's just get this over with." She was more than ready to be done with Argent.

☾

They flew out of the knothole with Cerise and Fall in the lead, with Indigo carrying Fluff and Cloud following her. Ruby, Tranquil, four other Umber Shadow warriors, and the warriors Fall had brought from Sunset Water trailed behind.

The air was cool and sweet, with an edge of damp to it and not much wind. It would have been a good day to go flying with the consorts, if the colony tree hadn't been surrounded by a number of curious, possibly hostile, possibly sympathetic representatives of other courts.

They swept in toward Emerald Twilight's camp. Cerise, Fall, Indigo, Fluff, and Cloud landed on the platform, while Ruby and the warriors settled on the next nearest garden platform, about fifty paces behind them.

The Emerald Twilight warriors watched them grimly. Silver stood with them, and Argent ducked out of the shelter with Beryl. Both queens had their spines held stiffly; Cerise guessed Beryl might have been talking over the realities of the situation with Argent, now that Sunset Water had arrived.

Indigo set Fluff down and he planted himself right in front of her and shifted to his groundling form. Indigo tried to nudge him aside but he refused to move. If Argent wanted to attack, she would have to go through him first. It wasn't an ideal situation, and the idea of Fluff in the path of an angry, overly aggressive queen made Cerise's scales itch. She reminded herself that there were just too many witnesses for Argent to risk any kind of attack, especially with a mentor in the middle of it.

Beryl and Silver watched them with wary resignation. They had clearly recognized Fall and knew this was over. Cerise caught movement from the right but it was only two sister queens from close allies landing on a nearer platform. From there they had a good view but were far enough away not to be included in the conversation. Their action seemed to spark similar ideas from every court present, and more queens took to the air to head toward adjacent platforms.

Ignoring them, her attention focused solely on Argent, Fall stepped forward. "I understand from my clutchmate that the match had some difficulties. I ask you to return Cloud to me."

Simple and to the point, Cerise thought. Fall was wise to keep to the essentials and not to try to air Cloud's grievances in front of all the courts. But watching Argent's expression, Cerise knew it wasn't going to be as simple as Fall hoped.

Argent bared her fangs. "You mean to hand him over to the one who stole him."

Fall twitched a little, an involuntary response to the threat, but said calmly enough, "It's none of your concern what I do with my clutchmate."

Argent jerked her head toward Indigo and Cerise. "Then why are they here with you?"

Fall tilted her head and her voice took on a harder edge. "You've called this judgment of the queens down on them. They are here to see it settled."

"The judgment was their idea." Argent glared at Indigo. "I'll settle it by fighting her."

Indigo surged forward, slammed into Fluff's back, and he thumped her solidly in the chest with an elbow.

Cloud took a step forward and Cerise caught his arm and tugged him back behind Fall. Undeterred, he said, "Argent, I lied to her and tricked her into taking me away. It was my fault, not hers."

Cerise hoped the queens on the other platforms had heard that. Cleverly, Cloud had pitched his voice to carry, and she thought she could see spines flicking on the next platform out of the corner of her eye. It would make Argent's refusal to release him look just as stubborn and pointless as it was.

But Argent didn't acknowledge Cloud with so much as a spine twitch. She said to Indigo, "Fight me, and you can have him."

Beryl hissed in frustration and Silver half turned away, her spines held at a furious angle. With a growl in her voice, Fall said, "He's not yours to give, not anymore."

Cerise tried to hold her spines down. This wasn't going well. Argent was determined to fight and she knew most of the queens here would see no reason to prevent her. *No, there's no way around this.* Cerise would have to challenge Argent herself and just try to keep the fight from going to the death or to serious injuries.

She took a breath to speak but Indigo said first, "I'll fight you, on one condition."

Cloud gasped in dismay. Cerise snarled under her breath. She had thought Indigo understood why her or Fall fighting Argent was out of the question. With a growl in her voice, she said, "Indigo—"

Indigo snatched up Fluff and tossed him toward Cerise. Whipping around to catch him, Cerise didn't get a chance to interrupt as Indigo said to Argent, "If I win, I take Cloud. If you win, you hand him back to Fall."

Cerise froze, Fluff cradled in her arms.

Argent snarled in triumph. "Agreed!"

Cerise and Fluff exchanged a look. Cerise thought, *She can't be about to do what I think she's about to do*—and Fluff shouted, "Witnessed by a mentor!" loud enough for the other courts on the nearby platforms to hear. "If Indigo wins, she takes the consort. If Argent wins, the consort is returned to his birthcourt!"

Voices sounded through the clearing as the words were passed on to the queens and warriors who had been too far away to hear. Some of the mentors present helpfully echoed Fluff's cry of "Witnessed!"

Beryl snapped, "Wait!" but it was too late. Indigo turned away and jumped off the platform. Argent crouched and leapt into the air. Fall grabbed Cloud's arm to keep him from following and pulled him back to Cerise's side. Cerise set Fluff on his feet. She thought, *I hope I'm right.*

The queens from the other courts leapt into flight too, but only to move closer, gliding across to the other outer platforms of the colony tree. Ruby hopped over from the platform the warriors waited on to land next to Cerise. She said, "Did I hear right?"

"Yes." Cerise kept her eyes on Indigo and Argent as they made wide circles around each other, gradually making their way out away from the platforms, into the open area where the colony tree's canopy intertwined with the surrounding mountain-trees. Her own pulse was starting to pound in syncopation with their wingbeats.

Ruby cast a sideways look toward Beryl and Silver and their warriors, standing across the platform, their eyes on the two queens. Beryl was fuming, furious, and Silver's spines flicked anxiously. Ruby said, "If it works, it's brilliant."

So Ruby had seen Indigo's plan as well. "If she can bring it off," Cerise said, sick with tension. Indigo and Argent circled closer now and the watching queens and warriors were silent, their spines moving in agitation like a field of tall grass in the wind. Paragon and Cinnabar and some of the others were probably watching from the consorts' door. They would have a good view from there. Cerise hoped she hadn't mistaken Indigo's intentions, that Paragon wasn't about to see his favorite daughter maimed or killed, and that this wouldn't spark a war with Emerald Twilight.

Still frantic, Cloud said, "I understand Argent only accepted because she doesn't want me, but—"

"But nothing. Be quiet." Fall glanced at Cerise.

Cloud continued stubbornly, "Argent won't give way. If Indigo wins, if Indigo has to kill her, Emerald Twilight will start a war." He turned to Cerise. "If she's injured, you won't let Argent kill her—"

Cerise said, "She knows what she's doing." She hoped Indigo knew what she was doing. In the air, Argent darted in and Indigo twisted away.

Lapis hopped over from the other platform, followed by Tranquil. Lapis pushed past Fluff, close to Cerise's side, her gaze on Indigo and Argent. Cerise asked her, "Did she discuss this with you?"

"No," Lapis whispered. "If she gets herself killed—"

Cerise squeezed her wrist. Argent circled to recover from her miss and darted in again. This time Indigo met her.

They spun together, claws flashing, then broke apart. Both fell away from each other and flapped to stay in the air. Cerise couldn't see any blood. Argent recovered first and dove toward Indigo. Indigo flapped like a fledgling finding her wings for the first time but somehow managed to drop and whip away at the last instant. Argent overshot and Indigo crossed her back, but the swipe was deflected by Argent's spines. Argent twisted to grab at Indigo and the two queens went into a close skirmish, locked together, clawing at each other.

Indigo, if you're going to do this—Cerise thought. Then Indigo broke from the skirmish and flapped awkwardly away, spiraled down toward a garden platform. "I yield!" she shouted.

There was a heartbeat of stunned, nonplussed silence from the watching courts. Then a whisper of voices as everyone turned to murmur to everyone else.

Argent broke off her dive and circled uncertainly above Indigo. Cerise saw her look down at her claws, checking for blood. Below her, Indigo dropped her spines submissively and shouted again, "I yield!"

"Go get her," Cerise told Tranquil and Lapis. They leapt off the platform and dove out of sight. Some warriors from the other courts followed them, either ordered by their queens to offer help or told to go over and find out what in the name of the Three Worlds had just happened. Argent circled around again, hesitating, but Tranquil and Lapis landed near Indigo. Argent gave in and angled away back toward the Emerald Twilight camp.

Cloud lunged forward to go to Indigo and Fall caught him around the waist and dragged him back. "This isn't over yet," Fall hissed in his ear, just loud enough for only Cerise to hear. "Don't ruin it!"

Cloud took a deep breath, seemed to regain his sense and self-control. He nodded. She let him go and stepped back. Cerise braced herself to catch him if it was a trick, but he stayed where he was.

Argent landed near Beryl and Silver, breathing hard. Her scales were scratched up a little and one spine was bent, but the injuries were minor at worst. Indigo had had excellent self-control, far better than Cerise would have given her credit for.

Beryl stepped forward, ignoring Argent to look toward the platform where Indigo had landed. Indigo was on her feet, shaking her spines out, while Lapis anxiously checked her back for injuries. Tranquil turned and raised one hand, a sign that all was well. Cerise had expected no less, but it was suddenly easier to breathe.

Argent's expression was still furious, but with an element of confusion. She must know by now how she had been bested but she clearly still couldn't believe it. Beryl turned toward her and said, dryly, "Well, you've won. Your pride is satisfied. Now hand the consort back over to his clutchmate, as agreed."

Argent shook her head, spines flaring. "I barely touched her! It wasn't fair."

"But it was witnessed," Fluff said, stepping forward.

Argent looked away and hissed in frustration. Cerise kept a grim smile to herself. Yes, Argent would never have sacrificed her pride just to get the best outcome for Cloud and all three courts involved.

Beryl just stood there, waiting, arms folded. Argent shook herself, shedding some of the tension in her spines. "She humiliated herself," she said finally, sullen. "Why would she do that?"

Because being born a queen isn't the only thing that makes a good leader, Cerise thought, but kept her mouth shut.

Fall, sensibly sticking to the most important point, said, "I mean to take my clutchmate home with me, as agreed. But a formal statement from you will go far to restore friendship between our courts."

A light thump near Cerise made all the warriors flinch. Cerise turned to see the Opal Night queen. She was an impressive sight, not much older than Cerise but a half a head taller, her scales a deep emerald overlaid with a web of gold. The Opal Night queen said, deceptively mild, "Is there a problem? Our mentor witnessed the agreement; should I bring her over?" She added, with a touch of irony in her voice, "We're assuming there is no need for a judgment now, but I am sure we're willing to offer one if it's still required."

It was a pointed reminder that the other courts had been called here for a judgment and that Emerald Twilight had agreed to accept it, whatever it was. Argent was trapped all around.

Silver stepped close to Argent. Keeping her voice low, she said, "Yes, she's humiliated herself and everyone has seen it. Be satisfied with that."

Argent flicked her spines in grudging agreement. She said, formally, to Fall, "I return your clutchmate to you." She didn't look at Cloud, but turned and walked back into the shelter.

Silver followed her, and Beryl stayed only to tell Cerise, "We'll leave as soon as we can."

Cerise flicked her spines in acknowledgement. Fluff sighed in relief. Fall tugged on Cloud's arm and together they leapt off the platform to fly back to the one where the Sunset Water warriors waited. Cerise flicked a glance at Ruby. Ruby nodded and leapt into flight too, signaling the Umber Shadow warriors to follow her as she curved down toward the knothole entrance.

The other courts were settling down, dispersing into groups to chat since it was clear the excitement was over and everyone would be leaving soon. The Opal Night queen was still standing there so Cerise said, "I'm not sure your intervention was needed, but it was timely. I thank you for it."

The Opal Night queen shrugged her spines. "It was an entertaining performance. I didn't want to see the ending ruined." She flipped backward off the platform.

Indigo was flying toward the knothole with Tranquil and Lapis. It was time for everyone to withdraw with dignity mostly intact. Cerise shook her head and held out a hand for Fluff. "Come on, old man. Let's go inside and get some tea."

Fluff hopped into her arms. "Excellent idea."

☾

Cerise and Fluff were the last ones to enter the greeting hall, which was so full of chattering Arbora and warriors the echo of their voices off the wood walls made her ears hurt. She set Fluff on his feet and sang the first long note of the colony's song. Everyone went instantly silent.

Cerise stalked over to where Indigo stood with Lapis and her other warriors. Indigo's wounds were as minor as Argent's had been; she had had worse from Lapis when the two had played too roughly as fledglings, before they knew how to control their claws. Fall and Cloud stood a little distance away with their warriors. Everyone, Aeriat and Arbora, radiated anxiety and relief. Except Indigo, who looked very satisfied with herself.

Arguably, she had a right to, but Cerise asked her, "When did you get the idea to do this?"

Indigo rubbed absently at a scratch on her arm. "A couple of days ago, I suppose. The goal was always to get Cloud free of Emerald Twilight. And this seemed the only way to avoid the thing that we were really worried about, that Argent just wanted to force someone to fight her, and would be too angry to fight like a rational person and someone would end up dead and we'd all go to war over it." She added, "You were right about that—it took everything I had to hold her off without ripping her throat out!"

Ruby snorted amusement. Cerise tilted her head toward her and said, "This is not funny."

"It wasn't earlier, but it is now," Ruby assured her.

"But I didn't think it would work," Indigo interposed hurriedly, as if that would make it better. "I had to wait for the right moment and I never thought I'd get the chance."

Cerise snarled, letting out all the pent emotion. "You little idiot, if you ever, ever think of trying something like that again, I'll kill you myself!"

Paragon landed in a rush of wings that sent several Arbora and warriors reeling. He stared down at Indigo, who had the sense to at least look chagrined. She said, "I'm sorry, but it was the only solution I could think of."

He hissed through his fangs, then said, "If you ever do anything like that again, I'll let your birthqueen kill you herself."

"Indigo was always very goal-oriented, as a fledgling," Fluff said reminiscently to Streak. "Watching her play flying games with the young warrior fledglings wore my nerves down to nubs."

Cloud left Fall's side and walked up to Indigo. He said, "Thank you. I know you didn't do it for me, but . . . thank you."

Indigo twitched her spines a little, in a gesture that was probably meant to be a shrug but that came across to Cerise as a release of tension. She said, "I got us into this trouble, I had to get us out of it."

"No," Cloud said, "I got us into this trouble, and you got us out."

Cerise met Paragon's gaze and nodded in relief. They were in for a busy evening. Many of the courts outside were bound to want to stay the night and would be asking permission to hunt, and some of the ones that weren't already allied with Umber Shadow would probably want to come in and at least be greeted. It was going to be a busy afternoon.

☾

It was sometime later, after everyone had settled down and the Arbora had provided a meal of fresh grasseater, flatbread, baked roots, citrus melon, and the baked snails that they brought out for every special occasion even though the warriors wouldn't eat them, that Cerise finally took a deep breath and felt her spines actually relax. It had been a month of nothing but tension, and she was glad to see it done.

Warriors and Arbora were scattered around the hall, some still talking and eating, others falling asleep. Cerise sat near the hearth with Ruby and Fall, while the consorts had all withdrawn to talk among themselves. Indigo sat a little distance away with Lapis and Tranquil and some of the other female warriors. Indigo looked far more relaxed too. When she looked at Cloud, she smiled, and he met her gaze.

Cerise and the other queens had been pretending not to notice this. Now Fall sniffed a bowl full of snail, blinked, and set it aside. With an effort to sound casual, she said, "Cloud has told me that he has enjoyed visiting with your consorts. I hope we can count on your hospitality for a few days."

Ruby smiled to herself and poured more tea. Cerise pretended that the request needed sober consideration, and after a suitable pause, said, "Of course. We can discuss trade, and so on." Sunset Water still wanted an alliance, and still had a now notorious trouble-causing young consort to settle somewhere. Umber Shadow had a consort-stealing young queen who had just ruined her prospects with most of the courts who had seen her humiliate herself and default on a challenge. It seemed a perfect match.

Fall's spines relaxed a little, relieved to have that settled. Then she ruined the subtlety of the moment by saying, "I'll have to consult with my reigning queen, but I expect no difficulty."

Cerise expected a great deal of difficulty, but she felt confident they would all get through it somehow.

☾

EPILOGUE: MANY TURNS LATER

The story came to them during a trade exchange with Sunset Water, in a packet with copies of other courts' books that the mentors had bargained for.

Moon sat on the floor of the teachers' hall, where Heart, Blossom, and Chime examined the new acquisitions. The bulk of the trade goods were spread out across the greeting hall floor on the level above, being picked over and admired by the rest of the court. They had brought the books down here to look them over where it was more quiet.

Moon's ability to read Raksuran was still rudimentary, but he had found a book with drawings and was carefully unrolling the pages, looking at delicately penned, detailed illustrations of plants from the suspended forest. He had no idea if the text was about their medicinal use or which ones were poisonous, or just describing them. Whatever it was, it had to come in handy.

Blossom stepped carefully across the book-littered floor, the list clutched in her hand. "Moon, what's that one?"

He showed her the writing in the front, which he assumed identified the book somehow. Blossom angled her head to peer at it. "Oh, I didn't think they'd send that one! Drawings like that are so hard to copy."

Chime picked up another book from the collection, frowning. "I didn't think Sunset Water would be so generous. I mean, there are more books here than what we asked for." The court had been trying to trade for books almost since they had arrived here. When Indigo Cloud had returned to their original colony tree in the Reaches, it had become obvious that there was a huge disparity between the number of books the court owned compared to the size of the library. Even Stone wasn't certain what had happened to them; there had been many disasters as the court had left the then-overcrowded Reaches and searched for a new colony. One by one, the missing books must have been lost or destroyed along the way.

Moon turned another page in the plant book. Blossom was right, someone had put a lot of effort into these drawings. "I wonder if they're setting us up for something."

Heart didn't seem convinced. "I think you two are too suspicious."

Blossom picked her way back across the room to hand Heart the list and added, "It just means that we're obligated to share the volumes in our collection with them. That's not a disadvantage."

Chime was still frowning, unrolling the pages of the book he had picked up. "Like this one, it isn't on the list. It looks like it's a story– Wait." He turned more pages, his expression becoming more and more incredulous.

Everyone was staring at him. Moon demanded impatiently, "Well, what is it?"

Chime looked up. "This is the story of Indigo and Cloud!"

Heart and Blossom hurried over, but Moon had no idea what Chime was talking about. "The court?"

"Yes, well, the queen and consort the court was named after, when it left the Reaches." Chime unrolled another page and bounced with excitement.

Heart leaned in to look. "It's the story of how Indigo led the court out of the Reaches? Some of that's in the histories, but we're missing—"

Chime waved a hand. "No, no, it's how Indigo stole Cloud from Emerald Twilight."

Blossom stared. "I thought Stone made that up!"

Moon had known Stone hadn't made it up. When they had arrived at Emerald Twilight hoping to find a replacement for the colony tree's missing seed, it had been pretty obvious that Emerald Twilight hadn't forgotten the incident. But Stone had been a fledgling when it happened, and hadn't remembered or never known about many of the details. As a line-grandfather, he was the court's oldest member, and his past was practically ancient history to this generation.

"No, it was true," Heart told Blossom. She tried to tug the book out of Chime's lap and he turned it so she could read it too. She said, "We found a mention of it in the histories later, but the whole story must have been in one of the books that was lost."

Chime said, "There's a note in the front." With a catch in his voice, he read, "'This is such an old story that no one remembers what happened anymore, and we know that in your travels you have lost some of the contents of your library and may not have it. But it is a favorite among our fledglings and young Arbora, and it should be among yours as well.'" He cleared his throat and managed to add, "It looks like Cloud's birthcourt was Sunset Water."

Moon carefully rolled up the plant book and set it aside. "So keep reading." The story wouldn't mean as much to him as it did to the others, but the idea of queens stealing consorts was intriguing for a number of reasons. It would be fascinating to hear what had actually happened.

"The whole court is going to want to hear this," Heart said. "Chime, give it to me. No, right now. I'll ask Pearl to call a gathering tonight and we can take turns reading it to everyone."

"All right, all right." Chime reluctantly released the book.

☾

They gathered in the greeting hall that evening, and Moon sat with Jade. They were surrounded by a group of her warriors including Balm, Root, and Song. The Arbora were mostly crowded up to the front, though there wasn't really any part of the hall where it was hard to hear and there was nothing to see as the book had no drawings in it. Chime, Heart, and Blossom would take turns reading.

It was a cool rainy evening, so it was a perfect time for a story. The older fledglings and Arbora children had been allowed to sit up for it but the younger ones who were unlikely to be able to stay still for the whole thing were down in the nurseries. The teachers who were watching them were going to be owed some big favors in trade for their sacrifice later, and had been promised a second private reading as soon as possible. Even Pearl, Ember, and their followers had settled a comfortable distance away. It was hard to tell if Pearl was as happy about the find as everyone else, but she did seem settled in, Ember curled by her side, and ready to stay for the whole story.

Jade, on the other hand, had made it clear she was almost as excited about this as Chime. As Moon leaned comfortably against her, she said, "I'm a little worried about Stone. Do you know if he's coming?"

Moon glanced around, realizing that Stone wasn't here. Late arrivals were still hurrying in, but most of the court had settled in and quieted down, ready for the story to start. "I thought he was. But he didn't say so specifically." Stone hadn't reacted much when Heart and Chime had run up to the greeting hall to tell everyone about the book, but then considering Stone, that didn't mean anything.

Balm leaned past Root to say, "I saw him down near the nurseries. I thought he was coming up here right behind us."

Jade grimaced. "I wish—Oh wait, there he is." Stone had just stepped out of the passage under the waterfall. He wound his way through the seated crowd, nudged a warrior aside with a foot and took a place about ten paces away from Moon and Jade. Root whispered loudly, "Stone's here!" and Balm shushed him, just as Heart started to read.

Moon missed the first bit, still distracted by Stone's late arrival. Though Jade clearly had, Moon hadn't thought about the fact that for Stone the figures in this story were all real people that he had memories of, friends and close relations, even though he must have been very young when the events took place. For the others in the court they were distant ancestors, and for Moon they weren't much different than the made-up characters in groundling tales. Of course Stone had been reluctant to listen to the story, especially with everyone else watching.

There was nothing to be done about it now, and Moon turned his attention to the reading. It was about how Indigo had gone on a trading trip to Emerald Twilight, where she had seen how Cloud was treated by his queen who no longer wanted him, and how he had asked her for help. They had fled Emerald Twilight for Umber Shadow, which was what the Indigo Cloud court had been called at the time. For a Raksuran story, it was almost romantic.

Moon had become acquainted with the idea of romance from hearing so many groundling stories, but it wasn't something he had encountered much among Raksuran courts. Aside from all the wrangling between queens and consorts about bloodlines and alliances, Raksuran relationships were very direct. If you wanted to have sex with someone, you just asked. It made things a lot less fraught.

But as the story progressed, Moon felt there was a lot left unsaid that had nothing to do with the attraction between Indigo and Cloud. It must have been the diplomatic disaster of a large part of the Reaches, considering all the intertwined alliances implied in the text. He thought the court would have had a hard time navigating that. He knew the current version of Indigo Cloud would have had a miserable time of it, even in this much less crowded and competitive Reaches.

Whether all the details were exactly what had happened or not, it was a very good story. Several of the younger warriors and Arbora got so excited they shifted involuntarily at a few dire moments. And it explained why Sunset Water had been inclined to be generous about the books; the two courts had had no contact until Indigo Cloud had returned to the Reaches, but the Sunset Water mentors must have still been aware of the connection between them. Moon got so caught up in it he forgot to watch Stone for reactions. Not that it would have provided any insight; Stone was excellent at not reacting.

The hall was silent until the end, when most of the court burst into immediate commentary. Heart and Blossom looked delighted by the reaction and Chime was clearly as pleased as if he had made up the story himself instead of just reading it.

Jade said thoughtfully, "I don't think she did it for him."

Moon knew she meant the part where Indigo had thrown the fight. It had sounded like common sense to him, but many of the others had reacted with shocked gasps. "Why not?"

Jade uncoiled from Moon so she could sit up and stretch. "The situation was so tense that agreeing to the fight and then losing it as quickly as possible, before any harm could be done, was the only way out."

"So she did the smartest thing," Moon said.

Jade eyed him, a little amused. "Some consorts wouldn't see it that way."

"Some consorts are idiots." Moon saw Stone was already on his feet and headed out of the hall. He wasn't stopping to speak to anyone, which wasn't necessarily unusual, but . . . he told Jade, "I'm going to—"

Jade had followed his gaze, frowning worriedly. "Yes, go on."

Most people were still sitting and talking so it was relatively easy to move quickly through the crowd without stepping on anyone or needing to shift and use his wings. Moon caught up with Stone near the waterfall. Stone threw him an opaque glance but didn't immediately object to his presence. Moon walked with him until they were past the noise of the rushing water, and into the smaller hall beyond it. "That was a good story," he said. "Was that how it really was?"

Stone said, "It's close enough."

He sounded so normal, he almost had Moon fooled. But there was just something in his voice. Moon stopped and said, "But it isn't. Stories aren't enough." That he knew from personal experience.

Stone kept walking, and for a moment Moon thought he wouldn't reply. Then he paused, one hand on the vine carving wrapped around the doorframe. "It's not like what the Fell did to Opal Night, or to Sky Copper. I was with them all a long time, till the end. It wasn't enough, but it was good."

Stone slipped through the doorway and Moon didn't try to follow. He knew from experience that there were just some things you had to go through alone.

THE FOREST BOY

A prequel to The Cloud Roads, *set many turns ago when Moon was still a fledgling.*

When Tren was younger, he had been afraid of the settlement's midden. He had imagined every monster from Ari's stories lurking in the piles of broken pottery and rotten fruit rinds.

Now going there was one of his more interesting chores, especially on a breezy summer day. The big flat leaves of the round-trees, stacked like plates all the way up the tall slim trunks, filtered the hot sun into cool green shade. Tren always went with Lua, his favorite foster sister, and they searched for thrown-away things that were still useful, like broken bits of carved wood and colorful glazed ceramic, and puzzled over strange objects that travelers on the Long Road had cast aside. They wound their way along the grass pathways between the piles of rubbish, and the white birds called and the treelings chirped and played high above them. They didn't go near the darker deeper forest beyond the fringe, where everyone knew the dangerous predators lurked.

Kaleb, Tren's foster father, had remarked on the change, noting how Tren now seemed to consider the trip to the midden an outing rather than a chore. "I'm not afraid of it anymore," Tren had told him, reluctantly honest. He hated to admit that he had been afraid in the first place, but he wanted Kaleb to know he was a grown-up of twelve seasonal turns now, past such childish fancies.

Instead of saying that Tren was now assuming his adult responsibilities, like Tren expected, Kaleb said, "You aren't afraid anymore because you've learned there was nothing to fear. Are you still afraid of the forest?" Tren had nodded, and Kaleb had said, "Good. That's a good fear, to keep you safe."

This morning Tren and Lua had dumped the basket of household refuse, and moved on to investigate a new pile of rubbish probably left by the trading caravan that had passed down the Long Road yesterday. It was mostly broken glass and looked as if someone had tossed out a whole wagonload. "Why would they leave all this?" Tren wondered, digging past unraveled grass baskets to uncover a store of pieces as blue as the sky at high summer. "Are they crazy?"

Lua held up a shard from another basket, red as blood, curved as if it had been part of a vase or funnel. "Maybe somebody died, and they didn't want to carry her trade goods anymore." She was small for a Mirani, a head shorter than Tren, and everyone assumed she was younger. The Mirani all had green-tinged skin and light-colored hair, blond or very light brown, like Tren. Lua had dark hair and her skin was closer to gray-green in winter, pale green in summer. She was a mix of Mirani and something else, and Tren had heard whispers in the settlement that that was why she had been dumped on the Long Road for Kaleb to find. Sometimes Tren thought she was older than him, just shorter than she should be for her age.

Noting that the glass all seemed to be shattered, nothing whole, he said more practically, "Or the baskets fell over and this is everything that broke." Tren had been with Kaleb and his wife Ari for four of his twelve turns, in their house under the biggest, oldest round-tree at the edge of the Mirani settlement. The house held six children, none of them actually birthed by Ari. The couple took in the unwanted young of this settlement and those further up the Long Road. And children like Tren, whose parents had died and left him with nowhere else to go.

He and Lua half-filled their basket with glass, with no clear idea of what to do with it except that such beauty shouldn't go to waste. Then something rustled somewhere in the piles about thirty paces away, toward a thicker stand of trees. Tren froze, glancing at Lua to see if she was afraid. Lua just cocked her head, intrigued. "What is it?" she whispered.

"A monster, from the deep forest." Tren dropped his voice to its lowest register, mocking their younger foster brother Melic, who liked to tell scare-you stories, badly and to excess. The only animals who came to the midden were the fringe scavengers, small flightless birds and harmless treelings.

Lua snorted, standing and shaking bits of glass out of her smock. "Let's find out."

They split up, Tren creeping one way, Lua the other. It was very like when they had both been younger, playing hunter by stalking the settlement's small sumptor herd. The sumptors were big and calm and had mostly eyed them without interest, refusing to cooperate by running and hiding.

The faint noise came from a big pile of old food trash. As Tren eased up on it, he caught a glimpse of Lua's dark hair as she made her way around the other side. Then Tren heard a metallic crash, and Lua called out, "Here, back here!"

Tren bolted around the pile and heard something flap, like one of the giant deep-forest birds. Only it was frighteningly close rather than high overhead. He slid to a halt, startled, but what he saw was Lua, standing and staring at a boy crouched in the grass.

The boy wasn't a Mirani. He had brown skin and short dark hair, and under his tattered dirty shirt and pants he looked as skinny as if he had been starved. He was staring back at Lua, dirt smudges on his face, his eyes terrified. At first Tren thought he was awkwardly crouched atop a broken metal plow shaft, and he couldn't think why anyone would choose such an uncomfortable seat. Then the boy collapsed and slumped forward; Tren saw the blood on his calf below the torn leg of his pants, the serrated metal clamping the bronze skin.

Tren gasped, shocked. The metal shaft wasn't part of a broken plow, it was the snap-bar of a trap. "Lua, run and get Kaleb!" he shouted, and she ran.

As her steps pounded away down the path, Tren edged a little closer to the unmoving boy, getting a better look at the metal teeth clamped into his leg. The bile rose in his throat; he had seen dead people, and broken limbs and sickness, but nothing like this, never a bloody wound caused by something so cruel. And what was the trap doing here anyway, in the midden where he or Lua might have been caught too? He wanted to do something for the boy, but the teeth of the trap were sunk in so deeply he was afraid to touch it.

Finally Tren heard people running down the grass path. Kaleb arrived in a frantic rush, two more men from the settlement on his heels. Tren pointed mutely at the boy; Kaleb saw the trap and used words Tren had never heard him speak before. He had never seen Kaleb look so furious and so horrified, and it made Tren feel even more sick. Kaleb pushed him toward the path and said, "Go on now, go back home," and Tren ran, grateful to escape.

He found Lua standing in the sunny patch of bellflowers just past the fringe, where the pathway curved back toward the settlement. He took a big gulp of air, the fresh breeze clearing the stench of blood and rotted food from his lungs. Lua had her arms tightly folded as if she was cold. Breathless, she said, "Did you see?"

Tren nodded. "It was a trap for predators. Who would put it there?"

Lua looked up at him, blinking, as if he wasn't making sense. "What?" Tren asked her, wondering what he had missed. He had been so shaken by the sight of the injured boy, he hadn't looked for anything else. "What did you see?"

She shook her head, and didn't answer. Then Kaleb came out of the midden, carrying the unconscious boy, and Tren forgot that he had ever asked her the question.

(

The Mirani settlement lay in a big clearing between the curve of the river and the Long Road, among flower-covered hills and scattered round-trees. The houses were wood and stone, built against the hills and dug into them where possible, surrounded by gardens and fruit bushes.

Kaleb carried the boy back to their home, to one of the sleeping rooms that was built half into the hill beside the house, the one that was always cool in the hot season and warm in the cool rains. None of the children were allowed in the room, and for three days there was no sight or sound of the boy.

On the first day the settlement's healer came and went twice, and Kaleb spoke to him outside. Their voices were low and serious, reminding Tren uncomfortably of the illness that had taken his parents. All the children were subdued, especially Lua, who watched the doorway of the sleeping room as if expecting something startling to come out of it. Ari carried in water and towels and spent most of the day with the boy.

Hearing how terrible the trap was, everyone in the settlement thought the boy would die, and neighbors brought them bread, pottage, and even some spicecakes, as if he had been part of the settlement instead of a stranger. There were angry mutters about the trap, and the stupidity of whoever had left it there. The chief hunter reported to Kaleb that it had probably been thrown away by someone on the Long Road who hadn't known how to use it, and hadn't realized it was still set. Tren and Lua and all the other children were forbidden to go back to the midden until it had been thoroughly searched, to make certain the same someone hadn't dumped anything else dangerous there. But the second day the healer came and went again, and afterward Kaleb, looking relieved, told them, "Not as bad as it looked, not nearly as bad. Fever's down and he's much better today."

"Who is he?" Sarin, the oldest boy in the house, asked what they had all been wondering. "Where did he come from?"

Ari, about to carry another bowl of water into the room, answered, "He won't tell us his name, poor thing. Kaleb asked if he was looking for food in the midden, and he nodded, but that's all we know."

On the third night, after supper, the boy was so much better Ari could spend more time with them. She felt like telling a story, and they all sat around on the grass mats on the floor of the main room to listen. Ari sat on her carved stool, Kaleb at her feet, and leaned forward, her eyes sparkling. "This is about the Ghobin, and the village of Mirani-Gedin."

Tren had heard the Ghobin story before, and shivered in anticipation. Ari told the best scare-you stories in the settlement. They all settled in to listen; Lua pulled her blanket around her and leaned against Tren, Melic climbed into Sarin's lap, and Lys and Klia edged closer together. The Ghobin were a predator species, who lived in burrows in the deep forest far to the west. When they attacked a settlement, they tunneled underground, up under the houses, breaking through the floors to swarm out and kill the inhabitants. They were small, so their preferred prey was children. The first time Ari had told this story, Tren had been afraid to set foot on the dirt floor of the stillroom for six days.

Even with repetition, the story of how the Mirani-Gedin defeated the Ghobin was so absorbing that everyone listened intently. They didn't notice someone else was listening until Ari paused; she touched Kaleb's shoulder and nodded toward the back of the room.

Tren twisted to look, dislodging Lua.

The new boy was huddled in the doorway of the sleeping room, watching them. He had crept out so quietly no one had heard a thing. He was as skinny and strange and wide-eyed and long-limbed as Tren remembered, but the blood and dirt had been washed away, and he wore an oversized shirt that belonged to Kaleb. His leg was wrapped in a clean bandage, and he should have looked much better. But his eyes were still afraid. He could have been facing a room full of Ghobin rather than harmless Mirani.

Suddenly Lua leapt to her feet and ran into the other sleeping room. Everyone stared after her, baffled. She couldn't be afraid of the injured boy; Lua was the bravest girl in the settlement. Besides, he was clearly the one who was afraid of them.

She reappeared almost immediately, holding her old doll, a battered collection of tied rags that Ari had given her turns ago when she had first arrived here. It hadn't changed much since the last time Tren had seen it, except it was even more dirty and tattered. She must have been keeping it stuffed under her sleeping mat.

Lua started toward the boy, moving slowly as if she was trying to approach a wounded animal. The boy watched her with wary mistrust. She stopped in front of him and sat on her heels; he was still taller than she was, even sitting down huddled against the doorframe. She held out the doll, pressed it against his hand until his fingers closed around it. Then she whispered, "I won't tell."

The boy's eyes widened. He looked at the doll and then at Lua. Something seemed to pass between them, something that made his shoulders slump and the tension leave his body.

"What's your name, little one?" Kaleb said softly. He was speaking Altanic, the trade language that everyone along the Long Road used.

The boy hesitated, bit his lip, and said, "Moon."

Ari asked, "Did you leave your family, Moon?"

Moon hesitated, so long Tren didn't think he would answer. But then he said, "They were killed." His grip on the doll tightened, as if it was giving him courage to trust them, and he added, "We lived in the forest. My mother, my sister and brothers."

"You lived in the forest? That's—" Kaleb began, then Ari caught his sleeve and gave him a meaningful glare. Tren supposed he had been about to say it was dangerous to go near the forest, which is what Kaleb always said. Tren was pretty certain that Moon would know that already, if his family had been killed in it. Kaleb cleared his throat and instead said, "Where did this happen?"

Moon sat up a little straighter. "Much further east."

"But where have you been living?" Ari asked.

Moon frowned down at the doll. Then Lua said, "You were alone on the Long Road, following caravans?"

Moon glanced at her, then told Kaleb, "That's it, that's what I was doing."

Tren thought Moon didn't want to say what he had been doing, and wondered if he had been a thief. That would be exciting. He tried to catch Lua's eye, but she was still watching Moon. Kaleb started to ask another question, but Ari said, "That's enough for now. He needs to rest."

☾

As his leg healed, Moon gradually grew more easy around them, and lost the tense look of someone who expected something terrible to happen at any moment. He was limping too badly to leave the house and yard, but he played pebble games with Melic and Klia and Lys, and helped them build miniature farms and towns out of sticks and dirt, ignoring the unspoken rule that said if you wanted to be grown-up, you didn't play with babies. He didn't talk much, but this didn't seem to bother the younger children. Tren saw Kaleb watching Moon play with them, and heard him say to Ari, "He's not a wild boy, he's been raised by someone."

"You had doubts?" she asked, scrubbing briskly at the big cooking pot.

"One or two," he admitted. "Living in the forest, after all."

Ari made a derisive noise, nodding to where Lys was ordering Moon to lay the game pieces out and he was complacently obeying her. Ari said, "Not likely."

Moon spent the most time with Lua. In the evening they sat in the corner beside the warming hearth and talked in quiet voices, more than Moon talked to anybody else. Lua had never talked to anybody that much before either, except Tren. Moon also watched her draw, apparently fascinated by it, though he never tried to do it himself, even when she offered to share her slate.

Watching them together, Tren felt the first stirrings of dislike. "Come down to the river," he urged her one evening. "The fisherwoman says the mudcrabs will be out."

She shook her head, bending over her slate, while Moon handed her the drawing stone. "We'll stay here."

Tren had gone with Sarin, not happily. Since they were much younger, Tren and Lua had always planned to marry and build a big house on the river, and be fishers, a chore they both enjoyed. Granted, sometimes they had planned to run away and be Road pirates, but age and time had suggested that that probably wouldn't be a very good way to live.

Lua's promise not to tell anyone that she had given Moon her doll was wasted. Once Ari judged him well enough to venture out into the rest of the settlement, Moon kept it with him, tucked through his belt under his borrowed shirt. Any other boy who did such a thing would have been teased unmercifully and there would have been fights, but Moon was so odd and different that everything he did seemed normal for him. Also, he was taller than any other boy close to his age. Tren noticed that the older boys who might have been inclined to start trouble always seemed to think better of it, when confronted with Moon's size, wiry strength, and direct gaze.

Moon's only failing was that he ate as much as Tren and Sarin put together. Despite that, Kaleb was growing pleased with him. "Boy's got big hands and feet for his size," he told a neighbor. "He's going to be the tallest man in the settlement."

The neighbor nodded agreement. "He'll come in handy when it's fruit-picking season."

Chores did go much faster once Moon was able to help, because he didn't seem to get tired as long as he could eat. He helped with everything, with digging the toba from the fields near the river, grinding grain so Ari could make bread, weeding root patches, carrying water, washing the clothes and blankets. The only thing he couldn't do was help tend the sumptors. The big slow creatures didn't like him, tending to growl and sidle whenever he came within their limited sight. The chief herder thought it was because Moon wasn't Mirani, that the beasts must be reacting to the different way he looked. But still, with Moon around, Tren found he and the other children had more time in the late afternoon for play.

That was when Tren really started to dislike him.

He wasn't a fool; he knew it was jealousy, like the jealous herder in one of Ari's stories who lost his herd by trying to make it bigger than those his neighbors owned. He had been hearing that story and more like it for four turns, he didn't need it spelled out any more clearly. Moon was big, strong, helpful, good to everyone, and everyone in the house liked him. He also had the added mystery of being a wild boy from the Long Road, without any of the dirty or violent habits a real wild boy might have.

But knowing it was jealousy didn't seem to help Tren make it go away, It just made it worse, since now he could feel guilty about being jealous.

Tren had suffered like this for nearly a month, when Kaleb called for him and Moon to help carry a load of medicine herbs to the Long Road, where a trader wagon from another settlement was waiting for it.

As Tren, Moon, and Kaleb carried the baskets, Kaleb said, "The herdman told me this morning that one of the sumptor bucks was killed and gutted down by the river, near the western fringe of the forest. You two take care and stay away from there for a while. It's not often something comes out of the forest, but when it does, it's always bad."

Tren nodded glumly, but Moon said, "Not everything in the forest is bad."

"But it's still dangerous." Kaleb's voice was stern. "You should know that better than anyone."

Moon looked away, and Tren saw his jaw tighten. Tren wondered if Moon would argue with Kaleb, and he felt guilty for hoping they might. But instead, Moon asked, "Why didn't Lua come?"

Tren simmered. It wasn't going to take long to deliver the herbs, surely Moon could stand to be separated from Lua for that long.

"Didn't need anyone else to carry this, with you two along," Kaleb answered.

Tren slowed his steps, let Kaleb get a little way ahead, then said in a low voice, "The boys from this settlement are mean to her, because she's not all the way Mirani." Moon had to know these things, if he was going to marry Lua as seemed inevitable at the moment.

Moon frowned. "She isn't?"

Tren wasn't surprised Moon hadn't noticed. Lua had pointed out to him that the children with the traders and travelers from other places didn't notice either, and didn't tease her for it. It had occurred to Tren that Lua might prefer to live somewhere like Kish, where according to Kaleb there were lots of different kinds of people mixed together, and no one would care what Lua was. The fact that Moon would probably be happy to go there with her didn't improve his mood any. He said, sullenly, "She's half Mirani. The other traders don't tease her, just these boys."

Moon watched him a long moment, brows knit with that thoughtful expression where you couldn't tell if he understood or not. Then his mouth quirked in a quick smile, and he said, "Do you think they'll tease me?"

This time it was Tren who tightened his jaw and looked away. It was worse that Moon was nice to him, too. He said, grimly, "You're not half anything, you're just you."

Moon didn't reply.

They reached the Road, the high gray wall of it emerging from the heavy green forest and cutting through a grassy meadow, the edge of the settlement's clearing. It was made of weathered stone and stood a good twenty paces high, and the top was nearly sixty paces wide.

The Long Road made it possible for traders and travelers to get through the forest, and for the settlement to trade roots and fruit and fish for things they couldn't make for themselves. It had been built so long ago no one remembered when or who or how. Kaleb had told them that the Road ran all the way east, to the sea which was called the Gulf of Abascene, and all the way west, to the edge of Kish. But those places were as distant as the clouds, as far as the Mirani were concerned.

A path led to the carved stairs that climbed the Road's side, and velvety little plants grew in the cracks between the huge stones. From here Tren could see the wagon waiting up on the Road, the four sumptors that pulled it standing patiently.

"Better stay down here," Kaleb reminded Moon. "You know how the beasts startle around you."

Moon stopped obediently at the bottom of the steps, and Tren continued up with Kaleb, his mood not improved by the fact that he was going to have to make a second trip for Moon's basket, too.

Kaleb greeted the adult traders, and moved around the bulk of the wagon with them to talk. The two older boys who caused the most trouble, Gavin and Nelit, were nowhere in sight. That was a small mercy.

Tren deposited his basket and went down the stairs again for the second load. But as he put it down beside the wagon, something shoved him from behind, and he fell against the wagon bed and scraped his arm on the rough wood. He whipped around, glaring, and found himself facing Gavin and Nelit. Gavin grinned and said, "Where's your half-breed girlfriend?"

There were a lot of replies Tren could have made, but he was in a bad mood already, and this was all he needed. He said, "She couldn't stand the stink of you and your brother the treeling," and spit at Gavin's feet.

Gavin shoved Tren again, hard, and his back thumped against the wagon bed.

Moon was suddenly there, right beside Tren. He must have hurtled up the steps, but he wasn't even breathing hard. He studied Gavin, head cocked to one side. He said, "Don't do that again."

"Or what?" Gavin grinned, and shoved Moon hard in the shoulder. Only Moon didn't shove. He just stood there. He didn't even sway backward. It was like Gavin had shoved a skinny tree instead of a skinny boy.

Moon stepped forward, eye to eye with Gavin. "Do you really want to find out?"

Gavin drew back, watching him with real fear. Nelit, never the brave one, had already retreated a dozen paces down the Road.

The wagon-sumptors lowed uneasily, and from behind the wagon, Kaleb yelled, "Moon, are you up here?"

"No," Tren called back, urging Moon toward the stairs.

Moon went, and Gavin, encouraged, said, "You'd better go!"

Moon laughed, and hopped down the stairs as if nothing had happened. Then he looked at Tren's grim face. "What's wrong?"

"I didn't need your help," Tren said through gritted teeth.

"Did you want to get beat up?" Moon clearly didn't see the problem. "You should have said something earlier."

Tren hit him in the chest. It was like hitting a rock. Moon just looked hurt, and Tren stamped off, feeling like the worst person in the settlement.

☾

The next day, after Kaleb had set them free from their chores, Lua said, "I want you to come to the midden with me and Moon. We want to show you something."

Obviously, they meant to tell him that they had planned to be married. Not immediately, of course, but in a few turns when Lua was old enough. Tren didn't want to hear that. He said, sulkily, "We're not supposed to go near the fringe for a while, because something killed that sumptor."

"That was toward the west, not the east where the midden is," she said impatiently. "Come on."

Tren went, reluctantly. Moon was waiting for them at the top of the path to the midden. For some reason, he seemed almost as reluctant as Tren. "This was your idea," Lua told him, prodding him along down the path.

Moon shrugged and dragged his feet all the way.

Once there, Tren and Moon, by an unspoken temporary accord, poked around through the piles, looking for anything new and interesting. There wasn't much of a breeze, but the late afternoon sun was filtered to a cool green by the big leaves, and the usual complement of treelings squealed and squeaked high in the branches.

"Well?" Lua folded her arms, determined to keep them from stalling any longer. "Nobody's here."

"Wait." Moon was looking toward the shadows under the thicker trees, the ones that marked the end of the fringe and the beginning of the forest. He frowned. "I smell something."

Of course he smelled something, they were standing in the trash heap. "It's rotting guts," Tren said, annoyed.

"No, under that."

"How do you smell something under another smell—"

It leapt down from a high branch, landing hard in the grass, barely twenty paces from them.

It stood up from a crouch. It was shaped like a man, and wore rough hide clothing, but its skin looked like hardened pale leather, ridged and scarred. Its face seemed to be all staring black eyes and huge round fanged mouth. Lua screamed. Tren's breath strangled in his throat. "It's a Tath," Moon said, his voice calm and tight.

Tath. Ari told stories about Tath. They lived in the forest, they climbed trees, and they ate whatever they could catch.

The Tath snarled and lunged toward Lua. Moon lunged for it, but in mid-motion, he changed.

It happened fast, but not so fast there was any doubt about what happened. One moment Moon was Moon, running toward the Tath, then the air around him blurred as if he passed through a dark cloud, and then he was . . . something else.

He landed between Lua and the Tath. He was taller, his shoulders broader. His skin had darkened from brown to black, a shiny black made up of tiny jewel-like scales. He had long curving claws on his hands and feet and a long tail, and a mane of spines around his head, running down between the lumpy ridges on his back.

The Tath recoiled with a snarl, and Moon leapt on it. They rolled in the grass, snarling and fighting. Then the Tath threw Moon off, leapt to its feet, and ran right toward Tren.

Tren turned to bolt and made it two steps before it reached him. It snatched him up and ran.

The Tath's arm around his chest squeezed the breath out of him, but Tren kicked and beat at its tough skin, half-blind with terror. It reached a tree and leapt ten paces up the trunk, sunk claws into the bark, and started to climb one-handed.

Tren struggled for breath to scream. The jolting violent motion of the climb knocked his head back against the creature's hard shoulder, and he clawed at its arm helplessly. Then he heard a vaguely familiar sound, like a giant bird flapping. Something black shot past them. The Tath stopped, its claws grasping a branch, and looked up.

Moon perched on the trunk just above them, spines bristled, tail flicking. The ridges down his back had turned into black scaled wings, now partly extended.

The Tath growled defiance, and Moon dropped on its head.

Looking up into the Tath's face, Tren saw its expression turn from anger to horror as black-bronze claws clamped onto its skull, sinking into the skin of its forehead. Moon's spiny head whipped around, fangs sinking into the Tath's neck. His weight jerked it off the tree, it lost its grip on Tren, and they were all tumbling toward the ground.

Except Tren wasn't tumbling, something had him from behind, and he was gliding down. He saw the Tath hit the roots at the base of the tree, bounce and sprawl like a broken doll. A moment later Tren dropped into soft grass. He stumbled and sat down hard, dazed.

Lua fell to her knees beside him. "Are you all right?" she demanded breathlessly.

He stared at her, grabbed her arm. She didn't look hurt, just flushed and wide-eyed. He looked for Moon.

Moon was himself again, standing beside the dead Tath, nudging it with a bare foot. He looked just like he always had, still dressed in an oversized shirt and rope-belted pants. His hair was mussed and there was a spray of dark blood across his chest and shoulder. The Tath's blood.

Tren stuttered, found his voice, and managed, "What are you?"

Moon glanced at him, then dropped his gaze uneasily. "I don't know. My family—I didn't lie about that. We were all like this. My mother never said where we came from." He nudged the Tath with his foot again. "I can't find any others like us."

Tren turned to Lua. She didn't look surprised. Scared, shaken, but not surprised. When she had given Moon her doll, he remembered, she had whispered, *I won't tell.* "You knew!"

She bit her lip, guilty. "I saw him in the trap. He changed, because he was afraid of what we'd do if we knew what he was. That's why he got so hurt."

He had thought they were his friends, and they had lied to him. Lua had been his friend first, and now she loved Moon better, enough to lie for him. Tren scrambled to his feet, furious. "I'll tell! I'll tell Kaleb, I'll tell everyone!"

"No, you can't!" Lua shook her head, appalled. "They won't understand! We were going to tell you, that's why we came here—"

Moon stared at him, stricken. "Don't."

Their reaction, the obvious accord between them, just made him angrier. "I will, you're from the forest, you're dangerous!" If he had had time to think he would have known he was being stupid, threatening this strange creature.

Except that Moon didn't look like a strange creature, he looked like the frightened hurt boy they had found in the trap. "I just want a place to live—"

Lua yelled, "You can't tell!"

Tren ran, pounding away down the path.

He didn't run home, he ran to one of the fruit gardens near the fringe, and hid in the damp tall grass near the rain cistern. Then he cried until his nose ran and his head ached and he couldn't cry anymore.

That was when he realized he wasn't really afraid of Moon. He sat alone near the fringe, the birds singing overhead, and he wasn't afraid Moon would come after him. He was afraid of the Tath, even though it was dead, and mad at Lua, mad at Moon for not telling him that he could fly, and angry at himself for crying. Kaleb's words came back to him: *You're not afraid . . . because you know there's nothing to fear.*

Moon had slept in their house for days and days, eaten meals with them, played with them. There were no stories where forest-monsters did things like that. They were like the Tath and Ghobin, killing everything for food. There were no stories about monsters who could make themselves look like ordinary people. *And he saved you,* Tren thought.

The image of the Tath's face filled his vision, and his skin burned like its hands were still on him. He leapt to his feet and ran toward home.

☾

Lua was there, but it was evident from Ari's calm demeanor and the unconcern of the other children that she hadn't said anything about what had happened. She was hiding in her corner by the hearth, scratching on her slate, and didn't look at Tren when he came in. That suited Tren, who didn't want to look at anyone either. He stamped back to the main sleeping room, rolled up in his blanket, and went to sleep.

He slept through the rest of the afternoon, waking only briefly when Ari came to feel his forehead, suspicious that he had taken sick. He woke for real at dusk, and stumbled out into the main room. Ari was carrying a pot in from the cistern, and the other children were gathering for supper. Guilty and self-conscious, Tren looked for Moon, expecting to see him with Lua in the corner.

Moon wasn't there.

Kaleb walked in from the stillroom, wiping his hands on a towel. He glanced around at them all, doing a quick head-count, and said, "Where's Moon?"

Lua looked up. Her eyes were red, but she wasn't crying. She said, "He's gone." That was when Tren saw she had her doll back. Tattered and dirty, it lay beside her on the hearth stone.

"Gone?" Kaleb glanced at her. "Gone where?"

"Gone away." Lua's voice was tight and sullen. "Down the Long Road."

Kaleb stared, and Ari stepped forward, frowning. "You mean, he's left the valley?"

Lua nodded. Kaleb and Ari exchanged a look, their faces puzzled, distressed. Ari said, "Whyever for?"

Lua looked down, pressed her lips together, and wouldn't answer.

Kaleb and Ari couldn't leave it at that. Kaleb took a lamp and rousted the neighbors and went out to search the settlement. Tren knew Kaleb was hoping that Moon had gone off to hide and sulk, like the other children did occasionally.

Everyone went outside, watching the neighbors walk around with lamps, as Kaleb gathered a group to go and search the fringe. Tren found Lua sitting on the stone of the garden boundary, out of earshot of the others. He eased up beside her and whispered, "Why did he go?" He knew exactly why Moon had left, the knowledge ate at him like a . . . like a monster, but he was hoping against hope there had been another reason.

Lua turned to him and even in the dark he knew what her expression was like. Her voice was bitter. "You said you'd tell. If people find out what he is, they'll try to kill him. He said that's what always happened before, when people see him."

Tren slumped in misery. "I didn't mean it."

"You sounded like you did!" Lua slapped him with the doll, with a fury that suggested that she would rather be slapping him with a rock. "You were jealous."

Tren looked away. There was no point in denying it. But the jealousy had fled, leaving him cold, empty, and guilty.

Lua said, "He was jealous of you." Tren stared at her, uncomprehending, and she continued, "He told me. He didn't come to the midden to look for food, he came to watch us. He came here a month before we found him, and he stayed to watch us, from high in the trees where no one could see him. He was jealous of the way Kaleb talked to you, and showed you how to do things. He was jealous because he thought I was your little sister, like the one he used to have. He was watching us play in the midden and he was so jealous he didn't see the trap."

"I'm sorry," Tren said, miserably, inadequately. Lua shoved to her feet and ran away, pelting down the hill back toward the house.

☾

They didn't find Moon, and Kaleb and Ari worried about him for months, hoping he would come back. Lua didn't speak to Tren for ten days, but when she did she admitted that Moon had said the Tath had probably tracked him to the settlement. That he had killed some of its pack a few valleys away, and it might have been waiting near the midden, having scented Moon's blood at the spot where the trap had been. That Moon had thought it was all his fault.

That didn't make Tren feel any better. But Lua also said, "He said he wanted to fly so much, but it was too dangerous to do it here, there were too many people who might see him. He said he couldn't live without flying, so he couldn't live here for long."

Tren hoped it was true, and not just Moon trying to make Lua feel better. Lua eventually forgave Tren, but he never forgot what had happened. And he never looked at the forest the same way again.

ADAPTATION

This is another prequel to The Cloud Roads, *set in the Indigo Cloud court at the eastern colony.*

Chime woke to dim dawn light falling through the air shaft high above his bower. He wanted to sleep more, but his curved basket bed was too hot and crowded. Rill was cuddled against his chest, and she had been here when he went to sleep. But he didn't remember inviting the third occupant. Squinting back over his shoulder, he identified Braid. Grumpy and still half-asleep, Chime nudged the hunter with an elbow. "What are you doing here?"

Braid yawned. "Oh, is this your bed?" he said. "I thought it was Blossom's."

That was annoying. If someone was going to invade Chime's bower, it could at least be for sex with him. He elbowed Braid again. "Get out."

Rill poked him in the chest. "If you're getting up, tell Petal I'm working in the gardens today."

"I'm not—all right, all right." Giving up, Chime pushed himself up and clambered over Rill to drop down out of the basket bed.

He pulled on his clothes, then picked his way through the stray belongings littering the floor to the doorway. His bower was at the top of the long open hall of the teachers' level of the colony. A faint breeze came down the air shafts, carrying the green scents of the jungle and the cool damp of the shallow river beyond the heavy stone walls. The groundlings who had originally built this structure turns and turns ago might have meant it to be a palace or temple, but it made a fine Raksuran colony, with lots of long passages and plenty of nooks and crannies for bowers. This hall had many tall doorways, opening to narrow stairways and bowers curtained off with long drapes of fabric, and there was a shallow pool of water down the center for drinking and washing.

Chime splashed water on his face to wake himself up, and made his way out of the hall and through the passages to the center well. It was a big airy chamber with a shaft open to the floors above and below, dawn light falling down it from openings in the upper part of the structure. Hanging beds with fruit vines hung down from the three levels above, their sweet scent lacing the cool morning air.

Chime was about to shift and climb down to the work areas below, when six warriors dropped down the shaft, their wings partially spread, spines flared, tails whipping around. Chime stumbled back as they flashed by, their bright scales blending into a rainbow of colors. "Watch it!" he shouted. This was just more confirmation for his private theory that wings made people stupid.

The only response was a laugh, echoing up from below.

Raksura were divided into winged Aeriat and wingless Arbora, and sometimes they were divided in more ways than that one. The four Arbora castes of teachers, hunters, soldiers, and mentors cared for the colony and took care of its children, and produced everything it needed. The Aeriat, warriors and the queens and consorts, protected and guided the court. Or that was the idea, anyway. In Indigo Cloud, the queens did the protecting and guiding and the warriors, especially the young male ones, mostly caused trouble.

"Stupid warriors," he muttered. "Oh, sorry, Balm." She was just climbing down from the open platform on the level above and dropped to land on the floor beside him. Balm was a warrior too, but a cut above the others; she was clutchmate to Jade, the court's daughter queen.

She waved away the comment with a distracted expression, and shifted to her groundling form. Like all the warriors she was tall and slim, with sharp features. She had the dark bronze-brown skin common to the main Indigo Cloud bloodline, but her curly hair was a lighter color, reminiscent of the gold scales she wore in her other body. "They're just excited. Jade suggested to Pearl that we send a group to visit Mist Silver, and they all want to go."

Visiting other courts for trade and to exchange news was part of the warriors' duties, though they hadn't done much of it lately. In fact, Chime couldn't remember the last time Indigo Cloud had sent an embassy to one of their allies, and he knew no one had visited them for a couple of turns except Sky Copper, their nearest neighbor. Arbora were sometimes taken on these trading visits too, and Chime had a moment of excitement himself, knowing that as a mentor he had an advantage in trying to wangle a spot on the trip. "You think Pearl will let them go? I'd think she'd send you and Vine, not any of those idiots."

Balm shrugged, her mouth set in an ironic line. "I don't think she'll send anybody."

Chime, in the middle of convincing himself that he actually wanted to leave the safety of the colony and visit another court, frowned. "Why not?"

"Because it was Jade's idea." Balm shook her head, frustrated. "We need allies, but Pearl just doesn't seem to care anymore."

It had been obvious for a while that Pearl, the reigning queen, hadn't been as attentive to the court's needs as she should have been, and that she also seemed to be resisting Jade's natural transition from daughter queen to sister queen. Everyone knew it, but no one talked about it. Chime found himself hesitant to talk about it with Balm, though she had brought it up. But he took the chance and asked the question that many of the younger Arbora had been whispering to each other when they thought the elders weren't listening. "If we don't start visiting other courts again, where is Jade going to get a consort?"

"Good question," Balm said, her expression somewhere between rueful and grim.

Jade couldn't take her place as sister queen without a consort. Chime didn't understand why Pearl was so set against it, if she was tired of ruling the court herself. "But—"

"I'd better go." Balm gave him a regretful smile. "We'll talk later."

Meaning Balm didn't want anyone to hear her criticize Pearl. Glumly, Chime watched her climb down the inner wall. For the first time that morning, he shifted to his scaled form.

And everything went dark.

He woke lying on his back, blinking up at the worried faces that hovered over him. Braid was here now, and Rill, and Petal, as well as Balm. But the person crouched next to him was Jade, the young daughter queen, the soft blue of her scales vivid against the gray walls. He stared at her, startled. She watched him with worry and some other emotion he couldn't quite place. Fear? *What's she afraid of?*

"What happened? Did I fall?" he tried to ask, but his voice was a strangled croak. He had shifted and he could feel the gritty stone floor under his scales. He started to lift a hand to his head.

"Just lie still." Petal caught his hand. She was leader of the teachers' caste, and she and Chime had been friends since the nurseries. He had never seen her look this disturbed. Her voice tight and tense, she said, "Flower's coming."

Chime stared at her. He cleared his throat. "Am I hurt?" He didn't feel hurt; stunned, maybe, and a little sore in the back. Nobody answered, they just looked at each other, like . . . like he didn't know what. Fear made his heart pound. "What is it? Tell me!"

They all looked at Jade. Jade took a sharp breath, as if about to plunge into something unpleasant. "Chime, something happened when you shifted. You don't look like yourself. I mean, we can still tell it's you, but it's you . . . if you were a warrior."

He stared up at her, incredulous. "That's not funny," he said weakly, but no one was laughing. "That can't . . . what? That's not . . . " He pulled his hand from Petal's grasp, stared at it. The scales of his shifted form should be gold-brown, a common color for Arbora in his line. But the light fell on dark blue scales, catching a gold undersheen. The blue was close to Jade's shade. There were blue Arbora, but it wasn't as common . . . "Oh, this can't be happening." Chime pushed away from them, shoved himself to his feet. He staggered; his balance was off, his body oddly light.

Someone must have carried him out of the central well; they were in one of the smaller side rooms, the one with a fountain pool fed by a channel in the wall. Chime stumbled to the pool and almost swayed over backwards. Catching himself on the rim, he stared down at his reflection.

He was looking at a Raksuran warrior, tall, lean, with blue scales. Horrified and fascinated, he raised his spines to see if they were longer, and something else extended out behind him. It took him a moment to realize he was looking at the edges of his wings as they unfolded from his back. "Oh, no."

Jade said sharply, "Chime, don't." She stepped up behind him to press on a spot between his shoulder blades. Some reflex he didn't understand made the wings fold back in at the pressure. "There's no room in here. If you extend your wings, you'll hurt yourself."

Your wings. That was why his back felt heavy, why his balance was gone, why his body felt light. Warriors had lighter bones than Arbora. He turned to Jade, saying helplessly, "What happened?"

She spread her hands. "I wish I knew."

"What's this?"

Chime turned to see Flower stood in the archway, Balm behind her. Flower was in her groundling form, a small woman with ragged white hair, dressed in a loose smock. She was thin for an Arbora, with the paling skin and white hair that signaled advanced age. She planted her hands on her hips, annoyed. "Balm said Chime was hurt and I don't even see . . . " She met his gaze, and blinked. "Chime," she finished. "Oh. Oh, my."

"It just happened," he blurted. Flower had been Chime's teacher since he had been a child, since they had first told him he was going to be a mentor. Back then, he had thought she could do anything. He still thought so. "Can you fix it?"

"Ah . . . " Her expression of growing consternation was not encouraging. "Give me some time."

Braid said, "Maybe he should try shifting again. That's how it happened."

Chime leapt on the idea. "Yes! Yes, I'll try—" Ignoring Jade, Flower, Petal, and Balm's chorus of "Wait!" Chime shifted.

The startling thing was that the change felt the same as it always had, no pain, no odd sensation of the world twisting around him. He whipped around to stare down into the pool, overbalanced and nearly pitched in headfirst. He caught himself and grimaced, waiting impatiently for the water to still again.

"I don't think it worked," Braid offered helpfully.

Chime groaned. As the ripples faded, he saw the groundling form of a warrior, tall, thin. He still felt too light, but not as if he was about to float off the floor. It was recognizably him—same eyes, same nose, same mouth, just arranged on a longer face. His skin was the same even bronze, his hair the same light brown. His pants and shirt were the same ones he had put on that morning, but now they were too short for his height and too wide or too tight in all the wrong places. He slumped on the fountain rim, miserable. "How could this happen?"

Jade looked at Flower, the scales on her brow furrowed. "It's a good question. How could this happen?"

Balm added quietly, "And is it going to happen to anyone else?"

In the ensuing worried silence, Braid said, "Are we all going to switch, Arbora into Aeriat and Aeriat into Arbora? Because that would be horrible."

Chime glared up at him, fury temporarily overcoming the humiliation. "Yes, that would be horrible! How could anybody possibly live like that?"

"Chime!" Flower's sharp voice didn't quell his hysteria, but it did make him shut up.

Flower sat on the rim beside him. She said, quietly, "Chime, hold still, and look at me."

His throat went dry. Powerful mentors like Flower could look into your mind, see sicknesses, other things that weren't supposed to be there. Chime was nearly as strong as Flower, but he had only done it once, to a younger mentor named Merit. He had had other mentors do it to him for practice, but this was different. He took a deep breath, and looked into Flower's eyes.

He blinked, and she was sitting back. Her expression was tight and closed. He said, "Did you do it? I didn't feel it." He should have felt something; he always had before.

She nodded, looked down and cleared her throat. "I didn't sense anything wrong. You're perfectly normal."

"Perfectly normal," Chime repeated. The words sounded hollow. He wasn't the only one who thought so. The others stirred uneasily, and Balm and Jade exchanged a worried look.

Flower hissed under her breath, and got to her feet. "Come with me."

☾

Flower took him to her bower, and made everyone wait outside.

Her bower was bigger but neater than his, with baskets holding extra blankets, cushions, and clothes stacked against the far wall, a pot and cups for tea neatly set out by the metal pan that held warming stones, and books and writing materials lay on every flat surface.

Chime sat on a fur mat, swallowing nervously. "What? Did you see something in my head you didn't want the others to know about?"

Taking a seat opposite him, Flower gave him a grim look. "No. But I wanted to do this in private." She took a deep breath. "Use your power."

Chime went still and a cold lump settled in his stomach. Aeriat couldn't be mentors. Queens and consorts mating with Arbora was what produced mentor births among the Arbora, but even queens didn't have mentor abilities.

His throat had gone so dry it hurt. He looked around, his mind going blank for a moment. *Something simple, something easy*, he thought. Something any mentor apprentice could do. He picked up a smooth river stone from beside the hearth.

He took a deep breath, focused on the stone, and borrowed some of the sunlight falling down the hall's airshafts. Carefully, he slid it into the stone.

Nothing happened.

I'm just panicking, he thought, and took a deep calming breath. He tried again, and again. Feeling tears prick his eyes, he looked up at Flower.

Her expression made his heart sink even further. She started to speak, hesitated, then said, "Maybe it will come back."

☾

Chime hid in Flower's bower most of the day, huddled miserably in a back corner behind the storage baskets for the winter blankets. He tried shifting back and forth, as fast as he could, then at longer intervals, but he was still a warrior.

By the time Rill and Blossom managed to coax him out that evening, he had a burst of optimism. Maybe his mentor's ability had only temporarily vanished, from the shock of changing into a warrior. Both Rill and Blossom agreed to a test, and he tried to put one, then the other, into a light healing sleep.

It didn't work.

"Maybe it worked a little?" Blossom said hopefully, as Chime slunk back into hiding. "I think I feel better."

His next visitors, sometime later, were Knell and Bell, his clutchmates. Knell was a soldier and Bell a teacher; Chime had been the only mentor to turn up in their main bloodline. Their hunter mother and the soldier who had sired them had died turns ago, taken by the same illness that had taken Rain, Pearl's consort. Chime was so depressed by this point that he could barely answer Knell and Bell's questions, and he didn't come out to talk. Bell tried coaxing and Knell eventually graduated to threats, but Chime didn't budge, and they finally gave in and left.

Time wore on. At some point that night, Flower wearily said the same thing she had been saying for most of the day, "Chime, come out. You can't hide from this."

As a mentor, Chime knew that lack of food and sleep could make Raksura overwrought and paranoid, and that warriors had always claimed to need more food and sleep than Arbora. This knowledge didn't help, because he still thought they were planning to kill him. "Are you going to kill me?"

Flower, who had apparently reached her limit, snarled and stamped out of the room. Sometime later, Chime sensed rather than heard someone else enter. He thought it might be Knell coming back to haul him out of hiding. Unexpectedly, it was Stone's voice that said, "Chime. Come out of there. Now."

Stone was the line-grandfather, the only consort left in the court. Indigo Cloud hadn't had good luck with consorts, the only fertile male Aeriat. In the past generation, they had died, of disease or from fighting when the court had been attacked. Several turns ago, Pearl had sent away the last of the young ones to other courts when her own consort had died.

Stone was so old his Raksuran form wouldn't fit into most of the rooms of the colony. That didn't matter, since Chime was pretty certain that even in groundling form, Stone could beat a warrior senseless. Especially him. Chime asked, "Are you going to kill me?" At this point, it would be something of a relief.

"Nobody's going to kill you, you little idiot." Stone's voice was flat and his tone suggested he had only a limited amount of patience for this, which Chime had just expended. "Don't make me come in there after you."

Stone wasn't known for making idle threats. He wouldn't have hurt an Arbora, but then Chime wasn't an Arbora anymore. Chime crawled out from behind the baskets, and eyed Stone warily. As a groundling Aeriat, Stone looked like a tall lean man, his face lined and weathered. Everything about him had faded to gray, his hair, his skin, even his clothes. The only spot of color was in his blue eyes, though the right one was dimmed and clouded. Even in his groundling form, Stone made the bower seem much smaller.

He tossed a skinned grasseater haunch down on the mat and said, "Eat."

"I'm not hungry."

Stone cocked his head. "Did I ask you if you were hungry?"

"Um, no." Chime sat on the mat, tore a strip off the haunch, and obediently stuffed it in his mouth. He had been sick all day, so he expected to just vomit it up, which would serve Stone right. Instead it sparked his appetite, and he finished the haunch and half of the basket of fruit sitting beside Flower's hearth before he stopped for breath. "Is there bread left?" he asked Stone.

"If you wanted bread, you should have eaten with the others." Stone sounded like he was talking to a sulky fledgling. Chime had never known if all line-grandfathers were like Stone or if he was unique to Indigo Cloud. Young consorts were sensitive delicate creatures, sheltered by the court. Since Indigo Cloud had none left, they would have to try to get one from another court, when it was time for Jade to take a mate . . .

Chime stared at Stone, letting the last piece of half-eaten fruit fall from suddenly nerveless fingers. "I can't make clutches, not anymore, not like this." Aeriat consorts and male Arbora were fertile; warriors, male and female, weren't.

There was possibly a trace of pity in Stone's expression. "No, you can't."

Chime took a deep breath and rubbed his eyes. He had never made a clutch, but it was important for mentors to pass on their bloodline. He had always planned to ask to have clutches with Rill or Blossom or both, when they were ready. Another part of who he was, gone. "I don't . . . I don't know . . ."

"Chime." Stone leaned forward. "I don't know why this happened to you, but I know you can't hide down here. You have to get up, go out, and take up your life."

Chime just sat there, pushing fruit pits around on the grainy floor. A part of him knew Stone was right. The rest of him still wanted to wail at the unfairness of it. "Can I hide down here for one more night, and come out tomorrow?"

Stone sighed, stretched out a long arm to ruffle Chime's hair, and said, "One more night. If you don't come out tomorrow, I'll come back here and make you regret it."

Chime nodded glumly. It was only fair.

Stone left, and Chime sat there a long time, listening to the quiet movements of the colony around him. He hadn't been paying attention before, but he thought most of the Arbora in this hall must be either asleep or off in one of the common areas talking. *Talking about me*, he thought, with that reflexive starvation paranoia. Then he realized he might be right. They might be talking about what had happened to him. Trying to understand why, fearing it might happen to them, too. Flower had said she would have the other mentors start searching the libraries, to see if there was any record of this happening before. He wondered if they had found anything yet. *You should get up, go up to the library chambers and see if they're still there, see what they found.* The thought of facing the others, knowing he was no longer one of them, made his heart twist.

He had just managed to overcome his depressed inertia and get to his feet, when he heard soft footfalls on the steps to the bower. He tasted the air automatically, hoping it was Flower coming back. But it was Balm who pushed the curtain aside, and said, "Chime, Pearl wants to see you."

☾

Walking up the central stair to the queens' chambers on the top level, Chime realized it hadn't been paranoia. The colony felt disturbed and too quiet all at the same time. Some of the light stones in the stairwell were fading, making shadows cluster more thickly in the big space. Automatically he reached up to brush his hand against one to renew it, and then let it drop. He slid a sideways look at Balm to see if she had noticed, but if she had she didn't comment on it. She hadn't objected to walking up the stairs in their groundling forms instead of climbing the inner well, either. He cleared his throat and waved a hand around, indicating the silence in the wrong places, the faint sounds of talking and movement in others. "Is this about me?"

Balm glanced at him and admitted, "Yes. Everyone's very disturbed."

They reached the top of the steps, and Chime was startled when Balm turned down the passage to the big chamber that was used as a gathering hall. Whenever Chime had been called up here with Flower for a private meeting, it had always been in either Pearl's or Jade's bowers. Using the gathering space felt . . . official.

The chamber was large, the only opening to the outside a shaft in the center of the high roof. The light from glowing moss baskets in the wall niches left most of the space in shadow. But Chime saw the fruit vines growing down through the open shaft were mottled and discolored. *When did that happen?* he wondered, shocked. If there was a plant blight on the vines growing on the outer walls, that could be a serious problem for their crops. *Why hasn't anyone done anything about it?*

There were a few warriors sitting up on the ledge around the upper perimeter of the chamber; Chime saw Floret, Vine, Sage, and Pearl's longtime favorite, River. It was too dark to read their expressions, but their body language looked nervous. Pearl herself was pacing on the raised stone platform at the back of the room. Even in the dim light, her scales were bright gold, the webbed pattern over them the deepest indigo; her mane of frills and spines was full and extended all the way down her back. She was at least a head taller than all the other Aeriat.

It took Chime a moment to notice that Jade was sitting on the edge of the platform with Flower. He realized the other Arbora caste leaders weren't here, not Bone, Knell, or Petal. That hit Chime suddenly like a blow to the stomach. He wasn't an Arbora anymore, and rules for warriors and Aeriat were different. He felt a lump grow in his throat and sweat break out all over his groundling skin.

Chime had never been afraid of Pearl, from the time when he was barely old enough to walk and she was just the big gold person who visited the nurseries. He was respectful of her temper and wary of her bad moods, but never afraid. She was a queen, he was an Arbora, and she was supposed to protect him. That was the way it worked.

Now he wasn't an Arbora, he was something else, and he was afraid.

Pearl glanced up, saw him, and went still. Chime dropped his gaze immediately.

She said, "Come here."

Chime made it to the bottom step, then collapsed in a heap and covered his head. He heard the whisper of Pearl's folded wings as she came toward him. Her claws clicked on the steps, then she crouched in front of him. Her hand lifted his chin, and he didn't resist. He looked up into her face, so beautiful even when she frowned. She said, "I'd hoped it was a lie. Shift."

Chime swallowed in a painfully dry throat, and shifted. Even kneeling on the steps, the unexpected weight of his wings forming on his back made him fall over. He sprawled, and awkwardly pushed himself back up into a sitting position.

Pearl stood, looking down at him, and hissed under her breath.

"I'm sorry," Chime said miserably.

One of her spines flicked in annoyance. "Did you do this on purpose?"

He sat back, aghast. "No!"

"Then be quiet." Pearl looked at Flower. "Well?"

Flower spread her hands. "We have some hope the change will reverse itself."

We do? Chime thought, startled into hope. Then he took a better look at Flower's face. She didn't look very hopeful.

Pearl didn't seem to think so, either. Her tail lashed, and she said with bitter amusement. "Let's hope it happens soon. Apparently our time is limited."

Silence sank over the room again. It was so quiet, Chime heard scales whisper as one of the warriors on the ledge changed position. Then Jade said, "Chime, is there anything you want to ask? About . . . being a warrior?"

Chime was too numb with relief that Pearl apparently wasn't going to kill him to form a coherent question. But he knew Jade had spoken to him to remind the others it was still him in this different body, and he shouldn't let the opportunity go by. He said, "Has anybody done anything about the blight?"

The room seemed to freeze and they all stared at him, as if he had asked something else. He realized no one knew what he meant, and pointed up to the discolored vines around the shaft. "The plant blight."

He wasn't sure what they all thought he had been referring to, but the room breathed in relief again. Pearl looked up at the vines, her spines folding down into her mane, and said, "They tried. Nothing helps."

Flower let out her breath in a long sigh. "You'd better go, Chime."

Chime started to stand, overbalanced and almost banged his head on the top step. He shifted back to groundling and stumbled to his feet. Balm took his wrist to steady him. She said, kindly, "I'll walk with you."

They left the gathering hall, but out in the stairwell foyer, a warrior dropped from the ceiling. It was River. He hissed at Chime and said, "You're not one of us, no matter what you look like."

"I know," Chime snapped. "That's the only thing that keeps me from killing myself."

Balm snorted in amusement, and shouldered River out of the way. Two landings down the stairs, she said, "Try not to mind that. They're not sure what your status is going to be, and it worries them."

It worried Chime, too.

(

Chime woke the next morning, curled up on a cushion behind Flower's baskets. Bleary and confused, he frowned at the hall's ceiling high overhead, wondering how he had ended up here.

Memory washed over him and he moaned. He still had his long, awkwardly light body; it hadn't just been an extended nightmare.

Flower leaned over the baskets and said, "Chime, remember what Stone told you."

He winced and buried his head in his arms. "I know, I know. I'll come out. In a while."

Flower sighed, and after a moment he heard her leave the bower.

He lay there, listening to the other inhabitants of the hall rustle around and talk quietly. Eventually, the hall went still.

Chime climbed slowly out, his legs cramping from disuse. He stumbled out of the bower and took the passage at the other end of the hall, headed for the other side of the colony. He managed to avoid running into anyone, and came out on a platform overlooking the river.

It was another cool damp morning, a few clouds dotting the blue sky to the south. The colony was built across a shallow river that cut through a narrow valley, jungle-clad hills rising to either side. Some of the lower hills had been turned into garden terraces, where the Arbora planted the crops that helped sustain the court. Raksura had built the terraces, but the building was a relic of some long-ago groundling empire. It was made of gray stone in the shape of a step pyramid, and this platform was one of many extending from the outer wall, and used mostly for sunning. It had a shallow square pool filled with rainwater, and Chime had chosen it for that and the fact that it faced away from the gardens where the Arbora would be working this morning, and the platforms that the warriors frequented.

Chime took a deep breath and shifted. He looked down at himself, unable to squelch the last spark of hope, but he was still a blue warrior. He swore wearily and started across to the pool.

Walking in this too-light body was odd; each step still felt as if he might lift right off the ground. He stepped carefully up onto the pool's edge. The water was strewn with blue lilies but mostly clear, and it gave him a fairly good view of himself. *All right*, he thought, *how do I do this?* He frowned, trying to figure out how to make the new muscles work. He lashed his tail, his spines lifted and flicked, and then his wings started to unfold. They stopped with only the outermost section extended, the way they had the first time. They seemed to be stuck there, in a resting position, and he rolled his shoulders, shook himself, and bounced up and down before he finally found the right combination of muscles.

His wings stretched and spread, unfolding to nearly eighteen paces, the weight of them making him hunch forward until he got the trick of balancing with his tail. The scaly membrane caught the light, reflecting an edge of gold under the blue. It wasn't as if he had never seen wings close-up before, but these were attached to him, and that was different.

Trying to move them was like suddenly having four arms. It took effort to make the muscles contract by themselves, without moving his arms, hands, spines, or tail. After a time, he managed to make the right one curl in toward him. The front edge of the wing looked razor-sharp, but the skin folded over the joints was smooth.

"You're going to have to work on that."

He twitched and his wings snapped in, a jolt that made him stumble forward and step into the pool.

Balm strolled forward, watching him critically. "You have to catch the wind and play it, mold it, with the surfaces. It's like . . . having sex with the air."

Chime grimaced. "When I'm having sex I'm not worried about falling to my death."

"If you fall to your death, I'll catch you," she said.

Chime stared at her. Balm apparently expected him to fly. "I'm not going to fall because I'm not going to be in the air. I was just . . . just . . . " He didn't really know why he had come out here, he had just been drawn to the sun and the wind.

Balm folded her arms. "Chime, you have to do this. This is what we are. If you won't fly, you won't be an Arbora, but you won't be an Aeriat either."

"I know that! I know." He took a deep breath. "I need more time."

"If you put it off today, you'll put it off forever."

"I will not."

"You will." Balm stepped forward, her expression stony. Her disapproval was much more intimidating than River's, mainly because he actually cared what she thought of him. "You'll let fear rule you."

"I won't." He hissed at her. "You think it's easy to be a mentor? Making simples that could kill if we get the slightest element wrong? Making light and heat with our hands? I won't let fear rule me because I never have before!"

She laughed. "That's easy enough to say."

Chime snarled, whipped around, and stepped to the edge of the platform. The river was below, and the green of the jungle, a flight of white water birds just lifting above the trees in the distance. Chime spread his wings, or his wings spread of their own accord, he wasn't sure. The wind caressed his scales and he wanted to lean into it.

Before he could change his mind, he did.

Suddenly he was gliding, the river and the spiral trees flashing below. *Don't panic,* he told himself, but Balm was right. He could feel the wind against the inner scales of his wings, and it was like nothing he had ever felt before. It was like folding paper with your fingers, or molding clay. Like the wind was a solid substance he could smooth or bend at will.

"Chime!" Balm was suddenly under him, and he stared at her. Her spines were flat, her wings fully spread. He had never seen her, or any other warrior, from this angle before. *We're beautiful,* he thought. She shouted, "Pull your wings in!"

"What?" That didn't sound like a good idea. "Why?"

"You don't know how to land!"

"Oh!" He concentrated and his wings snapped in, much faster than he had expected. He dropped like a rock, but Balm snapped her wings in and rolled, caught him as he fell, and twisted back around. Her wings unfolded and cupped the air, and they sank to a gentle landing on a sandbar in the river. Chime let go and stumbled away, ankle-deep in the cool shallow water. "That was . . . That was . . . "

"A good start." Balm smiled.

☾

They practiced most of the morning, and Chime never did manage to land on his own, mostly because he was afraid to try. But he could glide now with a degree of confidence. And he had admitted to himself that it was stupid to have wings and not be able to use them.

After that, Chime ate in the teachers' gathering room, then went back to Flower's bower and slept most of the afternoon. It surprised him how exhausted he was; flying was apparently more like work than it had always looked. He didn't wake until Flower walked into the bower and sat down beside the bowl hearth.

Chime sat up, rubbing his eyes blearily. Then he saw Flower was holding an old scroll-book, and that woke him up. His heart pounding, he said, "You found it."

Flower set the scroll aside. "Yes, we found a mention of it in the histories of other courts."

"You did?" From her expression, it was easy to see it wasn't good news. She looked tired and discouraged. His heart still sank, though by this point he hadn't really expected anything else. "I won't go back to normal. This is permanent."

"I think it must be, Chime."

He watched her face carefully. Flower looked far more upset than that news warranted. Everyone had pretty much expected it to be permanent; the idea that it might not be had been a last-ditch hope. *Uh oh,* Chime thought, suddenly convinced he was going to die. "But there's something else."

Flower pushed the hair out of her eyes, weary and discouraged. "This has happened before, in courts that were on the verge of collapse. Warriors can travel further, don't breed, so they're more useful than Arbora when a colony fails. It's a natural process." She sighed. "A natural process for colonies that are . . . dying out."

"But we're not—oh." A great many things flashed through Chime's mind. All the sicknesses that had come and gone over the last ten turns or so. The lack of young consorts, which had always seemed a temporary thing while Pearl was grieving for Rain, but Rain had been dead for so many turns now. The blight on the vines at the top of the colony, that no one could cure. *Pearl knows,* he thought, remembering her cryptic comment about "our time being limited." Jade knew, they all knew. "How long? I mean, how long have you known . . . "

"We didn't know." She shook her head. "We suspected. We feared. Now we know."

Chime sat back. His problems suddenly seemed small to the point of complete insignificance. "We have to do something," he said. "There's got to be a reason. There's got to be something we can do."

"Stone has some ideas," Flower said, but didn't explain. She reached over and squeezed his wrist. "Don't say anything to the others yet."

"I won't," he promised. Flower got to her feet and left. She had left the book, and he sat there for a time, his hand on the cover. As a mentor, it would be his job to study the histories and try to find solutions to offer the queens. As a warrior . . . Whatever his job as a warrior would be, it was going to involve flying.

Chime got to his feet and went to look for Balm again. It was time to learn how to land.

APPENDICES

APPENDIX I

The Court of Indigo Cloud
Aeriat

Queens

Pearl—Reigning Queen.

Jade—Sister Queen.

Amber—former Sister Queen of Pearl, now dead.

Azure—the queen who took Stone, now dead.

Frost—a fledgling queen of the court of Sky Copper, now adopted by Indigo Cloud.

Indigo—the Reigning Queen who originally led the court away from the Reaches to the east.

Solace—a Sister Queen in an earlier generation of the court, who was the first to visit the Golden Isles.

Cerise—a past Reigning Queen; Indigo's birthqueen.

Consorts

Stone—line-grandfather.

Rain—Pearl's last consort, now dead.

Moon—Jade's consort.

Thorn and Bitter—fledgling consorts of Sky Copper, now adopted by Indigo Cloud.

Cloud—the consort Indigo stole from Emerald Twilight.

Sable—Solace's consort.

Dust and Burn—young consorts given away by Pearl when Rain died. Dust became the second consort to the reigning queen of Wind Sun.

Warriors

River—leader of Pearl's faction of warriors. A product of one of Amber's royal clutches.

Drift—River's clutchmate.

Branch—River and Drift's clutchmate, killed in a Fell ambush.

Root—young warrior from an Arbora clutch; a member of Jade's faction.

Song—young female warrior; a member of Jade's faction.

Spring—fledgling female, one of only two survivors from Amber's last clutch of warriors.

Snow—fledgling male, Spring's clutchmate.

Balm—female warrior, and Jade's clutchmate. Jade's strongest supporter and leader of her faction.

Chime—former Arbora mentor, now a warrior; a member of Jade's faction.

Vine and Coil—male warriors of Pearl's faction, though they chafe under River's rule.

Floret—female warrior of Pearl's faction.

Sand—a young male warrior of Jade's faction.

Serene—a young female warrior of Jade's faction.

Band and Fair—young male warriors of Pearl's faction.

Sage—an older male warrior of Pearl's faction.

Serene—a young female warrior of Jade's faction.

Briar and Aura—young female warriors, inclining to Jade's faction, but currently unattached. Aura came from an Arbora clutch.

Sorrow—female warrior who took care of Moon as a fledgling, believed to be the last Aeriat survivor of his court, killed by Tath.

ARBORA

Mentors

Flower—leader of the Mentors' Caste.

Heart—young female mentor, one of the Arbora rescued from the Dwei Hive by Moon.

Merit—young male mentor, rescued with Heart.

Copper—a young male mentor, still in the nurseries.

Thistle—a young female mentor.

Teachers

Petal—former leader of the Teachers' Caste, killed in the Fell attack on the old Indigo Cloud colony.

Bell—new leader of the Teachers' Caste, and clutchmate to Chime.

Blossom—an older female, one of only two teachers to escape during the Fell attack on the colony. Later learned to pilot a Golden Isles Wind-ship.

Bead—a young female, she escaped the colony with Blossom.

Rill, Bark, and Weave—female teachers.

Gift, Needle, and Dream—young female teachers, rescued from the Dwei Hive by Moon.

Snap—young male teacher, also rescued from the Dwei Hive.

Dash—a very old male teacher.

Gold—an older female teacher, and the best artisan in the court.

Merry—a younger male teacher, and Gold's student.

Hunters

Bone—leader of the Hunters' Caste.

Braid, Salt, Spice, Knife—young male hunters.

Bramble, Blaze, Plum—young female hunters.

Wake—an older female hunter.

Strike—a very young hunter, male, who volunteered to test the Fell poison.

Soldiers

Knell—leader of Soldiers' Caste, and clutchmate to Chime.

Grain—the first Arbora to speak to Moon and to order him to leave Indigo Cloud.

Shell—Grain's clutchmate, killed in the Fell attack on the colony.

Sharp, Ginger, Sprout—young female soldiers.

THE COURT OF EMERALD TWILIGHT
AERIAT

Queens

Ice—reigning queen of Emerald Twilight.

Tempest—senior sister queen, Ash's birthqueen.

Ash—youngest daughter queen.

Halcyon—another sister queen, Tempest's clutchmate.

Consorts

Shadow—first consort to Ice.

Fade—second consort to Tempest, now dead.

Ember—consort sent to Indigo Cloud, from Tempest and Fade's only clutch.

Warriors

Willow—a female Warrior who greets visitors at Emerald Twilight.

Torrent—female warrior, from a queen's clutch with Tempest and Halcyon.

Beacon, Prize—female warriors of Tempest's faction.

Dart, Streak, Gust—male warriors of Tempest's faction.

The Court of Opal Night
Aeriat

Queens

Malachite—reigning queen of Emerald Twilight.

Onyx—sister queen.

Celadon—daughter queen, of Malachite's line.

Ivory—another daughter queen, of Onyx's line.

Consorts

Dusk—first consort to Malachite, killed after the attack on the eastern colony.

Umber—first consort to Onyx.

Shade—young consort, son of Malachite's consort Night.

Warriors

Rise—female warrior of Opal Night, of Malachite's faction.

Saffron—female warrior, clutchmate of Ivory.

Sorrow—female warrior who took care of Moon as a fledgling, killed by Tath.

Horn, Tribute—male warriors of Ivory's faction.

Gallant, Fleet—female warriors of Ivory's faction.

Dare, Rime—male warriors of Celadon's faction.

Arbora

Mentors

Lithe—female mentor, young but powerful.

Tear—older female mentor, now dead.

Reed—young female mentor

Auburn—an older male mentor.

Teachers

> *Feather*—female teacher, survivor of the eastern colony.
>
> *Russet*—female teacher, survivor of the eastern colony.
>
> *Twist, Yarrow*—two male teachers killed in the eastern colony.
>
> *Luster*—a male teacher.
>
> *Moss*—a young male teacher.

Hunters

> *Fair*—a female hunter killed in the eastern colony.

THE COURT OF VERIDIAN SEA

Amaranth—reigning queen.

Flint—her first consort.

THE COURT OF SUNSET WATER

Zephyr—a sister queen, daughter of an Emerald Twilight consort, Shadow's clutchmate, who was given to the reigning Sunset Water queen.

THE COURT OF OCEAN WINTER

Flame—a sister queen.

Garnet—a daughter queen.

Venture—a female warrior, clutchmate to the reigning queen.

Violet—a female mentor.

Appendix II

Excerpt from Observations of the Raksura:
Volume Thirty-Seven of A Natural History by
scholar-preeminent Delin-Evran-Lindel

The Two Breeds of the Raksura

ARBORA: Arbora have no wings but are agile climbers, and their scales appear in a variety of colors. They have long tails, sharp retractable claws, and manes of flexible spines and soft "frills," characteristics that are common to all Raksura. They are expert artisans and are dexterous and creative in the arts they pursue for the court's greater good. In their alternate form they are shorter than Aeriat Raksura and have stocky, powerful builds. Both male and female Arbora are fertile, and sometimes may have clutches that include warrior fledglings. This is attributed to queens and consorts blending their bloodlines with Arbora over many generations.

The four castes of the Arbora are:

Teachers—They supervise the nurseries and train the young of the court. They are also the primary artisans of the court, and tend the gardens that will be seen around any Raksuran colony.

Hunters—They take primary responsibility for providing food for the court. This includes hunting for game, and gathering wild plants.

Soldiers—They "guard the ground" and protect the colony and the surrounding area.

Mentors—They are Arbora born with arcane powers, who have skill in healing and augury. They also act as historians and record-keepers for the court, and usually advise the queens.

AERIAT: The winged Raksura. Like the Arbora, they have long tails, sharp retractable claws, and manes of flexible spines and soft frills.

Warriors—They act as scouts and guardians, and defend the colony from threats from the air, such as the Fell. Warriors are sterile and cannot breed, though they appear as male and female forms. Their scales are in any number of bright colors. Female warriors are usually somewhat stronger than male warriors. In their alternate form, they are always tall and slender. They are not as long-lived generally as queens, consorts, and Arbora.

Consorts—Consorts are fertile males, and their scales are always black, though there may be a tint or "undersheen" of gold, bronze, or blood red. At maturity they are stronger than warriors, and may be the longest lived of any Raksura. They are also the fastest and most powerful flyers, and this ability increases as they grow older. There is some evidence to suggest that consorts of great age may grow as large or larger than the major kethel of the Fell.

Queens—Queens are fertile females, and are the most powerful and deadly fighters of all the Aeriat. Their scales have two brilliant colors, the second in a pattern over the first. The queens' alternate form resembles an Arbora, with no wings, but retaining the tail, and an abbreviated mane of spines and the softer frills. Queens mate with consorts to produce royal clutches, composed of queens, consorts, and warriors.

Appendix III

Excerpt from Additions to the List of
Predatory Species by scholar-eminent-posthumous
Venar-Inram-Alil.

Fell are migratory and prey on other intelligent species.

The Known Classes of Fell

Major kethel—The largest of the Fell, sometimes called harbingers, major kethel are often the first sign that a Fell flight is approaching. Their scales are black, like that of all the Fell, and they have an array of horns around their heads. They have a low level of intelligence and are believed to be always under the control of the rulers.

Minor dakti—The dakti are small, with armor plates on the back and shoulders, and webbed wings. They are somewhat cunning, but not much more intelligent than kethel, and fight in large swarms.

Rulers—Rulers are intelligent creatures that are believed to have some arcane powers of entrancement over other species. Rulers related by blood are also believed to share memories and experiences through some mental bond. They have complete control of the lesser Fell in their flights, and at times can speak through dakti and see through their eyes. (*Addendum* by scholar-preeminent Delin-Evran-lindel: *Fell rulers in their winged form bear an unfortunate and superficial resemblance to Raksuran Consorts.*)

There is believed to be a fourth class, or possibly a female variant of the Rulers, called the *Progenitors.*

Common lore holds that if a Fell ruler is killed, its head must be removed and stored in a cask of salt or yellow mud and buried on land in order to prevent drawing other Fell rulers to the site of its death. It is possible that only removing the head from the corpse may be enough to prevent this, but burying it is held to be the safest course.